KT-499-547

English Fairy Tales

Retold by
FLORA ANNIE STEEL

Illustrated by
ARTHUR RACKHAM

WORDSWORTH CLASSICS

For my husband
ANTHONY JOHN RANSON
with love from your wife, the publisher.
Eternally grateful for your unconditional love.

Readers who are interested in other titles from
Wordsworth Editions are invited to visit our website at
www.wordsworth-editions.com

First published in 1994 by Wordsworth Editions Limited
8B East Street, Ware, Hertfordshire SG12 9HJ

ISBN 978 1 85326 133 6

Text © Wordsworth Editions Limited 1994

Wordsworth® is a registered trade mark of
Wordsworth Editions Limited

Wordsworth Editions
is the company founded in 1987 by
MICHAEL TRAYLER

All rights reserved. This publication may not be
reproduced, stored in a retrieval system or
transmitted, in any form or by any means, electronic,
mechanical, photocopying, recording or otherwise,
without the prior permission of the publishers.

Typeset in Great Britain by Antony Gray
Printed and bound by Clays Ltd, St Ives plc

ENGLISH FAIRY TALES

CONTENTS

St George of Merrie England

In the darksome depths of a thick forest lived Kalyb, the fell enchantress. Terrible were her deeds, and few there were who had the hardihood to sound the brazen trumpet which hung over the iron gate that barred the way to the Abode of Witchcraft. Terrible were the deeds of Kalyb; but above all things she delighted in carrying off innocent newborn babes, and putting them to death.

And this, doubtless, she meant to be the fate of the infant son of the Earl of Coventry, who long long years ago was Lord High Steward of England. Certain it is that the babe's father being absent, and his mother dying at his birth, the wicked Kalyb, with spells and charms, managed to steal the child from his careless nurses.

But the babe was marked from the first for doughty deeds, for on his breast was pictured the living image of a dragon, on his right hand was a blood-red cross and on his left leg showed the golden garter.

And these signs so affected Kalyb, the fell enchantress, that she stayed her hand; and the child growing daily in beauty and stature, he became to her as the apple of her eye. Now, when twice seven years had passed the boy began to thirst for honourable adventures, though the wicked enchantress wished to keep him as her own.

But he, seeking glory, utterly disdained so wicked a creature; thus she sought to bribe him. And one day, taking him by the hand, she led him to a brazen castle and showed him six brave knights, prisoners therein.

Then said she: 'Lo! These be the six champions of Christendom. Thou shalt be the seventh and thy name shall be St George of Merrie England if thou wilt stay with me.'

But he would not.

Then she led him into a magnificent stable where stood seven of the most beautiful steeds ever seen. 'Six of these,' said she, 'belong to the six champions. The seventh and the best, the swiftest and the most powerful in the world, whose name is Bayard, will I bestow on thee, if thou wilt stay with me.'

But he would not.

Then she took him to the armoury, and with her own hand buckled on a corselet of purest steel, and laced on a helmet inlaid with gold. Then, taking a mighty falchion, she gave it into his hand, and said: 'This armour which none can pierce, this sword called Ascalon, which will hew in sunder all it touches, are thine; surely now thou wilt stop with me?'

But he would not.

Then she bribed him with her own magic wand, thus giving him power over all things in that enchanted land, saying: 'Surely now wilt thou remain here?'

But he, taking the wand, struck with it a mighty rock that stood by; and lo! it opened, and laid in view a wide cave garnished with the bodies of a vast number of innocent newborn infants whom the wicked enchantress had murdered.

Thus, using her power, he bade the sorceress lead the way into the place of horror, and when she had entered, he raised the magic wand yet again, and smote the rock; and lo! it closed for ever, and the sorceress was left to bellow forth her lamentable complaints to senseless stones.

Thus was St George freed from the enchanted land, and taking with him the six other champions of Christendom on their steeds, he mounted Bayard and rode to the city of Coventry.

Here for nine months they abode, exercising themselves in all feats of arms. So when spring returned they set forth, as knights errant, to seek for foreign adventure.

And for thirty days and thirty nights they rode on, until, at the beginning of a new month, they came to a great wide plain. Now in the centre of this plain, where seven several ways met, there stood a great brazen pillar, and here, with high heart and courage, they bade each other farewell, and each took a separate road.

Hence, St George, on his charger Bayard, rode till he reached the seashore where lay a good ship bound for the land of Egypt. Taking passage in her, after long journeying he arrived in that land when the silent wings of night were outspread and darkness brooded on all things.

Here, coming to a poor hermitage, he begged a night's lodging, on which the hermit replied: 'Sir knight of Merrie England – for I see her arms graven on thy breastplate – thou hast come hither in an ill time, when those alive are scarcely able to bury the dead by reason of the cruel destruction waged by a terrible dragon, who ranges up and down the country by day and by night. If he have not an innocent maiden to devour each day, he sends a mortal plague amongst the people. And this has not ceased for twenty and four years, so that there is left throughout the land but one maiden, the beautiful Sâbia, daughter to the king. And tomorrow must she die, unless some brave knight will slay the monster. To such will the king give his daughter in marriage, and the crown of Egypt in due time.'

'For crowns I care not,' said St George boldly, 'but the beauteous maiden shall not die. I will slay the monster.'

So, rising at dawn of day, he buckled on his armour, laced his helmet, and with the falchion Ascalon in his hand, bestrode Bayard, and rode into the Valley of the Dragon. Now on the way he met a procession of old women weeping and wailing and in their midst the most beauteous damsel he had ever seen. Moved by compassion he dismounted, and bowing low before the lady entreated her to return to her father's palace, since he was about to kill the dreaded dragon. Whereupon the beautiful Sâbia, thanking him with smiles and tears, did as he requested and he, remounting, rode on his emprise.

Now, no sooner did the dragon catch sight of the brave knight than its leathern throat sent out a sound more terrible than thunder, and weltering from its hideous den, it spread its burning wings and prepared to assail its foe.

Its size and appearance might well have made the stoutest heart tremble. From shoulder to tail ran full forty feet, its body was covered with silver scales, its belly was as gold, and through its flaming wings the blood ran thick and red.

So fierce was its onset, that at the very first encounter the knight was nigh felled to the ground; but recovering himself he gave the dragon such a thrust with his spear that the latter shivered to a thousand pieces; whereupon the furious monster smote him so violently with its tail that both horse and rider were overthrown.

Now, by great good chance, St George was flung under the shade of a flowering orange tree, whose fragrance hath this virtue in it, that no poisonous beast dare come within the compass of its branches. So there the valiant knight had time to recover his senses, until with eager courage he rose, and rushing to the combat, smote the burning dragon on his burnished belly with his trusty sword Ascalon; and thereinafter spouted out such black venom, as, falling on the armour of the knight, burst it in twain. And ill might it have fared with St George of Merrie England but for the orange tree, which once again gave him shelter under its branches, where, seeing the issue of the fight was in the hands of the Most High, he knelt and prayed that such strength of body should be given him as would enable him to prevail. Then, with a bold and courageous heart, he advanced again, and smote the fiery dragon under one of his flaming wings, so that the weapon pierced the heart, and all the grass

around turned crimson with the blood that flowed from the
dying monster. So St George of England cut off the dreadful
head and hanging it on a truncheon made of the spear which at
the beginning of the combat had shivered against the beast's
scaly back, he mounted his steed Bayard, and proceeded to the
palace of the king.

Now the king's name was Ptolemy, and when he saw that the
dreaded dragon was indeed slain, he gave orders for the city to
be decorated. And he sent a golden chariot with wheels of ebony
and cushions of silk to bring St George to the palace, and
commanded a hundred nobles dressed in crimson velvet, and
mounted on milk-white steeds richly caparisoned, to escort him
thither with all honour, while musicians walked before and after,
filling the air with sweetest sounds.

Now the beautiful Sâbia herself washed and dressed the weary
knight's wounds, and gave him in sign of betrothal a diamond
ring of purest water. Then, after he had been invested by the
king with the golden spurs of knighthood and had been magnifi-
cently feasted, he retired to rest his weariness, while the beautiful Sâbia from her balcony lulled him to sleep with her golden
lute.

So all seemed happiness; but alas! dark misfortune was at hand.

Almidor, the black King of Morocco, who had long wooed the
Princess Sâbia in vain, without having the courage to defend her,
seeing that the maiden had given her whole heart to her
champion, resolved to compass his destruction.

So, going to King Ptolemy, he told him – what was perchance
true – namely that the beauteous Sâbia had promised St George
to become Christian, and follow him to England. Now the
thought of this so enraged the king that, forgetting his debt of
honour, he determined on an act of basest treachery.

Telling St George that his love and loyalty needed further
trial, he entrusted him with a message to the King of Persia, and
forbade him either to take with him his horse Bayard or his
sword Ascalon; nor would he even allow him to say farewell to
his beloved Sâbia.

St George then set forth sorrowfully, and surmounting many

dangers, reached the court of the King of Persia in safety; but what was his anger to find that the secret missive he bore contained nothing but an earnest request to put the bearer of it to death. But he was helpless, and when sentence had been passed upon him, he was thrown into a loathly dungeon, clothed in base and servile weeds, and his arms strongly fettered up to iron bolts, while the roars of the two hungry lions who were to devour him ere long deafened his ears. Now his rage and fury at this black treachery was such that it gave him strength, and with mighty effort he drew the staples that held his fetters; so being part free he tore his long locks of amber-coloured hair from his head and wound them round his arms instead of gauntlets. So prepared he rushed on the lions when they were let loose upon him, and thrusting his arms down their throats choked them, and thereinafter, tearing out their very hearts, held them up in triumph to the gaolers who stood by trembling with fear.

After this the King of Persia gave up the hopes of putting St George to death, and, doubling the bars of the dungeon left him to languish therein. And there the unhappy knight remained for seven long years, his thoughts full of his lost princess; his only companions rats and mice and creeping worms, his only food and drink bread made of the coarsest bran and dirty water.

At last one day, in a dark corner of his dungeon, he found one of the iron staples he had drawn in his rage and fury. It was half consumed with rust, yet it was sufficient in his hands to open a passage through the walls of his cell into the king's garden. It was the time of night when all things are silent; but St George, listening, heard the voices of grooms in the stables; entering, he found two grooms furnishing forth a horse against some business. Whereupon, taking the staple with which he had redeemed himself from prison, he slew the grooms, and mounting the palfrey rode boldly to the city gates where he told the watchman at the Bronze Tower, that St George having escaped from the dungeon, he was in hot pursuit of him. Whereupon the gates were thrown open and St George, clapping spurs to his horse, found himself safe from pursuit before the first red beams of the sun shot up into the sky.

Now, ere long, being most famished with hunger, he saw a tower set on a high cliff, and riding thitherward determined to ask for food. But as he neared the castle he saw a beauteous damsel in a blue and gold robe seated disconsolate at a window.

Whereupon, dismounting he called aloud to her: 'Lady! If thou hast sorrow of thine own, succour one also in distress, and give me, a Christian knight, now almost famished, one meal's meat.'

To which she replied quickly: 'Sir knight! Fly quickly an' thou canst, for my lord is a mighty giant, a follower of Mahomed, who hath sworn to destroy all Christians.'

Hearing this St George laughed loud and long. 'Go tell him then, fair dame,' he cried, 'that a Christian knight waits at his door, and will either satisfy his wants within his castle or slay the owner thereof.'

Now the giant no sooner heard this valiant challenge than he rushed forth to the combat, armed with a hugeous crowbar of iron. He was a monstrous giant, deformed, with a huge head, bristled like any boar's, with hot, glaring eyes and a mouth equalling a tiger's. At first sight of him St George gave himself up for lost, not so much for fear, but for hunger and faintness of body. Still, commending himself to the Most High, he also rushed to the combat with such poor arms as he had and with many a regret for the loss of his magic sword Ascalon. So they fought till noon, when, just as the champion's strength was nigh finished, the giant stumbled on the root of a tree, and St George, taking his chance, ran him through the mid-rib, so that he gasped and died.

After which St George entered the tower; whereat the beautiful lady, freed from her terrible lord, set before him all manner of delicacies and pure wine with which he sufficed his hunger, rested his weary body, and refreshed his horse.

So, leaving the tower in the hands of the grateful lady, he went on his way, coming ere long to the Enchanted Garden of the necromancer Ormadine, where, embedded in the living rock, he saw a magic sword, the like of which for beauty he had never seen, the belt being beset with jasper and sapphire stones, while the pommel was a globe of the purest silver chased in gold with these verses:

> My magic will remain most firmly bound
> Till that a knight from the far north be found
> To pull this sword from out its bed of stone.
> Lo! when he comes wise Ormadine muse fall.
> Farewell, my magic power, my spell, my all.

Seeing this St George put his hand to the hilt thinking to essay pulling it out by strength; but lo! he drew it out with as much ease as though it had hung by a thread of untwisted silk. And immediately every door in the Enchanted Garden flew open, and the magician Ormadine appeared, his hair standing on end; and he, after kissing the hand of the champion, led him to a cave where a young man wrapped in a sheet of gold lay sleeping, lulled by the songs of four beautiful maidens.

'The knight whom thou seest here,' said the necromancer in a hollow voice, 'is none other than thy brother-in-arms, the Christian champion St David of Wales. He also attempted to draw my sword but failed. Him hast thou delivered from my enchantments since they come to an end.'

Now, as he spoke, came such a rattling of the skies, such a lumbering of the earth as never was, and in the twinkling of an eye the Enchanted Garden and all in it vanished from view, leaving the Champion of Wales, roused from his seven years' sleep, giving thanks to St George, who greeted his ancient comrade heartily.

After this St George of Merrie England travelled far and travelled fast, with many adventures by the way, to Egypt where he had left his beloved Princess Sâbia. But, learning to his great grief and horror from the same hermit he had met on first landing, that, despite her denials, her father, King Ptolemy, had consented to Almidor the black King of Morocco carrying her off as one of his many wives, he turned his steps towards Tripoli, the capital of Morocco; for he was determined at all costs to gain a sight of the dear princess from whom he had been so cruelly rent.

To this end he borrowed an old cloak of the hermit, and,

disguised as a beggar, gained admittance to the gate of the
women's palace, where were gathered together on their knees
many others, poor, frail, infirm.

And when he asked them wherefore they knelt, they answered:
'Because good Queen Sâbia succours us that we may pray for the
safety of St George of England, to whom she gave her heart.'

Now when St George heard this his own heart was like to
break for very joy, and he could scarce keep on his knees when,
lovely as ever, but with her face pale and sad and wan from long
distress, the Princess Sâbia appeared clothed in deep mourning.

In silence she handed an alms to each beggar in turn; but when
she came to St George she started and laid her hand on her
heart. Then she said softly: 'Rise up, Sir beggar! Thou art too
like one who rescued me from death for it to be meet for thee to
kneel before me!'

Then St George rising, and bowing low, said quietly: 'Peerless
lady! Lo! I am that very knight to whom thou did'st condescend
to give this.'

And with this he slipped the diamond ring she had given him
on her finger. But she looked not at it, but at him, with love in
her eyes.

Then he told her of her father's base treachery and Almidor's part in it, so that her anger grew hot and she cried: 'Waste no more time in talk. I remain no longer in this detested place. Ere Almidor returns from hunting we shall have escaped.'

So she led St George to the armoury, where he found his trusty sword Ascalon, and to the stable, where his swift steed Bayard stood ready caparisoned.

Then, when her brave knight had mounted, and she, putting her foot on his, had leapt like a bird behind him, St George touched the proud beast lightly with his spurs, and, like an arrow from a bow, Bayard carried them together over city and plain, through woods and forests, across rivers, and mountains, and valleys, until they reached the land of Greece.

And here they found the whole country in festivity over the marriage of the king. Now amongst other entertainments was a grand tournament, the news of which had spread through the world. And to it had come all the other six champions of Christendom; so St George arriving made the seventh. And many of the champions had with them the fair lady they had rescued. St Denys of France brought beautiful Eglantine, St James of Spain sweet Celestine, while noble Rosalind accompanied St Anthony of Italy. St David of Wales, after his seven years' sleep, came full of eager desire for adventure. St Patrick of Ireland, ever cour-teous, brought all the six Swan-princesses who in gratitude had been seeking their deliverer St Andrew of Scotland; since he, leaving all worldly things, had chosen to fight for the faith.

So all these brave knights and fair ladies joined in the joyful jousting, and each of the seven champions was in turn Chief Challenger for a day.

Now in the midst of all the merriment appeared a hundred heralds from a hundred different parts of the paynim world, declaring war to the death against all Christians.

Whereupon the seven champions agreed that each should return to his native land to place his dearest lady in safety, and gather together an army, and that six months later they should meet, and, joining as one legion, go forth to fight for Christendom.

And this was done. So, having chosen St George as Chief General they marched on Tripoli with the cry:

'For Christendom we fight,
For Christendom we die.'

Here the wicked Almidor fell in single combat with St George, to the great delight of his subjects, who begged the champion to be king in his stead. To this he consented, and, after he was crowned, the Christian host went on towards Egypt where King Ptolemy, in despair of vanquishing such stalwart knights, threw himself down from the battlements of the palace and was killed. Whereupon, in recognition of the chivalry and courtesy of the Christian champions, the nobles offered the crown to one of their number, and they with acclaim chose St George of Merrie England.

Thence the Christian host journeyed to Persia, where a fearsome battle raged for seven days, during which two hundred thousand pagans were slain, beside many who were drowned in attempting to escape. Thus they were compelled to yield, the emperor himself happening into the hands of St George, and six other viceroys into the hands of the six other champions.

And these were most mercifully and honourably entreated after they had promised to govern Persia after Christian rules. Now the emperor, having a heart fraught with despite and tyranny, conspired against them, and engaged a wicked wizard named Osmond to so beguile six of the champions that they gave up fighting, and lived an easy slothful life. But St George would not be beguiled; neither would he consent to the enchantment of his brothers: and he so roused them that they never sheathed their swords nor unlocked their armour till the wicked emperor and his viceroys were thrown into that very dungeon in which St George had languished for seven long years.

Whereupon St George took upon himself the government of Persia, and gave the six other champions the six viceroyalties.

So, attired in a beautiful green robe, richly embroidered, over which was flung a scarlet mantle bordered with white fur and decorated with ornaments of pure gold, he took his seat on the throne which was supported by elephants of translucent alabaster. And the heralds at arms, amid the shouting of the people, cried: 'Long live St George of Merrie England, Emperor of Morocco, King of Egypt and Sultan of Persia!'

Now, after that he had established good and just laws to such effect that innumerable companies of pagans flocked to become Christians, St George, leaving the government in the hands of his trusted counsellors, took truce with the world and returned to England, where, at Coventry, he lived for many years with the Egyptian Princess Sâbia, who bore him three stalwart sons. So here endeth the tale of St George of Merrie England, first and greatest of the seven champions.

The Story of the Three Bears

Once upon a time there were Three Bears, who lived together in a house of their own, in a wood. One of them was a Little Wee Bear and one was a Middle-Sized Bear and the other was a Great Big Bear. They had each a bowl for their porridge: a little bowl for the Little Wee Bear and a middle-sized bowl for the Middle-Sized Bear and a great bowl for the Great Big Bear. And they had each a chair to sit in: a little chair for the Little Wee Bear and a middle-sized chair for the Middle-Sized Bear and a great chair for the Great Big Bear. And they had each a bed to sleep in: a little bed for the Little Wee Bear and a middle-sized bed for the Middle-Sized Bear and a great bed for the Great Big Bear.

One day, after they had made the porridge for their breakfast, and poured it into their porridge-bowls, they walked out into the wood while the porridge was cooling, that they might not burn their mouths by beginning too soon, for they were polite, well-brought-up Bears. And while they were away a little girl called Goldilocks, who lived at the other side of the wood and had been sent on an errand by her mother, passed by the house, and looked in at the window. And then she peeped in at the keyhole, for she was not at all a well-brought-up little girl. Then seeing nobody in the house she lifted the latch. The door was not fastened, because the Bears were good Bears, who did nobody any harm, and never suspected that anybody would harm them. So Goldilocks opened the door and went in; and well pleased was she when she saw the porridge on the table. If she had been a well-brought-up little girl she would have waited till the Bears came home, and then, perhaps, they would have asked her to breakfast; for they were good Bears – a little rough or so, as the manner of Bears is, but for all that very good-natured and hospitable. But she was an impudent, rude little girl, and so she set about helping herself.

First she tasted the porridge of the Great Big Bear, and that was too hot for her. Next she tasted the porridge of the Middle-Sized Bear, but that was too cold for her. And then she went to the porridge of the Little Wee Bear, and tasted it, and that was neither too hot nor too cold, but just right, and she liked it so well that she ate it all up, every bit!

Then Goldilocks, who was tired, for she had been catching butterflies instead of running on her errand, sat down in the chair of the Great Big Bear, but that was too hard for her. And then she sat down in the chair of the Middle-Sized Bear, and that was too soft for her. But when she sat down in the chair of the Little Wee Bear, that was neither too hard, nor too soft, but just right. So she seated herself in it, and there she sat till the bottom of the chair came out, and down she came, plump upon the ground; and that made her very cross, for she was a bad-tempered little girl.

Now, being determined to rest, Goldilocks went upstairs into the bedchamber in which the three Bears slept. And first she lay down upon the bed of the Great Big Bear, but that was too high at the head for her. And next she lay down upon the bed of the Middle-Sized Bear, and that was too high at the foot for her. And then she lay down upon the bed of the Little Wee Bear, and that was neither too high at the head, nor at the foot, but just right. So she covered herself up comfortably, and lay there till she fell fast asleep.

By this time the Three Bears thought their porridge would be cool enough for them to eat it properly: so they came home to breakfast. Now careless Goldilocks had left the spoon of the Great Big Bear standing in his porridge.

'Somebody has been at my porridge!'

said the Great Big Bear in his great, rough, gruff voice.

Then the Middle-Sized Bear looked at his porridge and saw the spoon was standing in it too.

'Somebody has been at my porridge!'

said the Middle-Sized Bear in his middle-sized voice.

'Somebody has been lying in my bed – and here she is still!'

Then the Little Wee Bear looked at his, and there was the spoon in the porridge-bowl, but the porridge was all gone!

'Somebody has been at my porridge, and has eaten it all up!'

said the Little Wee Bear in his little wee voice.

Upon this the Three Bears, seeing that someone had entered their house, and eaten up the Little Wee Bear's breakfast, began to look about them. Now the careless Goldilocks had not put the hard cushion straight when she rose from the chair of the Great Big Bear.

'Somebody has been sitting in my chair!'

said the Great Big Bear in his great, rough, gruff voice.

And the careless Goldilocks had squatted down the soft cushion of the Middle-Sized Bear.

'Somebody has been sitting in my chair!'

said the Middle-Sized Bear in his middle-sized voice.

'Somebody has been sitting in my chair, and has sat the bottom through!'

said the Little Wee Bear in his little wee voice.

Then the Three Bears thought they had better make further search in case it was a burglar, so they went upstairs into their bedchamber. Now Goldilocks had pulled the pillow of the Great Big Bear out of its place.

'Somebody has been lying in my bed!'

said the Great Big Bear in his great, rough, gruff voice.

And Goldilocks had pulled the bolster of the Middle-Sized Bear out of its place.

'Somebody has been lying in my bed!'

said the Middle-Sized Bear in his middle-sized voice.

But when the Little Wee Bear came to look at his bed, there was the bolster in its place!

And the pillow was in its place upon the bolster!

And upon the pillow – ?

There was Goldilocks' yellow head – which was not in its place, for she had no business there.

'Somebody has been lying in my bed – and here she is still!'

said the Little Wee Bear in his little wee voice.

Now Goldilocks had heard in her sleep the great, rough, gruff voice of the Great Big Bear; but she was so fast asleep that it was no more to her than the roaring of wind, or the rumbling of thunder. And she had heard the middle-sized voice of the Middle-Sized Bear, but it was only as if she had heard someone speaking in a dream. But when she heard the little wee voice of the Little Wee Bear, it was so sharp, and so shrill, that it awakened her at once. Up she started, and when she saw the Three Bears on one side of the bed, she tumbled herself out at the other, and ran to the window. Now the window was open, because the Bears, like good, tidy Bears, as they were, always opened their bedchamber window when they got up in the morning. So naughty, frightened little Goldilocks jumped; and whether she broke her neck in the fall, or ran into the wood and was lost there, or found her way out of the wood and got whipped for being a bad girl and playing truant no one can say. But the Three Bears never saw anything more of her.

Tom-Tit-Tot

Once upon a time there was a woman and she baked five pies. But when they came out of the oven they were over-baked, and the crust was far too hard to eat. So she said to her daughter: 'Daughter,' says she, 'put them pies on to the shelf and leave 'em there awhile. Surely they'll come again in time.'

By that, you know, she meant that they would become softer; but her daughter said to herself, 'If mother says the pies will come again, why shouldn't I eat these now?' So, having good, young teeth, she set to work and ate the lot, first and last.

Now when supper-time came the woman said to her daughter, 'Go you and get one of the pies. They are sure to have come again by now.'

Then the girl went and looked, but of course there was nothing but the empty dishes.

So back she came and said, 'No, mother they ain't come again.'

'Not one o' them?' asked the mother, taken aback like.

'Not one o' them,' says the daughter, quite confident.

'Well,' says the mother, 'come again, or not come again, I will have one of them pies for my supper.'

'But you can't,' says the daughter. 'How can you if they ain't come? And they ain't, as sure's sure.'

'But I can,' says the mother, getting angry. 'Go you at once, child, and bring me the best on them. My teeth must just tackle it.'

'Best or worst is all one,' answered the daughter quite sulky, 'for I've ate the lot, so you can't have one till it comes again – so there!'

Well, the mother she bounced up to see; but half an eye told her there was nothing save the empty dishes; so she was dished up herself and done for.

So, having no supper, she sat her down on the doorstep, and, bringing out her distaff, began to spin. And as she span she sang:

> 'My daughter ha' ate five pies today,
> My daughter ha' ate five pies today,
> My daughter ha' ate five pies today,'

for, see you, she was quite flabbergasted and fair astonished.

Now the king of that country happened to be coming down the street and he heard the song going on and on, but could not quite make out the words. So he stopped his horse, and asked: 'What is that you are singing, my good woman?'

Now the mother, though horrified at her daughter's appetite, did not want other folk, leastwise the king, to know about it, so she sang instead:

> 'My daughter ha' spun five skeins today,
> My daughter ha' spun five skeins today,
> My daughter ha' spun five skeins today.'

'Five skeins!' cried the king. 'By my garter and my crown, I never heard tell of anyone who could do that! Look you here, I have been searching for a maiden to wife and your daughter who can spin five skeins a day is the very one for me. Only, mind you, though for eleven months of the year she shall be queen indeed, and have all she likes to eat, all the gowns she likes to get, all the company she likes to keep, and everything her heart desires, in the twelfth month she must set to work and spin five skeins a day, and if she does not she must die. Come! is it a bargain?'

So the mother agreed. She thought what a grand marriage it was for her daughter. And as for the five skeins? Time enough to bother about them when the year came round. There was many a slip between cup and lip, and, likely as not, the king would have forgotten all about it by then.

Anyhow, her daughter would be queen for eleven months. So they were married, and for eleven months the bride was happy as happy could be. She had everything she liked to eat, and all the gowns she liked to get, all the company she cared to keep, and everything her heart desired. And her husband the king was kind as kind could be. But in the tenth month she began to think of those five skeins and wonder if the king remembered? And in the eleventh month she began to dream about them as well. But ne'er a word did the king, her husband, say about them; so she hoped he had forgotten.

But on the very last day of the eleventh month, the king, her husband, led her into a room she had never set eyes on before. It had one window, and there was nothing in it but a stool and a spinning-wheel.

'Now, my dear,' he said quite kind like, 'you will be shut in here tomorrow morning with some victuals and some flax, and if by evening you have not spun five skeins, your head will come off.'

Well, she was fair frightened, for she had always been such a gatless thoughtless girl that she had never learnt to spin at all. So what she was to do on the morrow she could not tell; for, see you, she had no one to help her; for, of course, now she was queen, her mother didn't live nigh her. So she just locked the door of her room, sat down on a stool and cried and cried and cried until her pretty eyes were all red.

Now as she sat sobbing and crying she heard a queer little noise at the bottom of the door. At first she thought it was a mouse. Then she thought it must be something knocking.

So she upped and opened the door and what did she see? Why! a small, little, black Thing with a long tail that whisked round and round ever so fast.

'What are you crying for?' said that Thing, making a bow, and twirling its tail so fast that she could scarcely see it.

'What's that to you?' said she, shrinking a bit, for that Thing was very queer like.

'Don't look at my tail if you're frightened,' says That, smirking. 'Look at my toes. Ain't they beautiful?'

And sure enough That had on buckled shoes with high heels and big bows, ever so smart.

So she kind of forgot about the tail, and wasn't so frightened, and when That asked her again why she was crying, she upped and said, 'It won't do no good if I do.'

'You don't know that,' says That, twirling its tail faster and faster, and sticking out its toes. 'Come, tell me, there's a good girl.'

'Well,' says she, 'it can't do any harm if it doesn't do good.' So she dried her pretty eyes and told That all about the pies, and the skeins, and everything from first to last.

And then that little, black Thing nearly burst with laughing. 'If that is all, it's easy mended!' it says. 'I'll come to your window every morning, take the flax and bring it back spun into five skeins at night. Come! shall it be a bargain?'

Now she, for all she was so gatless and thoughtless, said, cautious like: 'But what is your pay?'

Then That twirled its tail so fast you couldn't see it, and stuck out its beautiful toes, and smirked and looked out of the corners of its eyes. 'I will give you three guesses every night to guess my name, and if you haven't guessed it before the month is up, why –' and That twirled its tail faster and stuck out its toes further, and smirked and sniggered more than ever – 'you shall be mine, my beauty.'

Three guesses every night for a whole month! She felt sure she would be able for so much; and there was no other way out of the business, so she just said, 'Yes! I agree!'

And lor! how That twirled its tail, and bowed, and smirked, and stuck out its beautiful toes.

Well, the very next day her husband led her to the strange room again, and there was the day's food, and a spinning-wheel and a great bundle of flax.

'There you are, my dear,' says he as polite as polite. 'And remember! if there are not five whole skeins tonight, I fear your head will come off!'

At that she began to tremble, and after he had gone away and locked the door, she was just thinking of a good cry, when she heard a queer knocking at the window. She upped at once and opened it, and sure enough there was the small, little, black Thing sitting on the window-ledge, dangling its beautiful toes and twirling its tail so that you could scarcely see it.

'Good-morning, my beauty,' says That. 'Come! hand over the flax, sharp, there's a good girl.'

So she gave That the flax and shut the window and, you may be sure, ate her victuals, for, as you know, she had a good appetite, and the king, her husband, had promised to give her everything she liked to eat. So she ate to her heart's content, and when evening came and she heard that queer knocking at the window again, she upped and oped it, and there was the small, little, black Thing with five spun skeins on his arm!

And it twirled its tail faster than ever, and stuck out its beautiful toes, and bowed and smirked and gave her the five skeins.

Then That said, 'And now, my beauty, what is That's name?'

And she answered quite easy like: 'That is Bill.'

'No, it ain't,' says That, and twirled its tail.

'Then That is Ned,' says she.

'No, it ain't,' says That, and twirled its tail faster.

'Well,' says she a bit more thoughtful, 'That is Mark.'

'No, it ain't,' says That, and laughs and laughs and laughs, and twirls its tail so as you couldn't see it, as away it flew.

Well, when the king, her husband, came in, he was fine and pleased to see the five skeins all ready for him, for he was fond of his pretty wife.

'I shall not have to order your head off, my dear,' says he. 'And I hope all the other days will pass as happily.' Then he said good-night and locked the door and left her.

But next morning they brought her fresh flax and even more delicious foods. And the small, little, black Thing came knocking at the window and stuck out its beautiful toes and twirled its tail faster and faster, and took away the bundle of flax and brought it back all spun into five skeins by evening. Then That made her guess three times what That's name was; but she could not guess right, and That laughed and laughed and laughed as it flew away.

Now every morning and evening the same thing happened, and every evening she had her three guesses; but she never guessed right. And every day the small, little, black Thing laughed louder and louder and smirked more and more, and looked at her quite maliceful out of the corners of its eyes until she began to get frightened, and instead of eating all the fine foods left for her, spent the day in trying to think of names to say. But she never hit upon the right one.

So it came to the last day of the month but one, and when the small, little, black Thing arrived in the evening with the five skeins of flax all ready spun, it could hardly say for smirking: 'Ain't you got That's name yet?'

So says she – for she had been reading her Bible: 'Is That Nicodemus?'

'No, it ain't,' says That, and twirled its tail faster than you could see.

'Is That Samuel?' says she all of a flutter.

'No, it ain't, my beauty,' chuckles That, looking maliceful.

'Well – is That Methusaleh?' says she, inclined to cry.

Then That just fixes her with eyes like a coal a-fire, and says, 'No, it ain't that neither, so there is only tomorrow night and then you'll be mine, my beauty.'

And away the small, little, black Thing flew, its tail twirling and whisking so fast that you couldn't see it.

Well, she felt so bad she couldn't even cry; but she heard the king, her husband, coming to the door, so she made bold to be cheerful, and tried to smile when he said, 'Well done, wife! Five skeins again! I shall not have to order your head off after all, my dear, of that I'm quite sure, so let us enjoy ourselves.' Then he bade the servants bring supper, and a stool for him to sit beside his queen, and down they sat lover-like, side by side.

But the poor queen could eat nothing; she could not forget the small, little, black Thing. And the king hadn't eaten but a mouthful or two when he began to laugh, and he laughed so long and so loud that at last the poor queen, all lackadaisical as she was, said: 'Why do you laugh so?'

'At something I saw today, my love,' says the king. 'I was out a-hunting, and by chance I came to a place I'd never been in before. It was in a wood, and there was an old chalk-pit there, and out of the chalk-pit there came a queer kind of a sort of a humming, bumming noise. So I got off my hobby to see what made it, and went quite quiet to the edge of the pit and looked down. And what do you think I saw? The funniest, queerest, smallest, little, black Thing you ever set eyes upon. And it had a little spinning-wheel and it was spinning away for dear life, but the wheel didn't go so fast as its tail, and that span round and round – *ho-ho-ha-ha!* – you never saw the like. And its little feet had buckled shoes and bows on them, and they went up and down in a desperate hurry. And all the time that small, little, black Thing kept humming and booming away at these words:

> 'Name me, name me not,
> Who'll guess it's Tom-Tit-Tot.'

Well, when she heard these words the queen nearly jumped

out of her skin for joy; but she managed to say nothing, but ate her supper quite comfortably.

And she said no word when next morning the small, little, black Thing came for the flax, though it looked so gleeful and maliceful that she could hardly help laughing, knowing she had got the better of it. And when night came and she heard that knocking against the windowpanes, she put on a wry face, and opened the window slowly as if she was afraid. But That thing was as bold as brass and came right inside, grinning from ear to ear. And oh, my goodness! how That's tail was twirling and whisking!

'Well, my beauty,' says That, giving her the five skeins all ready spun, 'what's my name?'

Then she put down her lip, and says, tearful like, 'Is – is – That – Solomon?'

'No, it ain't,' laughs That, smirking out of the corner of That's eye. And the small, little, black Thing came further into the room.

So she tried again – and this time she seemed hardly able to speak for fright.

'Well – is That Zebedee?' she says.

'No, it ain't,' cried the impet, full of glee. And it came quite close and stretched out its little black hands to her, and O–oh, its tail . . . ! ! !

'Take time, my beauty,' says That, sort of jeering like, and its small, little, black eyes seemed to eat her up. 'Take time! Remember! next guess and you're mine!'

Well, she backed just a wee bit from it, for it was just horrible to look at; but then she laughed out and pointed her finger at it and said, says she:

> 'Name me, name me not,
> *Your* name is
>> *Tom*
>> TIT
>> *TOT*.'

And you never heard such a shriek as that small, little, black

Thing gave out. Its tail dropped down straight, its feet all crumpled up, and away That flew into the dark and she never saw it no more.

And she lived happy ever after with her husband, the king.

The Golden Snuff-Box

Once upon a time, and a very good time too, though it was not in my time, nor your time, nor for the matter of that in anyone's time, there lived a man and a woman who had one son called Jack, and he was just terribly fond of reading books. He read, and he read, and then, because his parents lived in a lonely house in a lonely forest and he never saw any other folk but his father and his mother, he became quite crazy to go out into the world and see charming princesses and the like.

So one day he told his mother he must be off, and she called him an air-brained addle-pate, but added that, as he was no use at home, he had better go seek his fortune. Then she asked him if he would rather take a small cake with her blessing to eat on his journey, or a large cake with her curse? Now Jack was a very hungry lad, so he just up and said: 'A big cake, if you please, 'm.'

So his mother made a great big cake, and when he started she took herself off to the top of the house and cast malisons on him, till he got out of sight. You see she had to do it, but after that she sat down and cried.

Well, Jack hadn't gone far till he came to a field where his father was ploughing. Now the goodman was dreadfully put out when he found his son was going away, and still more so when he heard he had chosen his mother's malison. So he cast about what to do to put things straight, and at last he drew out of his pocket a little golden snuff-box, and gave it to the lad saying: 'If ever you are in danger of sudden death you may open the box; but not till then. It has been in our family for years and years; but, as we have lived, father and son, quietly in the forest, none of us have ever been in need of help – perhaps you may.'

So Jack pocketed the golden snuff-box and went on his way.

Now, after a time, he grew very tired, and very hungry, for he had eaten his big cake first thing, and night closed in on him so that he could scarce see his way.

But at last he came to a large house and begged board and lodging at the back door. Now Jack was a good-looking young fellow, so the maidservant at once called him into the fireside and gave him plenty good meat and bread and beer. And it so happened that while he was eating his supper the master's gay young daughter came into the kitchen and saw him. So she went to her father and said that there was the prettiest young fellow she had ever seen in the back kitchen, and that if her father loved her he would give the young man some employment. Now the gentleman of the house was exceedingly fond of his gay young daughter, and did not want to vex her; so he went into the back kitchen and questioned Jack as to what he could do.

'Anything,' said Jack gaily, meaning, of course, that he could do any foolish bit of work about a house.

But the gentleman saw a way of pleasing his gay young daughter and getting rid of the trouble of employing Jack; so he laughs and says, 'If you can do anything, my good lad,' says he, 'you had better do this. By eight o'clock tomorrow morning you must have dug a lake four miles round in front of my mansion, and on it there must be floating a whole fleet of vessels. And they must range up in front of my mansion and fire a salute of guns. And the very last shot must break the leg of the four-post bed on which my daughter sleeps, for she it always late of a morning!'

Well! Jack was terribly flabbergasted, but he faltered out: 'And if I don't do it?'

'Then,' said the master of the house quite calmly, 'your life will be the forfeit.'

So he bade the servants take Jack to a turret-room and lock the door on him.

Well! Jack sat on the side of his bed and tried to think things out, but he felt as if he didn't know *b* from a battledore, so he decided to think no more, and after saying his prayers he lay down and went to sleep. And he did sleep! When he woke it was close on eight o'clock, and he had only time to fly to the window and look out, when the great clock on the tower began to whirr before it struck the hour. And there was the lawn in front of the house all set with beds of roses and stocks and marigolds! Well! all of a sudden he remembered the little golden snuff-box.

'I'm near enough to death,' quoth he to himself, as he drew it out and opened it.

And no sooner had he opened it than out hopped three funny little red men in red nightcaps rubbing their eyes and yawning; for, see you, they had been locked up in the box for years and years and years.

'What do you want, master?' they said between their yawns. But Jack heard that clock a-whirring and knew he hadn't a moment to lose, so he just gabbled off his orders. Then the clock began to strike, and the little men flew out of the window and suddenly

> 'Bang! bang! bang! bang! bang! bang!'

went the guns, and the last one must have broken the leg of the four-post bed, for there at the window was the gay young daughter in her nightcap, gazing with astonishment at the lake four miles round, with the fleet of vessels floating on it!

And so did Jack! He had never seen such a sight in his life, and he was quite sorry when the three little red men disturbed him by flying in at the window and scrambling into the golden snuff-box.

'Give us a little more time when you want us next, master,' they said sulkily. Then they shut down the lid, and Jack could hear them yawning inside as they settled down to sleep.

As you may imagine the master of the house was fair astonished, while as for the gay young daughter she declared at once that she would never marry anyone else but the young man who could do such wonderful things; the truth being that she and Jack had fallen in love with each other at first sight.

But her father was cautious. 'It is true, my dear,' says he, 'that the young fellow seems a bully boy; but for aught we know it may be chance, not skill, and he may have a broken feather in his wing. So we must try him again.'

Then he said to Jack, 'My daughter must have a fine house to live in. Therefore by tomorrow morning at eight o'clock there must be a magnificent castle standing on twelve golden pillars in the middle of the lake, and there must be a church beside it. And all things must be ready for the bride, and at eight o'clock precisely a peal of bells from the church must ring out for the wedding. If not you will have to forfeit your life.'

This time Jack intended to give the three little red men more time for their task; but what with having enjoyed himself so much all day, and having eaten so much good food, he overslept himself, so that the big clock on the tower was whirring before it struck eight when he woke, leapt out of bed, and rushed to the golden snuff-box. But he had forgotten where he had put it, and so the clock had *really* begun to strike before he found it under his pillow, opened it, and gabbled out his orders. And then you never saw how the three little red men tumbled over each other and yawned and stretched and made haste all at one time, so that Jack thought his life would surely be forfeit. But just as the clock struck its last chime, out rang a peal of merry bells, and there was the castle standing on twelve golden pillars and a church beside it in the middle of the lake. And the castle was all decorated for the wedding, and there were crowds and crowds of servants and retainers, all dressed in their Sunday best.

Never had Jack seen such a sight before; neither had the gay young daughter who, of course, was looking out of the next window in her nightcap. And she looked so pretty and so gay that Jack felt quite cross when he had to step back to let the three little red men fly to their golden snuff-box. But they were far crosser than he was, and mumbled and grumbled at the hustle, so that Jack was quite glad when they shut the box down and began to snore.

Well, of course, Jack and the gay young daughter were married, and were as happy as the day is long; and Jack had fine clothes to wear, fine food to eat, fine servants to wait on him, and as many fine friends as he liked.

So he was in luck; but he had yet to learn that a mother's malison is sure to bring misfortune sometime or another.

Thus it happened that one day when he was going a-hunting

with all the ladies and gentlemen, Jack forgot to change the
golden snuff-box (which he always carried about with him for
fear of accidents) from his waistcoat pocket to that of his scarlet
hunting-coat; so he left it behind him. And what should happen
but that the servant let it fall on the ground when he was folding
up the clothes, and the snuff-box flew open and out popped the
three little red men yawning and stretching.

Well! when they found out that they hadn't really been
summoned and that there was no fear of death, they were in a
towering temper and said they had a great mind to fly away with
the castle, golden pillars and all.

On hearing this the servant pricked up his ears.

'Could you do that?' he asked.

'Could we?' they said, and they laughed loud. 'Why, we can do
anything.'

Then the servant said ever so sharp, 'Then move me, this
castle, and all it contains right away over the sea where the
master can't disturb us.'

Now the little red men need not really have obeyed the order,
but they were so cross with Jack that hardly had the servant said
the words before the task was done; so when the hunting-party
came back, lo, and behold! the castle, and the church, and the
golden pillars, had all disappeared!

At first all the rest set upon Jack for being a knave and a cheat;
and, in particular, his wife's father threatened to have at him for
deceiving the gay young daughter; but at last he agreed to let
Jack have twelve months and a day to find the castle and bring it
back.

So off Jack starts on a good horse with some money in his
pocket.

And he travelled far and he travelled fast, and he travelled east
and west, north and south, over hills, and dales, and valleys, and
mountains, and woods, and sheepwalks, but never a sign of the
missing castle did he see. Now at last he came to the palace of
thE KIng of all the Mice in the Wide World. And there was a
little mousie in a fine hauberk and a steel cap doing sentry at the
front gate, and he was not for letting Jack in until he had told his

errand. And when Jack had told it, he passed him on to the next mouse-sentry at the inner gate; so by degrees he reached the king's chamber where he sat surrounded by mice courtiers.

Now the King of the Mice received Jack very graciously, and said that he himself knew nothing of the missing castle, but, as he was King of all the Mice in the Wide World, it was possible that some of his subjects might know more than he. So he ordered his chamberlain to command a Grand Assembly for the next morning, and in the meantime he entertained Jack right royally.

But the next morning, though there were brown mice, and black mice, and grey mice, and white mice, and piebald mice, from all parts of the world, they all answered with one breath: 'If it please your majesty, we have not seen the missing castle.'

Then the king said, 'You must go and ask my elder brother the King of all the Frogs. He may be able to tell you. Leave your horse here and take one of mine. It knows the way and will carry you safe.'

So Jack set off on the king's horse, and as he passed the outer gate he saw the little mouse sentry coming away, for its guard was up. Now Jack was a kind-hearted lad, and he had saved some crumbs from his dinner in order to recompense the little sentry for his kindness. So he put his hand in his pocket and pulled out the crumbs.

'Here you are, mousekin,' he said. 'That's for your trouble!'

Then the mouse thanked him kindly and asked if he would take him along to the King of the Frogs.

'Not I,' says Jack. 'I should get into trouble with your king.'

But the mousekin insisted. 'I may be of some use to you,' it said. So it ran up the horse's hind leg and up by its tail and hid in Jack's pocket. And the horse set off at a hand gallop, for it didn't half like the mouse running over it.

So at last Jack came to the palace of the King of all the Frogs, and there at the front gate was a frog doing sentry in a fine coat of mail and a brass helmet. And the frog sentry was for not letting Jack in; but the mouse called out that they came from the King of all the Mice and must be let in without delay. So they were taken to the king's chamber where he sat surrounded by frog courtiers in fine clothes; but alas! he had heard nothing of the castle on golden pillars, and though he summoned all the frogs of all the world to a Grand Assembly next morning, they all answered his question with:

'*Kro kro, Kro kro,*'

which everyone knows stands for 'No' in frog language.

So the king said to Jack, 'There remains but one thing. You must go and ask my eldest brother the King of all the Birds. His subjects are always on the wing, so mayhap, they have seen something. Leave the horse you are riding here, and take one of mine. It knows the way, and will carry you safe.'

So Jack set off, and being a kind-hearted lad he gave the frog sentry, whom he met coming away from his guard, some crumbs he had saved from his dinner. And the frog asked leave to go with him, and when Jack refused to take him he just gave one hop on to the stirrup, and a second hop on to the crupper, and the next hop he was in Jack's other pocket.

Then the horse galloped away like lightning, for it didn't like the slimy frog coming down 'plop' on its back.

Well, after a time, Jack came to the palace of the King of all the Birds, and there at the front gate were a sparrow and a crow marching up and down with matchlocks on their shoulders. Now at this Jack laughed fit to split, and the mouse and the frog from his pockets called out: 'We come from the king! Sirrahs! Let us pass.'

So that the sentries were right mazed, and let them pass in without more ado.

But when they came to the king's chamber, where he sat surrounded by all manner of birds, tomtits, wrens, cormorants, turtledoves, and the like, the king said he was sorry, but he had no news of the missing castle. And though he summoned all the birds of all the world to a Grand Assembly next morning, not one of them had seen or heard tell of it.

So Jack was quite disconsolate till the king said, 'But where is the eagle? I don't see my eagle.'

Then the chamberlain – he was a tomtit – stepped forward

with a bow and said: 'May it please your majesty he is late.'

'Late?' says the king in a fume. 'Summon him at once.'

So two larks flew up into the sky till they couldn't be seen and sang ever so loud, till at last the eagle appeared all in a perspiration from having flown so fast.

Then the king said, 'Sirrah! Have you seen a missing castle that stands upon twelve pillars of gold?'

And the eagle blinked its eyes and said, 'May it please your majesty that is where I've been.'

Then everybody rejoiced exceedingly, and when the eagle had eaten a whole calf so as to be strong enough for the journey, he spread his wide wings, on which Jack stood, with the mouse in one pocket and the frog in the other, and started to obey the king's order to take the owner back to his missing castle as quickly as possible.

And they flew over land and they flew over sea, until at last in the far distance they saw the castle standing on its twelve golden pillars. But all the doors and windows were fast shut and barred, for, see you, the servant-master who had run away with it had gone out for the day a-hunting, and he always bolted doors and windows while he was absent lest someone else should run away with it.

Then Jack was puzzled to think how he should get hold of the golden snuff-box, until the little mouse said: 'Let me fetch it. There is always a mouse-hole in every castle, so I am sure I shall be able to get in.'

So it went off, and Jack waited on the eagle's wings in a fume; till at last mousekin appeared.

'Have you got it?' shouted Jack, and the little mousie cried:

'Yes!'

So everyone rejoiced exceedingly, and they set off back to the palace of the King of all the Birds, where Jack had left his horse; for now that he had the golden snuff-box safe he knew he could get the castle back whenever he chose to send the three little red men to fetch it. But on the way over the sea, while Jack, who was dead tired with standing so long, lay down between the eagle's wings and fell asleep, the mouse and the eagle fell to quarrelling as to which of them had helped Jack the most, and they quarrelled so much that at last they laid the case before the frog. Then the frog, who made a very wise judge, said he must see the whole affair from the very beginning; so the mouse brought out the golden snuff-box from Jack's pocket, and began to relate where it had been found and all about it. Now, at that very moment Jack awoke, kicked out his leg, and plump went the golden snuff-box down to the very bottom of the sea!

'I thought my turn would come,' said the frog, and went plump in after it

Well, they waited, and waited, and waited for three whole days and three whole nights; but froggie never came up again, and they had just given him up in despair when his nose showed above the water.

'Have you got it?' they shouted.

'No!' says he, with a great gasp.

'Then what do you want?' they cried in a rage.

'My breath,' says froggie, and with that he sinks down again.

Well, they waited two days and two nights more, and at last up comes the little frog with the golden snuff-box in its mouth.

Then they all rejoiced exceedingly, and the eagle flew ever so fast to the palace of the King of the Birds.

But alas and alack a day! Jack's troubles were not ended; his mother's malison was still bringing him ill-luck, for the King of the Birds flew into a fearsome rage because Jack had not brought the castle of the golden pillars back with him. And he said that unless he saw it by eight o'clock next morning Jack's head should come off as a cheat and a liar.

Then Jack being close to death opened the golden snuff-box, and out tumbled the three little red men in their three little red caps. They had recovered their tempers and were quite glad to be back with a master who knew that they would only, as a rule, work under fear of death; for, see you, the servant-master had been for ever disturbing their sleep with opening the box to no purpose.

So before the clock struck eight next morning, there was the palace on its twelve golden pillars, and the King of the Birds was fine and pleased, and let Jack take his horse and ride to the palace of the King of the Frogs. But there exactly the same thing happened, and poor Jack had to open the snuff-box again and order the castle to come to the palace of the King of the Frogs. At this the little red men were a wee bit cross; but they said they supposed it could not be helped; so, though they yawned, they brought the castle all right, and Jack was allowed to take his horse and go to the palace of the King of all the Mice in the Wide World. But here the same thing happened, and the little red men tumbled out of the golden snuff-box in a real rage, and said fellows might as well have no sleep at all! However, they did as they were bidden; they brought the castle of the golden pillars from the palace of the King of the Frogs to the palace of the King of all the Mice in the Wide World, and Jack was allowed to take his own horse and ride home.

But the year and a day which he had been allowed was almost gone, and even his gay young wife, after almost weeping her eyes out after her handsome young husband, had given up Jack for lost; so everyone was astounded to see him, and not over-pleased either to see him come without his castle. Indeed his father-in-law swore with many oaths that if it were not in its proper place by eight o'clock next morning Jack's life should be forfeit.

Now this, of course, was exactly what Jack had wanted and intended from the beginning; because when death was nigh he could open the golden snuff-box and order about the little red men. But he had opened it so often of late and they had become so cross that he was in a stew what to do; whether to give them time to show their temper, or to hustle them out of it. At last he decided to do half and half. So just as the hands of the clock were at five minutes to eight he opened the box, and stopped his ears!

Well! you never heard such a yawning, and scolding, and threatening, and blustering. What did he mean by it? Why should he take four bites at one cherry? If he was always in fear of death why didn't he die and have done with it?

In the midst of all this the tower clock began to whirr –

'Gentlemen!' says Jack – he was really quaking with fear – 'do as you are told.'

'For the last time,' they shrieked. 'We won't stay and serve a master who thinks he is going to die every day.'

And with that they flew out of the window.

AND THEY NEVER CAME BACK.

The gold snuff-box remained empty for evermore.

But when Jack looked out of window there was the castle in the middle of the lake on its twelve golden pillars, and there was his young wife ever so pretty and gay in her nightcap looking out of the window too.

So they lived happily ever after.

Tattercoats

In a great palace by the sea there once dwelt a very rich old lord, who had neither wife nor children living, only one little grand-daughter, whose face he had never seen in all her life. He hated her bitterly, because at her birth his favourite daughter died; and when the old nurse brought him the baby he swore that it might live or die as it liked, but he would never look on its face as long as it lived.

So he turned his back, and sat by his window looking out over the sea, and weeping great tears for his lost daughter, till his white hair and beard grew down over his shoulders and twined round his chair and crept into the chinks of the floor, and his tears, dropping on to the window-ledge, wore a channel through the stone, and ran away in a little river to the great sea. Meanwhile, his granddaughter grew up with no one to care for her, or clothe her; only the old nurse, when no one was by, would sometimes give her a dish of scraps from the kitchen, or a torn petticoat from the rag-bag; while the other servants of the palace would drive her from the house with blows and mocking words, calling her 'Tattercoats', and pointing to her bare feet and shoulders, till she ran away, crying, to hide among the bushes.

So she grew up, with little to eat or to wear, spending her days out of doors, her only companion a crippled gooseherd, who fed his flock of geese on the common. And this gooseherd was a queer, merry, little chap and, when she was hungry, or cold, or tired, he would play to her so gaily on his little pipe, that she forgot all her troubles, and would fall to dancing with his flock of noisy geese for partners.

Now one day people told each other that the king was travelling through the land, and was to give a great ball to all the lords and ladies of the country in the town near by, and that the prince, his only son, was to choose a wife from amongst the maidens in the company. In due time one of the royal invitations to the ball was brought to the palace by the sea, and the servants carried it up to the old lord, who still sat by his window, wrapped in his long white hair and weeping into the little river that was fed by his tears.

But when he heard the king's command, he dried his eyes and bade them bring shears to cut him loose, for his hair had bound him a fast prisoner, and he could not move. And then he sent them for rich clothes, and jewels, which he put on; and he ordered them to saddle the white horse, with gold and silk, that he might ride to meet the king; but he quite forgot he had a granddaughter to take to the ball.

Meanwhile Tattercoats sat by the kitchen-door weeping, because she could not go to see the grand doings. And when the old nurse heard her crying she went to the lord of the palace, and begged him to take his granddaughter with him to the king's ball.

But he only frowned and told her to be silent; while the servants laughed and said, 'Tattercoats is happy in her rags, playing with the gooseherd! Let her be – it is all she is fit for.'

A second, and then a third time, the old nurse begged him to let the girl go with him, but she was answered only by black looks and fierce words, till she was driven from the room by the jeering servants, with blows and mocking words.

Weeping over her ill-success, the old nurse went to look for Tattercoats; but the girl had been turned from the door by the cook, and had run away to tell her friend the gooseherd how unhappy she was because she could not go to the king's ball.

Now when the gooseherd had listened to her story, he bade her cheer up and proposed that they should go together into the town to see the king, and all the fine things; and when she looked sorrowfully down at her rags and bare feet he played a note or two upon his pipe, so gay and merry, that she forgot all about her tears and her troubles, and before she well knew, the gooseherd had taken her by the hand, and she, and he, and the geese before them, were dancing down the road towards the town.

'Even cripples can dance when they choose,' said the gooseherd.

Before they had gone very far a handsome young man, splendidly dressed, riding up, stopped to ask the way to the castle where the king was staying, and when he found that they too were going thither, he got off his horse and walked beside them along the road.

'You seem merry folk,' he said, 'and will be good company.'

'Good company, indeed,' said the gooseherd, and played a new tune that was not a dance.

It was a curious tune, and it made the strange young man stare and stare and stare at Tattercoats till he couldn't see her rags. Till he couldn't, to tell the truth, see anything but her beautiful face.

Then he said, 'You are the most beautiful maiden in the world. Will you marry me?'

Then the gooseherd smiled to himself, and played sweeter than ever.

But Tattercoats laughed. 'Not I,' said she, 'you would be finely put to shame, and so would I be, if you took a goose-girl for your wife! Go and ask one of the great ladies you will see tonight at the king's ball and do not flout poor Tattercoats.'

But the more she refused him the sweeter the pipe played, and the deeper the young man fell in love; till at last he begged her to come that night at twelve to the king's ball, just as she was, with the gooseherd and his geese, in her torn petticoat and bare feet, and see if he wouldn't dance with her before the king, and the lords and ladies, and present her to them all, as his dear and honoured bride.

Now at first Tattercoats said she would not; but the gooseherd said, 'Take fortune when it comes, little one.'

So when night came, and the hall in the castle was full of light and music, and the lords and ladies were dancing before the king, just as the clock struck twelve, Tattercoats and the gooseherd, followed by his flock of noisy geese, hissing and swaying their heads, entered at the great doors, and walked straight up the ballroom, while on either side the ladies whispered, the lords laughed, and the king seated at the far end stared in amazement.

But as they came in front of the throne Tattercoats' lover rose from beside the king, and came to meet her. Taking her by the hand, he kissed her thrice before them all, and turned to the king.

'Father!' he said – for it was the prince himself – 'I have made my choice, and here is my bride, the loveliest girl in all the land, and the sweetest as well!'

Before he had finished speaking the gooseherd had put his pipe to his lips and played a few notes that sounded like a bird singing far off in the woods; and as he played Tattercoats' rags were changed to shining robes sewn with glittering jewels, a golden crown lay upon her golden hair, and the flock of geese behind her became a crowd of dainty pages, bearing her long train.

And as the king rose to greet her as his daughter the trumpets sounded loudly in honour of the new princess, and the people outside in the street said to each other: 'Ah! now the prince has chosen for his wife the loveliest girl in all the land!'

But the gooseherd was never seen again, and no one knew what became of him; while the old lord went home once more to his palace by the sea, for he could not stay at court when he had sworn never to look on his granddaughter's face.

So there he still sits by his window – if you could only see him, as you may someday – weeping more bitterly than ever. And his white hair has bound him to the stones, and the river of his tears runs away to the great sea.

The Three Feathers

Once upon a time there lived a girl who was wooed and married by a man she never saw; for he came a-courting her after nightfall, and when they were married he never came home till it was dark, and always left before dawn.

Still he was good and kind to her, giving her everything her heart could desire, so she was well content for a while. But, after a bit, some of her friends, doubtless full of envy for her good luck, began to whisper that the unseen husband must have something dreadful the matter with him which made him averse to being seen.

Now from the very beginning the girl had wondered why her lover did not come a-courting her as other girls' lovers came, openly and by day, and though, at first, she paid no heed to her neighbours' nods and winks, she began at last to think there might be something in what they said. So she determined to see for herself, and one night when she heard her husband come into her room, she lit her candle suddenly and saw him.

And lo, and behold! he was handsome as handsome; beautiful enough to make every woman in the world fall in love with him on the spot. But even as she got her glimpse of him, he changed into a big brown bird which looked at her with eyes full of anger and blame.

'Because you have done this faithless thing,' it said, 'you will see me no more, unless for seven long years and a day you serve for me faithfully.'

And she cried with tears and sobs, 'I will serve seven times seven years and a day if you will only come back. Tell me what I am to do.'

Then the bird husband said, 'I will place you in service, and there you must remain and do good work for seven years and a day, and you must listen to no man who may seek to beguile you to leave that service. If you do I will never return.'

To this the girl agreed, and the bird, spreading its broad brown wings, carried her to a big mansion.

'Here they need a laundry-maid,' said the bird-husband. 'Go in, ask to see the mistress, and say you will do the work; but remember you must do it for seven years and a day.'

'But I cannot do it for seven days,' answered the girl. 'I cannot wash or iron.'

'That matters nothing,' replied the bird. 'All you have to do is to pluck three feathers from under my wing close to my heart, and these feathers will do your bidding whatever it may be. You will only have to put them on your hand, and say, "By virtue of these three feathers from over my true love's heart may this be done," and it will be done.'

So the girl plucked three feathers from under the bird's wing, and after that the bird flew away.

Then the girl did as she was bidden, and the lady of the house engaged her for the place. And never was such a quick laundress; for, see you, she had only to go into the wash-house, bolt the door and close the shutters, so that no one should see what she was at; then she would out with the three feathers and say, 'By virtue of these three feathers from over my true love's heart may the copper be lit, the clothes sorted, washed, boiled, dried, folded, mangled, ironed,' and lo! there they came tumbling on to the table, clean and white, quite ready to be put away. So her mistress set great store by her and said there never was such a good laundry-maid. Thus four years passed and there was no talk of her leaving. But the other servants grew jealous of her, all the more so because, being a very pretty girl, all the menservants fell in love with her and wanted to marry her.

But she would have none of them, because she was always waiting and longing for the day when her bird-husband would come back to her in man's form.

Now one of the men who wanted her was the stout butler, and one day as he was coming back from the ciderhouse he chanced to stop by the laundry, and he heard a voice say, 'By virtue of these three feathers from over my true love's heart may the copper be lit, the clothes sorted, boiled, dried, folded, mangled, and ironed.'

He thought this very queer, so he peeped through the keyhole. And there was the girl sitting at her ease in a chair, while all the clothes came flying to the table ready and fit to put away.

Well, that night he went to the girl and said that if she turned up her nose at him and his proposal any longer, he would up and tell the mistress that her fine laundress was nothing but a witch; and then, even if she were not burnt alive, she would lose her place.

Now the girl was in great distress what to do, since if she were not faithful to her bird-husband or if she failed to serve her seven years and a day in one service, he would alike fail to return; so she made an excuse by saying she could think of no one who could give her enough money to satisfy her.

At this the stout butler laughed. 'Money?' said he, 'I have seventy pounds laid by with master. Won't that satisfy thee?'

'Happen it would,' she replied.

So the very next night the butler came to her with the seventy pounds in golden sovereigns, and she held out her apron and took them, saying she was content; for she had thought of a plan. Now as they were going upstairs together she stopped and said: 'Mr Butler, excuse me for a minute. I have left the shutters of the wash-house open, and I must shut them, or they will be banging all night and disturb master and missus!'

Now though the butler was stout and beginning to grow old, he was anxious to seem young and gallant; so he said at once: 'Excuse me, my beauty, you shall not go. I will go and shut them. I shan't be a moment!'

So off he set, and no sooner had he gone than she out with her three feathers, and putting them on her hand, said in a hurry: 'By virtue of the three feathers from over my true love's heart may the shutters never cease banging till morning, and may Mr Butler's hands be busy trying to shut them.'

And so it happened.

Mr Butler shut the shutters, but – bru–u–u! there they were

hanging open again. Then he shut them once more, and this time they hit him on the face as they flew open. Yet he couldn't stop; he had to go on. So there he was the whole livelong night. Such a cursing, and banging, and swearing, and shutting, never was, until dawn came and, too tired to be really angry, he crept back to his bed, resolving that come what might he would not tell what had happened to him and thus get the laugh on him. So he kept his own counsel, and the girl kept the seventy pounds, and laughed in her sleeve at her would-be lover.

Now after a time the coachman, a spruce middle-aged man, who had long wanted to marry the clever, pretty laundry-maid, going to the pump to get water for his horses overheard her giving orders to the three feathers, and peeping through the keyhole as the butler had done, saw her sitting at her ease in a chair while the clothes, all washed, and ironed, and mangled came flying to the table.

So, just as the butler had done, he went to the girl and said, 'I have you now, my pretty. Don't dare to turn up your nose at me, for if you do I'll tell mistress you are a witch.'

Then the girl said quite calmly, 'I look on no one who has no money.'

'If that is all,' replied the coachman, 'I have forty pounds laid by with master. That I'll bring and ask for payment tomorrow night.'

So when the night came the girl held out her apron for the money, and as she was going up the stairs, she stopped suddenly and said, 'Goody me! I've left my clothes on the line. Stop a bit till I fetch them in.'

Now the coachman was really a very polite fellow, so he said at once: 'Let me go. It is a cold, windy night and you'll be catching your death.'

So off he went, and the girl out with her feathers and said: 'By virtue of the three feathers from over my true love's heart may the clothes slash and blow about till dawn, and may Mr Coachman not be able to gather them up or take his hand from the job.'

And when she had said this she went quietly to bed, for she

knew what would happen. And sure enough it did. Never was such a night as Mr Coachman spent with the wet clothes flittering and fluttering about his ears, and the sheets wrapping him into a bundle, and tripping him up, while the towels slashed at his legs. But though he smarted all over he had to go on till dawn came, and then a very weary woebegone coachman couldn't even creep away to his bed, for he had to feed and water his horses! And he, also, kept his own counsel for fear of the laugh going against him; so the clever laundry-maid put the forty pounds with the seventy in her box, and went on with her work gaily.

But after a time the footman, who was quite an honest lad and truly in love, going by the laundry peeped through the keyhole to get a glimpse of his dearest dear, and what should he see but her sitting at her ease in a chair, and the clothes coming all ready folded and ironed on to the table.

Now when he saw this he was greatly troubled. So he went to his master and drew out all his savings; and then he went to the girl and told her that he would have to tell the mistress what he had seen, unless she consented to marry him.

'You see!' he said, 'I have been with master this while back, and have saved up this bit, and you have been here this long while back and must have saved as well. So let us put the two together and make a home, or else stay on in service as pleases you.'

Well, she tried to put him off; but he insisted so much that at last she said: 'James! there's a dear, run down to the cellar and fetch me a drop of brandy. You've made me feel so queer!'

And when he had gone she out with her three feathers, and said, 'By virtue of the three feathers from over my true love's heart may James not be able to pour the brandy straight, except down his throat.'

Well! so it happened. Try as he would, James could not get the brandy into the glass. It splashed a few drops into it, then it trickled over his hand, and fell on the floor. And so it went on and on till he grew so tired that he thought he needed a dram himself. So he tossed off the few drops and began again; but he fared no better. So he took another little dram, and went on, and on and on, till he got quite fuddled. And who should come down into the cellar but his master to know what the smell of brandy meant!

Now James the footman was truthful as well as honest, so he told the master how he had come down to get the sick laundry-maid a drop of brandy, but that his hand had shaken so that he could not pour it out, and it had fallen on the ground, and that the smell of it had got to his head.

'A likely tale,' said the master, and beat James soundly.

Then the master went to the mistress, his wife, and said: 'Send away that laundry-maid of yours. Something has come over my men. They have all drawn out their savings as if they were going to be married, yet they don't leave, and I believe that girl is at the bottom of it.'

But his wife would not hear of the laundry-maid being blamed; she was the best servant in the house, and worth all the rest of them put together; it was his men who were at fault. So they quarrelled over it: but in the end the master gave in, and after this there was peace, since the mistress bade the girl keep herself to herself, and none of the men would say ought of what had happened for fear of the laughter of the other servants.

So it went on until one day when the master was going a-driving, the coach was at the door, and the footman was standing to hold the coach open, and the butler on the steps all ready, when who should pass through the yard, so saucy and bright, with a great basket of clean clothes, but the laundry-maid. And the sight of her was too much for James, the footman, who began to blub.

'She is a wicked girl,' he said. 'She got all my savings, and got me a good thrashing besides.'

Then the coachman grew bold. 'Did she?' he said. 'That was nothing to what she served me.' So he up and told all about the wet clothes and the awful job he had had the livelong night. Now the butler on the steps swelled with rage until he nearly burst, and at last he out with his night of banging shutters.

'And one,' he said, 'hit me on the nose.'

This settled the three men, and they agreed to tell their master the moment he came out, and get the girl sent about her business. Now the laundry-maid had sharp ears and had paused behind a door to listen; so when she heard this she knew she must do something to stop it. So she out with her three feathers and said, 'By virtue of the three feathers from over my true love's heart may there be striving as to who suffered most between the men so that they get into the pond for a ducking.'

Well! no sooner had she said the words than the three men began disputing as to which of them had been served the worst; then James up and hit the stout butler, giving him a black eye, and the fat butler fell upon James and pummelled him hard, while the coachman scrambled from his box and belaboured them both, and the laundry-maid stood by laughing.

So out comes the master, but none of them would listen, and each wanted to be heard, and fought, and shoved, and pummelled away until they shoved each other into the pond, and all got a fine ducking.

Then the master asked the girl what it was all about, and she said: 'They all wanted to tell a story against me because I won't marry them, and one said his was the best, and the next said his was the best, so they fell a-quarelling as to which was the likeliest story to get me into trouble. But they are well punished, so there is no need to do more.'

Then the master went to his wife and said, 'You are right. That laundry-maid of yours is a very wise girl.'

So the butler and the coachman and James had nothing to do but look sheepish and hold their tongues, and the laundry-maid went on with her duties without further trouble.

Then when the seven years and a day were over who should drive up to the door in a fine gilded coach but the bird-husband restored to his shape as a handsome young man. And he carried the laundry-maid off to be his wife again, and her master and mistress were so pleased at her good fortune that they ordered all the other servants to stand on the steps and give her good luck. So as she passed the butler she put a bag with seventy pounds in it into his hand and said sweetly, 'That is to recompense you for shutting the shutters.' And when she passed the coachman she put a bag with forty pounds into his hand and said, 'That is your reward for bringing in the clothes.' But when she passed the footman she gave him a bag with a hundred pounds in it, and laughed, saying, 'That is for the drop of brandy you never brought me!'

So she drove off with her handsome husband, and lived happy ever after.

Lazy Jack

Once upon a time there was a boy whose name was Jack, and he lived with his mother on a common. They were very poor, and the old woman got her living by spinning, but Jack was so lazy that he would do nothing but bask in the sun in the hot weather, and sit by the corner of the hearth in the wintertime. So they called him Lazy Jack. His mother could not get him to do anything for her, and at last told him, one Monday, that if he did not begin to work for his porridge she would turn him out to get his living as he could.

This roused Jack, and he went out and hired himself for the next day to a neighbouring farmer for a penny; but as he was coming home, never having had any money before, he lost it in passing over a brook.

'You stupid boy,' said his mother, 'you should have put it in your pocket.'

'I'll do so another time,' replied Jack.

Well, the next day, Jack went out again and hired himself to a cowkeeper, who gave him a jar of milk for his day's work. Jack took the jar and put it into the large pocket of his jacket, spilling it all, long before he got home.

'Dear me!' said the old woman; 'you should have carried it on your head.'

'I'll do so another time,' said Jack.

So the following day, Jack hired himself again to a farmer, who agreed to give him a cream cheese for his services. In the evening Jack took the cheese, and went home with it on his head. By the time he got home the cheese was all spoilt, part of it being lost, and part matted with his hair.

'You stupid lout,' said his mother, 'you should have carried it very carefully in your hands.'

'I'll do so another time,' replied Jack.

Now the next day, Lazy Jack again went out, and hired himself to a baker, who would give him nothing for his work but a large tomcat. Jack took the cat, and began carrying it very carefully in his hands, but in a short time pussy scratched him so much that he was compelled to let it go.

When he got home, his mother said to him, 'You silly fellow, you should have tied it with a string, and dragged it along after you.'

'I'll do so another time,' said Jack.

So on the following day, Jack hired himself to a butcher, who rewarded him by the handsome present of a shoulder of mutton. Jack took the mutton, tied it to a string, and trailed it along after him in the dirt, so that by the time he had got home the meat was completely spoilt. His mother was this time quite out of patience with him, for the next day was Sunday, and she was obliged to do with cabbage for her dinner.

'You ninney-hammer,' said she to her son; 'you should have carried it on your shoulder.'

'I'll do so another time,' replied Jack.

Well, on the Monday, Lazy Jack went once more, and hired himself to a cattle-keeper, who gave him a donkey for his trouble. Now though Jack was strong he found it hard to hoist the donkey on his shoulders, but at last he did it, and began walking home slowly with his prize. Now it so happened that in the course of his journey he passed a house where a rich man lived with his only daughter, a beautiful girl, who was deaf and dumb. And she had never laughed in her life, and the doctors said she would never speak till somebody made her laugh. So the father had given out that any man who made her laugh would receive her hand in marriage. Now this young lady happened to be looking out of the window when Jack was passing by with the donkey on his shoulders; and the poor beast with its legs sticking up in the air was kicking violently and hee-hawing with all its might. Well, the sight was so comical that she burst out into a great fit of laughter, and immediately recovered her speech and hearing. Her father was overjoyed, and fulfilled his promise by marrying her to Lazy Jack, who was thus made a rich gentleman. They lived in a large house, and Jack's mother lived with them in great happiness until she died.

Jack the Giant-Killer

I

When good King Arthur reigned with Guinevere his queen, there lived, near the Land's End in Cornwall, a farmer who had one only son called Jack. Now Jack was brisk and ready; of such a lively wit that none nor nothing could worst him.

In those days, the Mount of St Michael in Cornwall was the fastness of a hugeous giant whose name was Cormoran.

He was full eighteen feet in height, some three yards about his middle, of a grim fierce face, and he was the terror of all the countryside. He lived in a cave amidst the rocky Mount, and when he desired victuals he would wade across the tides to the mainland and furnish himself forth with all that came in his way. The poor folk and the rich folk alike ran out of their houses and hid themselves when they heard the swish-swash of his big feet in the water; for if he saw them, he would think nothing of broiling half a dozen or so of them for breakfast. As it was, he seized their cattle by the score, carrying off half a dozen fat oxen on his back at a time, and hanging sheep and pigs to his waistbelt like bunches of dip-candles. Now this had gone on for long years, and the poor folk of Cornwall were in despair, for none could put an end to the giant Cormoran.

It so happened that one market day Jack, then quite a young lad, found the town upside down over some new exploit of the giant's. Women were weeping, men were cursing, and the magistrates were sitting in council over what was to be done. But none could suggest a plan. Then Jack, blithe and gay, went up to the magistrates, and with a fine courtesy – for he was ever polite – asked them what reward would be given to him who killed the giant Cormoran?

'The treasures of the Giant's cave,' quoth they.

'Every whit of it?' quoth Jack, who was never to be done.

'To the last farthing,' quoth they.

'Then will I undertake the task,' said Jack, and forthwith set about the business.

It was wintertime, and having got himself a horn, a pickaxe, and a shovel, he went over to the Mount in the dark evening, set to work, and before dawn he had dug a pit no less than twenty-two feet deep and nigh as big across. This he covered with long thin sticks and straw, sprinkling a little loose mould over all to make it look like solid ground. So, just as dawn was breaking, he planted himself fair and square on the side of the pit that was farthest from the giant's cave, raised the horn to his lips, and with full blast sounded:

'Tantivy! Tantivy! Tantivy!'

just as he would have done had he been hunting a fox.

Of course this woke the giant, who rushed in a rage out of his cave, and seeing little Jack, fair and square blowing away at his horn, as calm and cool as may be, he became still more angry, and made for the disturber of his rest, bawling out, 'I'll teach you to wake a giant, you little whippersnapper. You shall pay dearly for your tantivys. I'll take you and broil you whole for break – '

He had only got as far as this when crash – he fell into the pit! So there was a break indeed; such an one that it caused the very foundations of the Mount to shake.

But Jack shook with laughter. 'Ho, ho!' he cried, 'how about breakfast now, sir giant? Will you have me broiled or baked? And will no diet serve you but poor little Jack? Faith! I've got you in Lob's pound now! You're in the stocks for bad behaviour, and I'll plague you as I like. Would I had rotten eggs; but this will do as well.' And with that he up with his pickaxe and dealt the giant Cormoran such a most weighty knock on the very crown of his head, that he killed him on the spot.

Whereupon Jack calmly filled the pit with earth again and went to search the cave, where he found much treasure.

Now when the magistrates heard of Jack's great exploit, they proclaimed that henceforth he should he known as –

Jack the Giant-Killer.

And they presented him with a sword and belt, on which these words were embroidered in gold:

Here's the valiant Cornishman,
Who slew the giant Cormoran.

II

Of course the news of Jack's victory soon spread over all England, so that another giant named Blunderbore, who lived to the north, hearing of it, vowed if ever he came across Jack he would be revenged upon him. Now this giant Blunderbore was lord of an enchanted castle that stood in the middle of a lonesome forest.

It so happened that Jack, about four months after he had killed Cormoran, had occasion to journey into Wales, and on the road he passed this forest. Weary with walking, and finding a pleasant fountain by the wayside, he lay down to rest and was soon fast asleep.

Now the giant Blunderbore, coming to the well for water, found Jack sleeping, and knew by the lines embroidered on his belt that here was the far-famed giant-killer. Rejoiced at his luck the giant, without more ado, lifted Jack to his shoulder and began to carry him through the wood to the enchanted castle.

But the rustling of the boughs awakened Jack, who, finding himself already in the clutches of the giant, was terrified; nor was his alarm decreased by seeing the courtyard of the castle all strewn with men's bones.

'Yours will be with them ere long,' said Blunderbore as he locked poor Jack into an immense chamber above the castle gateway. It had a high-pitched, beamed roof, and one window that looked down the road. Here poor Jack was to stay while Blunderbore went to fetch his brother-giant who lived in the same wood, that he might share in the feast.

Now, after a time, Jack, watching through the window, saw the two giants tramping hastily down the road, eager for their dinner.

'Now,' quoth Jack to himself, 'my death or my deliverance is at hand.' For he had thought out a plan. In one corner of the room he had seen two strong cords. These he took, and making a cunning noose at the end of each, he hung them out of the window, and as the giants were unlocking the iron door of the gate managed to slip them over their heads without their noticing it. Then, quick as thought, he tied the other ends to a beam, so that as the giants moved on the nooses tightened and throttled them until they grew black in the face. Seeing this, Jack slid down the ropes, and drawing his sword, slew them both.

So, taking the keys of the castle, he unlocked all the doors and set free three beauteous ladies who, tied by the hair of their heads, he found almost starved to death.

'Sweet ladies,' quoth Jack kneeling on one knee – for he was ever polite – 'here are the keys of this enchanted castle. I have destroyed the giant Blunderbore and his brutish brother, and thus have restored to you your liberty. These keys should bring you all else you require.'

So saying he proceeded on his journey to Wales.

III

He travelled as fast as he could; perhaps too fast, for, losing his way he found himself benighted and far from any habitation. He wandered on always in hopes, until on entering a narrow valley he came on a very large, dreary-looking house standing alone. Being anxious for shelter he went up to the door and knocked. You may imagine his surprise and alarm when the summons was answered by a giant with two heads. But though this monster's look was exceedingly fierce, his manners were quite polite. The truth being that he was a Welsh giant, and as such double-faced and smooth, given to gaining his malicious ends by show of false friendship.

So he welcomed Jack heartily in a strong Welsh accent, and

prepared a bedroom for him, where he was left with kind wishes for a good rest. Jack, however, was too tired to sleep well, and as he lay awake, he overheard his host muttering to himself in the next room. Having very keen ears he was able to make out these words or something like them:

> 'Though here you lodge with me this night,
> You shall not see the morning light.
> My club shall dash your brains outright.'

'Say'st thou so!' quoth Jack to himself, starting up at once. 'So that is your Welsh trick, is it? But I will be even with you.' Then, leaving his bed, he laid a big billet of wood among the blankets and, taking one of these to keep himself warm, made himself snug in a corner of the room, pretending to snore, so as to make Mr Giant think he was asleep.

And sure enough, after a little time in came the monster on tiptoe as if treading on eggs, and carrying a big club. Then –

Whack! Whack! Whack!

Jack could hear the bed being belaboured until the giant thinking every bone of his guest's skin must be broken, stole out of the room again; whereupon Jack went calmly to bed once more and slept soundly! Next morning the giant couldn't believe his eyes when he saw Jack coming down the stairs fresh and hearty.

'Odds splutter hur nails!' he cried astonished. 'Did ye sleep well? Was there not nothing felt in the night?'

'Oh,' replied Jack, laughing in his sleeve, 'I think a rat did come and give me two or three flaps of his tail.'

On this the giant was dumbfoundered, and led Jack to breakfast, bringing him a bowl which held at least four gallons of hasty-pudding, and bidding him, as a man of such mettle, eat the lot. Now Jack when travelling wore under his cloak a leathern bag to carry his things withal; so, quick as thought, he hitched this round in front with the opening just under his chin; thus, as he ate, he could slip the best part of the pudding into it without the giant's being any the wiser. So they sat down to breakfast, the giant gobbling down his own measure of hasty-pudding, while Jack made away with his.

'See,' says crafty Jack when he had finished. 'I'll show you a trick worth two of yours,' and with that he up with a carving-knife and ripping up the leathern bag out fell all the hasty-pudding on the floor!

'Odds splutter hur nails!' cried the giant, not to be outdone. 'Hur can do that hurself!' Whereupon he seized the carving-knife, and ripping open his own belly fell down dead.

Thus was Jack quit of the Welsh giant.

IV

Now it so happened that in those days when gallant knights were always seeking adventures, King Arthur's only son, a very valiant prince, begged of his father a large sum of money to enable him to journey to Wales, and there strive to set free a certain beautiful lady who was possessed by seven evil spirits. In vain the king denied him; so at last he gave way and the prince set out with two horses, one of which he rode, the other he had laden with gold pieces. Now after some days' journey the prince came to a market-town in Wales where there was a great commotion. On asking the reason for it he was told that, according to law, the corpse of a very generous man had been arrested on its way to the grave, because, in life, it had owed large sums to the moneylenders.

'That is a cruel law,' said the young prince. 'Go, bury the dead in peace, and let the creditors come to my lodgings; I will pay the debts of the dead.'

So the creditors came, but they were so numerous that by evening the prince had but twopence left for himself, and could not go further on his journey.

Now it so happened that Jack the Giant-Killer on his way to Wales passed through the town, and, hearing of the prince's plight, was so taken with his kindness and generosity that he determined to be the prince's servant. So this was agreed upon, and next morning, after Jack had paid the reckoning with his last farthing, the two set out together. But as they were leaving the town, an old woman ran after the prince and called out, 'Justice! Justice! The dead man owed me twopence these seven years. Pay me as well as the others.'

And the prince, kind and generous, put his hand to his pocket and gave the old woman the twopence that was left to him. So now they had not a penny between them, and when the sun grew low the prince said: 'Jack! Since we have no money how are we to get a night's lodging?'

Then Jack replied, 'We shall do well enough, master; for

within two or three miles of this place there lives a huge and monstrous giant with three heads who can fight four hundred men in armour and make them fly from him like chaff before the wind.'

'And what good will that be to us?' quoth the prince. 'He will for sure chop us up in a mouthful.'

'Nay,' said Jack, laughing. 'Let me go and prepare the way for you. By all accounts this giant is a dolt. Mayhap I may manage better than that.'

So the prince remained where he was, and Jack pricked his steed at full speed till he came to the giant's castle, at the gate of which he knocked so loud that he made the neighbouring hills resound.

On this the giant roared from within in a voice like thunder: 'Who's there?'

Then said Jack as bold as brass, 'None but your poor cousin Jack.'

'Cousin Jack!' quoth the giant astounded. 'And what news with my poor cousin Jack?' For, see you, he was quite taken aback; so Jack made haste to reassure him.

'Dear coz, heavy news, God wot!'

'Heavy news,' echoed the giant, half afraid. 'God wot no heavy news can come to me. Have I not three heads? Can I not fight five hundred men in armour? Can I not make them fly like chaff before the wind?'

'True,' replied crafty Jack, 'but I came to warn you because the great King Arthur's son with a thousand men in armour is on his way to kill you.'

At this the giant began to shiver and to shake. 'Ah! Cousin Jack! Kind cousin Jack! This is heavy news indeed,' quoth he. 'Tell me, what am I to do?'

'Hide yourself in the vault,' says crafty Jack, 'and I will lock and bolt and bar you in, and keep the key till the prince has gone. So you will be safe.'

Then the giant made haste and ran down into the vault and Jack locked and bolted and barred him in. Then, having him thus secure, he went and fetched his master, and the two made

themselves heartily merry over what the giant was to have had for supper, while the miserable monster shivered and shook with fright in the underground vault.

Well, after a good night's rest Jack woke his master in early morn, and having furnished him well with gold and silver from the giant's treasure, bade him ride three miles forward on his journey. So when Jack judged that the prince was pretty well out of the smell of the giant, he took the key and let his prisoner out. He was half dead with cold and damp, but very grateful; and he begged Jack to let him know what he would be given as a reward for saving the giant's life and castle from destruction, and he should have it.

'You're very welcome,' said Jack, who always had his eyes about him. 'All I want is the old coat and cap, together with the rusty old sword and slippers which are at your bed-head.'

When the giant heard this he sighed, and shook his head. 'You don't know what you are asking,' quoth he. 'They are the most precious things I possess, but as I have promised, you must have them. The coat will make you invisible, the cap will tell you all you want to know, the sword will cut asunder whatever you strike, and the slippers will take you wherever you want to go in the twinkling of an eye!'

So Jack, overjoyed, rode away with the coat and cap, the sword and the slippers, and soon overtook his master; and they rode on together until they reached the castle where the beautiful lady lived whom the prince sought.

Now she was very beautiful, for all she was possessed of seven devils, and when she heard the prince sought her as a suitor, she smiled and ordered a splendid banquet to be prepared for his reception. And she sat on his right hand, and plied him with food and drink.

And when the repast was over she took out her own handkerchief and wiped his lips gently, and said with a smile: 'I have a task for you, my lord! You must show me that kerchief tomorrow morning or lose your head.'

And with that she put the handkerchief in her bosom and said, 'Good-night!'

The prince was in despair, but Jack said nothing till his master was in bed. Then he put on the old cap he had got from the giant, and lo! in a minute he knew all that he wanted to know. So, in the dead of the night, when the beautiful lady called on one of her familiar spirits to carry her to Lucifer himself, Jack was beforehand with her, and putting on his coat of darkness and his slippers of swiftness, was there as soon as she was. And when she gave the handkerchief to the Devil, bidding him keep it safe, and he put it away on a high shelf, Jack just up and nipped it away in a trice!

So the next morning when the beauteous enchanted lady looked to see the prince crestfallen, he just made a fine bow and presented her with the handkerchief.

At first she was terribly disappointed, but as the day drew on, she ordered another and still more splendid repast to be got ready. And this time when the repast was over, she kissed the prince full on the lips and said: 'I have a task for you, my lover. Show me tomorrow morning the last lips I kiss tonight or you lose your head.'

Then the prince, who by this time was head over ears in love, said tenderly, 'If you will kiss none but mine, I will.'

Now the beauteous lady for all she was possessed by seven

devils could not but see that the prince was a very handsome young man; so she blushed a little, and said: 'That is neither here nor there: you must show me them, or death is your portion.'

So the prince went to his bed, sorrowful as before; but Jack put on the cap of knowledge and knew in a moment all he wanted to know.

Thus when, in the dead of the night, the beauteous lady called on her familiar spirit to take her to Lucifer himself, Jack in his coat of darkness and his shoes of swiftness was there before her.

'Thou hast betrayed me once,' said the beauteous lady to Lucifer, frowning, 'by letting go my handkerchief. Now will I give thee something none can steal, and so best the prince, king's son though he be.'

With that she kissed the loathly demon full on the lips, and left him. Whereupon Jack with one blow of the rusty sword of strength, cut off Lucifer's head and, hiding it under his coat of darkness, brought it back to his master.

Thus next morning when the beauteous lady, with malice in her beautiful eyes, asked the prince to show her the lips she had last kissed, he pulled out the demon's head by the horns. On that the seven devils, which possessed the poor lady, gave seven dreadful shrieks and left her. Thus the enchantment being broken, she appeared in all her perfect beauty and goodness.

So she and the prince were married the very next morning. After which they journeyed back to the court of King Arthur, where Jack the Giant-Killer, for his many exploits, was made one of the Knights of the Round Table.

V

This, however, did not satisfy our hero, who was soon on the road again searching for giants. Now he had not gone far when he came upon one, seated on a huge block of timber near the entrance to a dark cave. He was a most terrific giant. His goggle eyes were as coals of fire, his countenance was grim and gruesome; his cheeks, like huge flitches of bacon, were covered with a stubbly beard, the bristles of which resembled rods of iron wire, while the locks of hair that fell on his brawny shoulders showed like curled snakes or hissing adders. He held a knotted iron club, and breathed so heavily you could hear him a mile away. Nothing daunted by this fearsome sight, Jack alighted from his horse and putting on his coat of darkness went close up to the giant and said softly: 'Hallo! is that you? It will not be long before I have you fast by your beard.'

So saying he made a cut with the sword of strength at the giant's head, but, somehow, missing his aim, cut off the nose instead, clean as a whistle! My goodness! How the giant roared! It was like claps of thunder, and he began to lay about him with the knotted iron club, like one possessed. But Jack in his coat of darkness easily dodged the blows, and running in behind, drove the sword up to the hilt into the giant's back, so that he fell stone dead.

Jack then cut off the head and sent it to King Arthur by a wagoner whom he hired for the purpose. After which he began to search the giant's cave to find his treasure. He passed through many windings and turnings until he came to a huge hall paved and roofed with freestone. At the upper end of this was an immense fireplace where hung an iron cauldron, the like of which, for size, Jack had never seen before. It was boiling and gave out a savoury steam; while beside it, on the right hand, stood a big massive table set out with huge platters and mugs. Here it was that the giants used to dine. Going a little further he came upon a sort of window barred with iron, and looking within beheld a vast number of miserable captives.

'Alas! Alack!' they cried on seeing him. 'Art come young man, to join us in this dreadful prison?'

'That depends,' quoth Jack; 'but first tell me wherefore you are thus held imprisoned?'

'Through no fault,' they cried at once. 'We are captives of the cruel giants and are kept here and well nourished until such time as the monsters desire a feast. Then they choose the fattest and sup off them.'

On hearing this Jack straightway unlocked the door of the prison and set the poor fellows free. Then, searching the giants'

coffers ·he divided the gold and silver equally amongst the
captives as some redress for their sufferings, and taking them to
a neighbouring castle gave them a right good feast.

VI

Now as they were all making merry over their deliverance, and
praising Jack's prowess, a messenger arrived to say that one
Thunderdell, a huge giant, with two heads, having heard of the
death of his kinsman was on his way from the northern dales to
be revenged, and was already within a mile or two of the castle,
the country folk with their flocks and herds flying before him
like chaff before the wind.

Now the castle with its gardens stood on a small island that
was surrounded by a moat twenty feet wide and thirty feet deep,
having very steep sides. And this moat was spanned by a

drawbridge. This, without a moment's delay, Jack ordered should be sawn on both sides at the middle, so as to leave only one plank uncut over which he in his invisible coat of darkness passed swiftly to meet his enemy, bearing in his hand the wonderful sword of strength.

Now though the giant could not, of course, see Jack, he could smell him, for giants have keen noses. Therefore Thunderdell cried out in a voice like his name:

> 'Fee, fi, fo, fum!
> I smell the blood of an Englishman.
> Be he alive, or be he dead,
> I'll grind his bones to make my bread!'

'Is that so?' quoth Jack, cheerful as ever. 'Then art thou a monstrous miller for sure!'

On this the giant peering round everywhere for a glimpse of his foe, shouted out: 'Art thou, indeed, the villain who hath killed so many of my kinsmen? Then, indeed, will I tear thee to pieces with my teeth, suck thy blood, and grind thy bones to powder.'

'Thou'lt have to catch me first,' quoth Jack, laughing, and throwing off his coat of darkness and putting on his slippers of swiftness he began nimbly to lead the giant a pretty dance, he leaping and doubling light as a feather, the monster following heavily like a walking tower, so that the very foundations of the earth seemed to shake at every step. At this game the onlookers nearly split their sides with laughter, until Jack, judging there had been enough of it, made for the drawbridge, ran neatly over the single plank, and reaching the other side waited in teasing fashion for his adversary.

On came the giant at full speed, foaming at the mouth with rage, and flourishing his club. But when he came to the middle of the bridge his great weight, of course, broke the plank, and there he was fallen headlong into the moat, rolling and wallowing like a whale, plunging from place to place yet unable to get out and be revenged.

The spectators greeted his efforts with roars of laughter, and Jack himself was at first too overcome with merriment to do more than scoff. At last, however, he went for a rope, cast it over the giant's two heads, and so with the help of a team of horses drew them shorewards, where two blows from the sword of strength settled the matter.

VII

After some time spent in mirth and pastimes, Jack began once more to grow restless, and taking leave of his companions set out for fresh adventures.

He travelled far and fast, through woods, and vales, and hills, till at last he came, late at night, on a lonesome house set at the foot of a high mountain.

He knocked at the door, and it was opened by an old man whose head was white as snow.

'Father,' said Jack, ever courteous, 'can you lodge a benighted traveller?'

'Ay, that will I, and welcome to my poor cottage,' replied the old man.

Whereupon Jack came in, and after supper they sat together chatting in friendly fashion. Then it was that the old man, seeing by Jack's belt that he was the famous Giant-Killer, spoke in this wise: 'My son! You are the great conqueror of evil monsters. Now close by there lives one well worthy of your prowess. On the top of yonder high hill is an enchanted castle kept by a giant named Galligantua, who, by the help of a wicked old magician, inveigles many beautiful ladies and valiant knights into the castle, where they are transformed into all sorts of birds and beasts, yea, even into fishes and insects. There they live pitiably in confinement; but most of all do I grieve for a duke's daughter whom they kidnapped in her father's garden, bringing her hither in a burning chariot drawn by fiery dragons. Her form is that of a white hind; and though many valiant knights have tried their utmost to break the spell and work her deliverance, none have succeeded; for, see you, at the entrance to the castle are two dreadful griffins who destroy everyone who attempts to pass them by.'

Now Jack bethought him of the coat of darkness which had served him so well before, and he put on the cap of knowledge, and in an instant he knew what had to be done. Then the very next morning, at dawn-time, Jack arose and put on his invisible coat and his slippers of swiftness. And in the twinkling of an eye there he was on the top of the mountain! And there were the two griffins guarding the castle gates – horrible creatures with forked tails and tongues.

But they could not see him because of the coat of darkness, so he passed them by unharmed.

And hung to the doors of the gateway he found a golden trumpet on a silver chain, and beneath it was engraved in red lettering:

> 'Whoever shall this trumpet blow
> Will cause the giant's overthrow.
> The black enchantment he will break,
> And gladness out of sadness make.'

No sooner had Jack read these words than he put the horn to his lips and blew a loud

> 'Tantivy! Tantivy! Tantivy!'

Now at the very first note the castle trembled to its vast foundations, and before he had finished the measure, both the giant and the magician were biting their thumbs and tearing their hair, knowing that their wickedness must now come to an end. But the giant showed fight and took up his club to defend himself; whereupon Jack, with one clean cut of the sword of strength, severed his head from his body, and would doubtless have done the same to the magician, but that the latter was a coward, and, calling up a whirlwind, was swept away by it into the air, nor has he ever been seen or heard of since. The enchantments being thus broken, all the valiant knights and beautiful ladies who had been transformed into birds and beasts and fishes and reptiles and insects, returned to their proper shapes, including the duke's daughter, who, from being a white hind, showed as the most beauteous maiden upon whom the sun ever shone. Now, no sooner had this occurred than the whole castle vanished away in a cloud of smoke, and from that moment giants vanished also from the land.

So Jack, when he had presented the head of Galligantua to King Arthur, together with all the lords and ladies he had delivered from enchantment, found he had nothing more to do. As a reward for past services, however, King Arthur bestowed the hand of the duke's daughter upon honest Jack the Giant-Killer. So married they were, and the whole kingdom was filled with joy at their wedding. Furthermore, the king bestowed on Jack a noble castle with a magnificent estate belonging thereto, whereon he, his lady and their children lived in great joy and content for the rest of their days.

The Three Sillies

Once upon a time, when folk were not so wise as they are nowadays, there lived a farmer and his wife who had one daughter. And she, being a pretty lass, was courted by the young squire when he came home from his travels.

Now every evening he would stroll over from the hall to see her and stop to supper in the farmhouse, and every evening the daughter would go down into the cellar to draw the cider for supper.

So one evening when she had gone down to draw the cider and had turned the tap as usual, she happened to look up at the ceiling, and there she saw a big wooden mallet stuck in one of the beams.

It must have been there for ages and ages, for it was all covered with cobwebs; but somehow or another she had never noticed it before, and at once she began thinking how dangerous it was to have the mallet just there.

'For,' thought she, 'supposing him and me was married, and supposing we was to have a son, and supposing he were to grow up to be a man, and supposing he were to come down to draw cider like as I'm doing, and supposing the mallet were to fall on his head and kill him, how dreadful it would be!'

And with that she put down the candle she was carrying and seating herself on a cask began to cry. And she cried and cried and cried.

Now, upstairs, they began to wonder why she was so long drawing the cider; so after a time her mother went down to the cellar to see what had come to her and found her, seated on the cask, crying ever so hard, and the cider running all over the floor.

'Lawks a mercy me!' cried her mother, 'whatever is the matter?'

'Oh, mother!' says she between her sobs, 'it's that horrid mallet. Supposing him and me was married and supposing we was to have a son, and supposing he was to grow up to be a man, and supposing he was to come down to draw cider like as I'm doing, and supposing the mallet were to fall on his head and kill him, how dreadful it would be!'

'Dear heart!' said the mother, seating herself beside her daughter and beginning to cry: 'How dreadful it would be!'

So they both sat a-crying.

Now after a time, when they did not come back, the farmer began to wonder what had happened, and going down to the cellar found them seated side by side on the cask, crying hard, and the cider running all over the floor.

'Zounds!' says he, 'whatever is the matter?'

'Just look at that horrid mallet up there, father,' moaned the mother. 'Supposing our daughter was to marry her sweetheart, and supposing they was to have a son, and supposing he was to grow to man's estate, and supposing he was to come down to draw cider like as we're doing, and supposing that there mallet was to fall on his head and kill him, how dreadful it would be!'

'Dreadful indeed!' said the father, and seating himself beside his wife and daughter started a-crying too.

Now upstairs the young squire wanted his supper; so at last he lost patience and went down into the cellar to see for himself what they were all after. And there he found them seated side by side on the cask a-crying, with their feet all a-wash in cider, for the floor was fair flooded. So the first thing he did was to run straight and turn off the tap. Then he said:

'What are you three after, sitting there crying like babies, and letting good cider run over the floor?'

Then they all three began with one voice. 'Look at that horrid mallet! Supposing you and $\frac{me}{she}$ was married, and supposing $\frac{we}{you}$ had a son, and supposing he was to grow to man's estate and supposing he was to come down here to draw cider like as we be, and supposing that there mallet was to fall down on his head and kill him, how dreadful it would be!'

Then the young squire burst out a-laughing, and laughed till he was tired. But at last he reached up to the old mallet and pulled it out, and put it safe on the floor. And he shook his head and said, 'I've travelled far, and I've travelled fast, but never have I met with three such sillies as you three. Now I can't marry one of the three biggest sillies in the world. So I shall start again on my travels, and if I can find three bigger sillies than you three, then I'll come back and be married – not otherwise.'

So he wished them goodbye and started again on his travels, leaving them all crying; this time because the marriage was off!

Well, the young man travelled far and he travelled fast, but never did he find a bigger silly, until one day he came upon an old woman's cottage that had some grass growing on the thatched roof.

And the old woman was trying her best to cudgel her cow into going up a ladder to eat the grass. But the poor thing was afraid and durst not go. Then the old woman tried coaxing, but it wouldn't go. You never saw such a sight! The cow getting more and more flustered and obstinate, the old woman getting hotter and hotter.

At last the young squire said, 'It would be easier if *you* went up the ladder, cut the grass, and threw it down for the cow to eat.'

'A likely story that,' says the old woman. 'A cow can cut grass for herself. And the foolish thing will be quite safe up there, for I'll tie a rope round her neck, pass the rope down the chimney, and fasten t'other end to my wrist, so as when I'm doing my bit o' washing, she can't fall off the roof without my knowing it. So mind your own business, young sir.'

Well, after a while the old woman coaxed and codgered and bullied and badgered the cow up the ladder, and when she got it on to the roof she tied a rope round its neck, passed the rope down the chimney, and fastened t'other end to her wrist. Then she went about her bit of washing, and young squire he went on his way.

But he hadn't gone but a bit when he heard the awfullest hullabaloo. He galloped back and found that the cow had fallen off the roof and got strangled by the rope round its neck, while the weight of the cow had pulled the old woman by her wrist up the chimney, where she had got stuck half-way and been smothered by the soot!

'That is one bigger silly,' quoth the young squire as he journeyed on. 'So now for two more!'

He did not find any, however, till late one night he arrived at a little inn. And the inn was so full that he had to share a room with another traveller. Now his room-fellow proved quite a pleasant fellow, and they foregathered, and each slept well in his bed.

But next morning when they were dressing what does the stranger do but carefully hang his breeches on the knobs of the tallboy.

'What are you doing?' asks young squire.

'I'm putting on my breeches,' says the stranger; and with that he goes to the other end of the room, takes a little run, and tries to jump into the breeches.

But he didn't succeed, so he took another run and another try, and another and another and another, until he got quite hot and flustered, as the old woman had got over her cow that wouldn't go up the ladder. And all the time young squire was laughing fit to split, for never in his life did he see anything so comical.

Then the stranger stopped a while and mopped his face with his handkerchief, for he was all in a sweat. 'It's very well laughing,' says he, 'but breeches are the most awkwardest things to get into that ever were. It takes me the best part of an hour every morning before I get them on. How do you manage yours?'

Then young squire showed him, as well as he could for laughing, how to put on his breeches, and the stranger was ever so grateful and said he never should have thought of that way.

'So that,' quoth young squire to himself, 'is a second bigger silly.' But he travelled far, and he travelled fast without finding the third, until one bright night when the moon was shining right overhead he came upon a village. And outside the village was a pond, and round about the pond was a great crowd of villagers. And some had got rakes, and some had got pitchforks, and some had got brooms. And they were as busy as busy, shouting out, and raking, and forking, and sweeping away at the pond.

'What is the matter?' cried young squire, jumping off his horse to help. 'Has anyone fallen in?'

'Aye! Matter enough,' says they. 'Can't ee see moon's fallen into the pond, an' we can't get her out nohow?'

And with that they set to again raking, and forking, and sweeping away. Then the young squire burst out laughing, told them they were fools for their pains, and bade them look up over their heads where the moon was riding broad and full. But they wouldn't, and they wouldn't believe that what they saw in the water was only a reflection. And when he insisted they began to abuse him roundly and threaten to duck him in the pond. So he got on his horse again as quickly as he could, leaving them raking and forking and sweeping away; and for all we know they may be at it yet!

But the young squire said to himself, 'There are many more sillies in this world than I thought for; so I'll just go back and marry the farmer's daughter. She is no sillier than the rest.'

So they were married, and if they didn't live happy ever after, that has nothing to do with the story of the three sillies.

The Golden Ball

Once upon a time there lived two lasses, who were sisters, and as they came from the fair they saw a right handsome young man standing at a house door before them. They had never seen such a handsome young man before. He had gold on his cap, gold on his finger, gold on his neck, gold at his waist! And he had a golden ball in each hand. He gave a ball to each lass, saying she was to keep it; but if she lost it, she was to be hanged.

Now the younger of the lasses lost her ball, and this is how. She was by a park-paling, and she was tossing her ball, and it went up, and up, and up, till it went fair over the paling; and when she climbed to look for it, the ball ran along the green grass, and it ran right forward to the door of a house that stood there, and the ball went into the house and she saw it no more.

So she was taken away to be hanged by the neck till she was dead, because she had lost her ball.

But the lass had a sweetheart, and he said he would go and get the ball. So he went to the park-gate, but 'twas shut; then he climbed the railing, and when he got to the top of it an old woman rose up

out of the ditch before him and said that if he wanted to get the ball he must sleep three nights in the house: so he said he would.

Well! when it was evening, he went into the house, and looked everywhere for the ball, but he could not find it, nor anyone in the house at all; but when night came on he thought he heard bogles moving about in the courtyard; so he looked out o' the window, and, sure enough, the yard was full of them!

Presently he heard steps coming upstairs, so he hid behind the door, and was as still as a mouse. Then in came a big giant five times as tall as the lad, and looked around; but seeing nothing he went to the window and bowed himself to look out; and as he bowed on his elbows to see the bogles in the yard, the lad stepped behind him, and with one blow of his sword he cut him in twain, so that the top part of him fell in the yard, and the bottom part remained standing looking out of the window.

Well! There was a great cry from the bogles when they saw half the giant come tumbling down to them, and they called out, 'There comes half our master, give us the other half.'

Then the lad said, 'It's no use, thou pair of legs, standing alone at the window, as thou hast no eye to see with, so go join thy brother;' and he cast the lower part of the giant after the top part. Now when the bogles had gotten all the giant they were quiet.

Next night the lad went to sleep in the house again, and this time a second giant came in at the door, and as he came in the lad cut him in twain; but the legs walked on to the fire and went straight up the chimney.

'Go, get thee after thy legs,' said the lad to the head, and he cast the other half of the giant up the chimney.

Now the third night nothing happened, so the lad got into bed; but before he went to sleep he heard the bogles striving under the bed, and he wondered what they were at. So he peeped, and saw that they had the ball there, and were playing with it, casting it to and fro.

Now after a time one of them thrust his leg out from under the bed, and quick as anything the lad brings his sword down, and cuts it off. Then another bogle thrust his arm out at t'other side of the bed, and in a twinkling the lad cuts that off too. So it went on, till at last he had maimed them all, and they all went off, crying and wailing, and forgot the ball! Then the lad got out of bed, found the ball, and went off at once to seek his true love.

Now the lass had been taken to York to be hanged; she was brought out on the scaffold, and the hangman said, 'Now, lass, thou must hang by the neck till thou be'st dead.' But she cried out:

> 'Stop, stop, I think I see my mother coming!
> O mother, hast thou brought my golden ball
>   And come to set me free?'

And the mother answered:

> 'I've neither brought thy golden ball
>   Nor come to set thee free,
> But I have come to see thee hung
>   Upon this gallows tree.'

Then the hangman said, 'Now, lass, say thy prayers, for thou must die.' But she said:

> 'Stop, stop, I think I see my father coming!
> O father, hast thou brought my golden ball
>   And come to set me free?'

And the father answered:

> 'I've neither brought thy golden ball
>   Nor come to set thee free,
> But I have come to see thee hung
>   Upon this gallows tree.'

Then the hangman said, 'Hast thee done thy prayers? Now, lass, put thy head into the noose.'

But she answered, 'Stop, stop, I think I see my brother coming!' And again she sang her little verse, and the brother sang back the same words. And so with her sister, her uncle, her aunt, and her cousin. But they all said the same:

> 'I've neither brought thy golden ball
>   Nor come to set thee free,
> But I have come to see thee hung
>   Upon this gallows tree.'

Then the hangman said, 'I will stop no longer, thou'rt making game of me. Thou must be hung at once.'

But now, at long last, she saw her sweetheart coming through the crowd, so she cried to him:

> 'Stop, stop, I see my sweetheart coming!
> Sweetheart, has thou brought my golden ball
>   And come to set me free?'

Then her sweetheart held up her golden ball and cried:

> 'Aye, I have brought to thee thy golden ball
>   And come to set thee free,
> I have not come to see thee hung
>   Upon this gallows tree.'

So he took her home, then and there, and they lived happy ever after.

The Two Sisters

Once upon a time there were two sisters who were as like each other as two peas in a pod; but one was good, and the other was bad-tempered. Now their father had no work, so the girls began to think of going into service.

'I will go first and see what I can make of it,' said the younger sister, ever so cheerfully, 'then you, sis, can follow if I have good luck.'

So she packed up a bundle, said goodbye, and started to find a place; but no one in the town wanted a girl, and she went farther afield into the country. And as she journeyed she came upon an oven in which a lot of loaves were baking. Now, as she passed, the loaves cried out with one voice: 'Little girl! Little girl! Take us out! Please take us out! We have been baking for seven years, and no one has come to take us out. Do take us out or we shall soon be burnt!'

Then, being a kind, obliging little girl, she stopped, put down her bundle, took out the bread, and went on her way, saying: 'You will be more comfortable now.'

After a time she came to a cow lowing beside an empty pail, and the cow said to her: 'Little girl! Little girl! Milk me! Please milk me! Seven years have I been waiting, but no one has come to milk me!'

So the kind girl stopped, put down her bundle, milked the cow into the pail, and went on her way, saying: 'Now you will be more comfortable.'

By and by she came to an apple tree so laden with fruit that its branches were nigh to break, and the apple tree called to her: 'Little girl! Little girl! Please shake my branches. The fruit is so heavy I can't stand straight!'

Then the kind girl stopped, put down her bundle, and shook

the branches so that the apples fell off, and the tree could stand straight. Then she went on her way, saying: 'You will be more comfortable now.'

So she journeyed on till she came to a house where an old witch-woman lived. Now this witch-woman wanted a servant-maid, and promised good wages. Therefore the girl agreed to stop with her and try how she liked service. She had to sweep the floor, keep the house clean and tidy, the fire bright and cheery. But there was one thing the witch-woman said she must never do, and that was look up the chimney!

'If you do,' said the witch-woman, 'something will fall down on you, and you will come to a bad end.'

Well! the girl swept, and dusted, and made up the fire; but ne'er a penny of wages did she see. Now the girl wanted to go home as she did not like witch-service, for the witch used to have boiled babies for supper, and bury the bones under some stones in the garden. But she did not like to go home penniless; so she stayed on, sweeping, and dusting, and doing her work, just as if she was pleased. Then one day, as she was sweeping up the hearth, down tumbled some soot, and, without remembering she was forbidden to look up the chimney, she looked up to see where the soot came from. And lo! and behold, a big bag of gold fell plump into her lap.

Now the witch happened to be out on one of her witch errands; so the girl thought it a fine opportunity to be off home.

So she kilted up her petticoats and started to run home but she had gone only a little way when she heard the witch-woman coming after her on her broomstick. Now the apple tree she had helped to stand straight happened to be quite close; so she ran to it and cried:

> 'Apple tree! Apple tree, hide me
> So the old witch can't find me,
> For if she does she'll pick my bones,
> And bury me under the garden stones.'

Then the apple tree said, 'Of course I will. You helped me to stand straight, and one good turn deserves another.'

So the apple tree hid her finely in its green branches; and when the witch flew past saying:

> 'Tree of mine! O Tree of mine!
> Have you seen my naughty little maid
> With a willy willy wag and a great big bag,
> She's stolen my money – all I had?'

the apple tree answered:

> 'No, mother dear,
> Not for seven year!'

So the witch flew on the wrong way, and the girl got down, thanked the tree politely, and started again. But just as she got to where the cow was standing beside the pail, she heard the witch coming again, so she ran to the cow and cried:

> 'Cow! Cow, please hide me
> So the witch can't find me,
> If she does she'll pick my bones,
> And bury me under the garden stones!'

'Certainly I will,' answered the cow. 'Didn't you milk me and make me comfortable? Hide yourself behind me and you'll be quite safe.'

And when the witch flew by and called to the cow:

> 'O Cow of mine! Cow of mine!
> Have you seen my naughty little maid
> With a willy willy wag and a great big bag,
> Who stole my money – all that I had?'

she just said politely:

> 'No, mother dear,
> Not for seven year!'

Then the old witch went on in the wrong direction, and the girl started afresh on her way home; but just as she got to where the oven stood, she heard that horrid old witch coming behind her again; so she ran as fast as she could to the oven and cried:

> 'O Oven! Oven! hide me
> So as the witch can't find me,
> For if she does she'll pick my bones,
> And bury them under the garden stones.'

Then the oven said, 'I am afraid there is no room for you, as another batch of bread is baking; but there is the baker – ask him.'

So she asked the baker, and he said, 'Of course I will. You saved my last batch from being burnt; so run in to the bakehouse, you will be quite safe there, and I will settle the witch for you.'

So she hid in the bakehouse, only just in time, for there was the old witch calling angrily:

> 'O Man of mine! Man of mine!
> Have you seen my naughty little maid
> With a willy willy wag and a great big bag,
> Who's stole my money – all I had?'

Then the baker replied, 'Look in the oven. She may be there.'

And the witch alighted from her broomstick and peered into the oven: but she could see no one.

'Creep in and look in the farthest corner,' said the baker slyly, and the witch crept in when –

> Bang! –

he shut the door in her face, and there she was roasting. And when she came out with the bread she was all crisp and brown and had to go home as best she could and put cold cream all over her!

But the kind, obliging little girl got safe home with her bag of money.

Now the ill-tempered elder sister was very jealous of this good luck, and determined to get a bag of gold for herself. So she in her turn packed up a bundle and started to seek service by the same road. But when she came to the oven, and the loaves begged her to take them out because they had been baking seven years and were nigh to burning, she tossed her head and said: 'A likely story indeed, that I should burn my fingers to save your crusts. No, thank you!'

And with that she went on till she came across the cow standing waiting to be milked beside the pail. But when the cow said: 'Little girl! Little girl! Milk me! Please milk me, I've waited seven years to be milked – '

She only laughed and replied, 'You may wait another seven years for all I care. I'm not your dairymaid!'

And with that she went on till she came to the apple tree all overburdened by its fruit. But when it begged her to shake its branches, she only giggled, and plucking one ripe apple, said: 'One is enough for me: you can keep the rest yourself.'

And with that she went on munching the apple, till she came to the witch-woman's house.

Now the witch-woman, though she had got over being crisp and brown from the oven, was dreadfully angry with all little maidservants, and made up her mind this one should not trick her. So for a long time she never went out of the house; thus the ill-tempered sister never had a chance of looking up the chimney, as she had meant to do at once. And she had to dust, and clean, and brush, and sweep ever so hard, until she was quite tired out.

But one day, when the witch-woman went into the garden to bury her bones, she seized the moment, looked up the chimney, and, sure enough, a bag of gold fell plump into her lap!

Well! she was off with it in a moment, and ran and ran till she came to the apple tree, when she heard the witch-woman behind her. So she cried as her sister had done:

> 'Apple tree! Apple tree, hide me
> So the old witch can't find me,
> For if she does she'll break my bones,
> Or bury me under the garden stones.'

But the apple tree said: 'No room here! I've too many apples.'

So she had to run on; and when the witch-woman on her broomstick came flying by and called:

> 'O Tree of mine! Tree of mine!
> Have you seen a naughty little maid
> With a willy willy wag and a great big bag,
> Who's stolen my money – all I had?'

the apple tree replied:

> 'Yes, mother dear,
> She's gone down there.'

Then the witch-woman went after her, caught her, gave her a thorough good beating, took the bag of money away from her, and sent her home without a penny payment for all her dusting, and sweeping, and brushing, and cleaning.

The Laidly Worm

In Bamborough Castle there once lived a king who had two children, a son named Childe Wynde, and a daughter who was called May Margret. Their mother, a fair woman, was dead, and the king mourned her long and faithfully. But, after his son Childe Wynde went to seek his fortune, the king, hunting in the forest, came across a lady of such great beauty that he fell in love with her at once and determined to marry her.

Now Princess May Margret was not over-pleased to think that her mother's place should be taken by a strange woman, nor was she pleased to think that she would have to give up keeping house for her father the king. For she had always taken a pride in her work. But she said nothing, though she stood long on the castle walls looking out across the sea wishing for her dear brother's return; for, see you, they had mothered each other.

Still no news came of Childe Wynde; so on the day when the old king was to bring the new queen home, May Margret counted over the keys of the castle chambers, knotted them on a string, and after casting them over her left shoulder for luck – more for her father's sake than for the new queen's regard – she stood at the castle gate ready to hand over the keys to her stepmother.

Now as the bridal procession approached with all the lords of the north countrie, and some of the Scots lords in attendance, she looked so fair and so sweet, that the lords whispered to one another of her beauty. And when, after saying in a voice like a mavis –

> 'Oh welcome, welcome, father,
> Unto your halls and towers!
> And welcome too, my stepmother,
> For all that's here is yours!' –

she turned upon the step and tripped into the yard, the Scots lords said aloud:

> 'Forsooth! May Margret's grace
> Surpasses all that we have met, she has so fair a face!'

Now the new queen overheard this, and she stamped her foot and her face flushed with anger as she turned her about and called:

> 'You might have excepted me,
> But I will bring May Margret to a Laidly Worm's degree;
> I'll bring her low as a Laidly Worm
> That warps about a stone,
> And not till the Childe of Wynde come back
> Will the witching be undone.'

Well! hearing this May Margret laughed, not knowing that her new stepmother, for all her beauty, was a witch; and the laugh made the wicked woman still more angry. So that same night she left her royal bed, and, returning to the lonely cave where she had ever done her magic, she cast Princess May Margret under a spell with charms three times three, and passes nine times nine. And this was her spell:

> 'I weird ye to a Laidly Worm
>   And such sall ye ever be
> Until Childe Wynde, the king's dear son,
>   Comes home across the sea.
> Until the world comes to an end
>   Unspelled ye'll never be,
> Unless Childe Wynde of his own free will
>   Sall give you kisses three!'

So it came to pass that Princess May Margret went to her bed a beauteous maiden, full of grace, and rose next morning a Laidly Worm; for when her tire-women came to dress her they found coiled up in her bed an awesome dragon, which uncoiled itself and came towards them. And when they ran away terrified, the Laidly Worm crawled and crept, and crept and crawled down to the sea till it reached the rock of the Spindlestone which is called the Heugh. And there it curled itself round the stone, and lay basking in the sun.

Then for seven miles east and seven miles west and seven miles north and south the whole countryside knew the hunger of the Laidly Worm of Spindlestone Heugh, for it drove the awesome beast to leave its resting-place at night and devour everything it came across.

At last a wise warlock told the people that if they wished to be quit of these horrors, they must take every drop of the milk of seven white milch kine every morn and every eve to the trough of stone at the foot of the Heugh, for the Laidly Worm to drink. And this they did, and after that the Laidly Worm troubled the countryside no longer; but lay warped about the Heugh looking out to sea with its terrible snout in the air.

But the word of its doings had gone east and had gone west; it had even gone over the sea and had come to Childe Wynde's ears; and the news of it angered him; for he thought perchance it had something to do with his beloved sister May Margret's disappearance. So he called his men-at-arms together and said: 'We must sail to Bamborough and land by Spindlestone, so as to quell and kill this Laidly Worm.'

Then they built a ship without delay, laying the keel with wood from the rowan tree. And they made masts of rowan wood also, and oars likewise; and, so furnished, set forth.

Now the wicked queen knew by her arts they were coming, so she sent out her imps to still the winds so that the fluttering sails of silk hung idle on the masts. But Childe Wynde was not to be bested; so he called out the oarsmen. Thus it came to pass that one morn the wicked queen, looking from the keep, saw the gallant ship in Bamborough Bay, and she sent out all her witch-wives and her impets to raise a storm, and sink the ship; but they came back unable to hurt it, for, see you, it was built of rowan wood, over which witches have no power.

Then, as a last device, the Witch queen laid spells upon the Laidly Worm, saying:

> 'Oh! Laidly Worm! Go make their topmast heel,
> Go! Worm the sand, and creep beneath the keel.'

Now the Laidly Worm had no choice but to obey. So:

> 'The Worm leapt up, the Worm leapt down,
>   And plaited round each plank,
> And aye as the ship came close to shore
>   She heeled as if she sank.'

Three times three did Childe Wynde attempt to land, and three times three the Laidly Worm kept the good ship from the shore. At last Childe Wynde gave the word to put the ship about, and the Witch queen, who was watching from the keep, thought he had given up: but he was not to be bested: for he only rounded the next point to Budley sands. And there, jumping into the shoal water, he got safely to land, and drawing his sword of proof, rushed up to fight the awesome Worm. But as he raised his sword to strike he heard a voice, soft as the western wind:

> 'Oh quit thy sword, unbend thy bow,
>   And give me kisses three,
> For though I seem a Laidly Worm
>   No harm I'll do to thee!'

And the voice seemed to him like the voice of his dear sister May Margret. So he stayed his hand. Then once again the Laidly Worm said:

> 'Oh quit thy sword, unbend thy bow,
>   My laidly form forget.
> Forgive the wrong and kiss me thrice
>   For love of May Margret.'

Then Childe Wynde, remembering how he had loved his sister, put his arms round the Laidly Worm and kissed it once. And he kissed the loathly thing twice. And he kissed it yet a third time as he stood with the wet sand at his feet.

Then with a hiss and a roar the Laidly Worm sank to the sand, and in his arms was May Margret!

He wrapped her in his mantle, for she trembled in the cold sea air, and carried her to Bamborough Castle, where the wicked queen, knowing her hour was come, stood, all deserted by her imps and witch-wives, on the stairs, twisting her hands.

Then Childe Wynde looking at her cried:

> 'Woe! Woe to thee, thou wicked witch!
>   An ill fate shalt thine be!
> The doom thou dreed on May Margret
>   The same doom shalt thou dree.
>
> Henceforth thou'lt be a Laidly Toad
>   That in the clay doth wend,
> And unspelled thou wilt never be
>   Till this world hath an end.'

And as he spoke the wicked queen began to shrivel, and she shrivelled and shrivelled to a horrid wrinkled toad that hopped down the castle steps and disappeared in a crevice.

But to this day a loathsome toad is sometimes seen haunting Bamborough Keep; and that Laidly Toad is the wicked Witch queen!

But Childe Wynde and Princess May Margret loved each other as much as ever, and lived happily ever after.

Titty Mouse and Tatty Mouse

Titty Mouse and Tatty Mouse both lived in a house.

Titty Mouse went a-gleaning, and Tatty Mouse went a-gleaning.

So they both went a-gleaning.

Titty Mouse gleaned an ear of corn and Tatty Mouse gleaned an ear of corn.

So they both gleaned an ear of corn.

Titty Mouse made a pudding and Tatty Mouse made a pudding.

So they both made a pudding.

And Tatty Mouse put her pudding into the pot to boil.

But when Titty went to put hers in, the pot tumbled over, and scalded her to death, and Tatty sat down and wept.

Then the three-legged stool said, 'Tatty, why do you weep?'

'Titty's dead,' said Tatty, 'and so I weep.'

'Then,' said the stool, 'I'll hop,' so the stool hopped.

Then a broom in the corner of the room said, 'Stool, why do you hop?'

'Oh!' said the stool, 'Titty's dead, and Tatty weeps, and so I hop.'

'Then,' said the broom, 'I'll sweep,' so the broom began to sweep.

Then said the door, 'Broom, why do you sweep?'

'Oh!' said the broom, 'Titty's dead, and Tatty weeps, and the stool hops, and so I sweep.'

'Then,' said the door, 'I'll jar,' so the door jarred.

Then the window said, 'Door, why do you jar?'

'Oh!' said the door, 'Titty's dead, and Tatty weeps, and the stool hops, and the broom sweeps, and so I jar.'

'Then,' said the window, 'I'll creak,' so the window creaked.

Now there was an old form outside the house, and when the window creaked, the form said, 'Window, why do you creak?'

'Oh!' said the window, 'Titty's dead, and Tatty weeps, and the stool hops, and the broom sweeps, the door jars, and so I creak!'

'Then,' said the old form, 'I'll gallop round the house.' So the old form galloped round the house.

Now there was a fine large walnut tree growing by the cottage, and the tree said to the form, 'Form, why do you gallop round the house?'

'Oh!' says the form, 'Titty's dead, and Tatty weeps, and the stool hops, and the broom sweeps, the door jars, and the window creaks, and so I gallop round the house.'

'Then,' said the walnut tree, 'I'll shed my leaves.' So the walnut tree shed all its beautiful green leaves.

Now there was a little bird perched on one of the boughs of the tree, and when all the leaves fell, it said, 'Walnut tree, why do you shed your leaves?'

'Oh!' said the tree, 'Titty's dead, and Tatty weeps, the stool hops, and the broom sweeps, the door jars, and the window creaks, the old form gallops round the house, and so I shed my leaves.'

'Then,' said the little bird, 'I'll moult all my feathers,' so he moulted all his gay feathers.

Now there was a little girl walking below, carrying a jug of milk for her brothers' and sisters' supper, and when she saw the poor little bird moult all its feathers, she said, 'Little bird, why do you moult all your feathers?'

'Oh!' said the little bird, 'Titty's dead, and Tatty weeps, the stool hops, and the broom sweeps, the door jars, and the window creaks, the old form gallops round the house, the walnut tree sheds its leaves, and so I moult all my feathers.'

'Then,' said the little girl, 'I'll spill the milk.' So she dropt the pitcher and spilt the milk.

Now there was an old man just by on the top of a ladder thatching a rick, and when he saw the little girl spill the milk, he said, 'Little girl, what do you mean by spilling the milk, your little brothers and sisters must go without their suppers.'

Then said the little girl, 'Titty's dead, and Tatty weeps, the stool hops, and the broom sweeps, the door jars, and the window creaks, the old form gallops round the house, the walnut tree sheds all its leaves, the little bird moults all its feathers, and so I spill the milk.'

'Oh!' said the old man, 'then I'll tumble off the ladder and break my neck.'

So he tumbled off the ladder and broke his neck; and when the old man broke his neck, the great walnut tree fell down with a crash and upset the old form and the house, and the house falling knocked the window out, and the window knocked the door down, and the door upset the broom, and the broom upset the stool, and poor little Tatty Mouse was buried beneath the ruins.

Jack and the Beanstalk

A long long time ago, when most of the world was young and folk did what they liked because all things were good, there lived a boy called Jack.

His father was bedridden, and his mother, a good soul, was busy early morns and late eves planning and placing how to support her sick husband and her young son by selling the milk and butter which Milky-White, the beautiful cow, gave them without stint. For it was summertime. But winter came on; the herbs of the fields took refuge from the frosts in the warm earth, and though his mother sent Jack to gather what fodder he could get in the hedgerows, he came back as often as not with a very empty sack; for Jack's eyes were so often full of wonder at all the things he saw that sometimes he forgot to work!

So it came to pass that one morning Milky-White gave no milk at all – not one drain! Then the good hard-working mother threw her apron over her head and sobbed: 'What shall we do? What shall we do?'

Now Jack loved his mother; besides, he felt just a bit sneaky at being such a big boy and doing so little to help, so he said, 'Cheer up! Cheer up! I'll go and get work somewhere.' And he felt as he spoke as if he would work his fingers to the bone; but the good woman shook her head mournfully.

'You've tried that before, Jack,' she said, 'and nobody would keep you. You are quite a good lad but your wits go a-woolgathering. No, we must sell Milky-White and live on the money. It is no use crying over milk that is not here to spill!'

You see, she was a wise as well as a hard-working woman, and Jack's spirits rose.

'Just so,' he cried. 'We will sell Milky-White and be richer than ever. It's an ill wind that blows no one good. So, as it is market-day, I'll just take her there and we shall see what we shall see.'

'But – ' began his mother.

'But doesn't butter parsnips,' laughed Jack. 'Trust me to make a good bargain.'

So, as it was washing-day, and her sick husband was more ailing than usual, his mother let Jack set off to sell the cow.

'Not less than ten pounds,' she bawled after him as he turned the corner.

Ten pounds, indeed! Jack had made up his mind to twenty! Twenty solid golden sovereigns!

He was just settling what he should buy his mother as a fairing out of the money, when he saw a queer, little, old man on the road who called out, 'Good-morning, Jack!'

'Good-morning,' replied Jack, with a polite bow, wondering how the queer, little, old man happened to know his name; though, to be sure, Jacks were as plentiful as blackberries.

'And where may you be going?' asked the queer little old man. Jack wondered again – he was always wondering, you know – what the queer, little, old man had to do with it; but, being always polite, he replied:

'I am going to market to sell Milky-White – and I mean to make a good bargain.'

'So you will! So you will!' chuckled the queer, little, old man. 'You look the sort of chap for it. I bet you know how many beans make five?'

'Two in each hand and one in my mouth,' answered Jack readily. He really was sharp as a needle.

'Just so, just so!' chuckled the queer little old man; and as he spoke he drew out of his pocket five beans. 'Well, here they are, so give us Milky-White.'

Jack was so flabbergasted that he stood with his mouth open as if he expected the fifth bean to fly into it.

'What!' he said at last. 'My Milky-White for five common beans! Not if I know it!'

'But they aren't common beans,' put in the queer little old man, and there was a queer little smile on his queer little face. 'If

you plant these beans overnight, by morning they will have grown up right into the very sky.'

Jack was too flabbergasted this time even to open his mouth; his eyes opened instead.

'Did you say right into the very sky?' he asked at last; for, see you, Jack had wondered more about the sky than about anything else.

'*Right up into the very sky*,' repeated the queer old man, with a nod between each word. 'It's a good bargain, Jack; and, as fair play's a jewel, if they don't – Why! meet me here tomorrow morning and you shall have Milky-White back again. Will that please you?'

'Right as a trivet,' cried Jack, without stopping to think, and the next moment he found himself standing on an empty road.

'Two in each hand and one in my mouth,' repeated Jack. 'That is what I said, and what I'll do. Everything in order, and if what the queer little old man said isn't true, I shall get Milky-White back tomorrow morning.'

So whistling and munching the bean he trudged home cheerfully, wondering what the sky would be like if he ever got there.

'What a long time you've been!' exclaimed his mother, who was watching anxiously for him at the gate. 'It is past sun-setting; but I see you have sold Milky-White. Tell me quick how much you got for her.'

'You'll never guess,' began Jack.

'Laws-a-mercy! You don't say so,' interrupted the good woman. 'And I worritting all day lest they should take you in. What was it? Ten pounds – fifteen – sure it *can't* be twenty!'

Jack held out the beans triumphantly.

'There,' he said. 'That's what I got for her, and a jolly good bargain too!'

It was his mother's turn to be flabbergasted; but all she said was: 'What! Them beans!'

'Yes,' replied Jack, beginning to doubt his own wisdom; 'but they're *magic* beans. If you plant them overnight, by morning they – grow – right up – into – the – sky – Oh! Please don't hit so hard!'

For Jack's mother for once had lost her temper, and was belabouring the boy for all she was worth. And when she had finished scolding and beating, she flung the miserable beans out of window and sent him, supperless, to bed.

If this was the magical effect of the beans, thought Jack ruefully, he didn't want any more magic, if you please.

However, being healthy and, as a rule, happy, he soon fell asleep and slept like a top.

When he woke he thought at first it was moonlight, for everything in the room showed greenish. Then he stared at the little window. It was covered as if with a curtain by leaves. He was out of bed in a trice, and the next moment, without waiting to dress, was climbing up the biggest beanstalk you ever saw. For what the queer little old man had said was true! One of the beans which his mother had chucked into the garden had found soil, taken root, and grown in the night . . .

Where? . . .

Up to the very sky? Jack meant to see at any rate.

So he climbed, and he climbed, and he climbed. It was easy work, for the big beanstalk with the leaves growing out of each side was like a ladder; for all that he soon was out of breath. Then he got his second wind, and was just beginning to wonder if he had a third when he saw in front of him a wide, shining white road stretching away, and away, and away.

So he took to walking, and he walked, and walked, and walked, till he came to a tall shining white house with a wide white doorstep.

And on the doorstep stood a great big woman with a black porridge-pot in her hand. Now Jack, having had no supper, was hungry as a hunter, and when he saw the porridge-pot he said quite politely: 'Good-morning, 'm. I wonder if you *could* give me some breakfast?'

'Breakfast!' echoed the woman, who, in truth, was an ogre's wife. 'If it is breakfast you're wanting, it's breakfast you'll likely be; for I expect my man home every instant, and there is nothing he likes better for breakfast than a boy – a fat boy grilled on toast.'

Now Jack was not a bit of a coward, and when he wanted a thing he generally got it, so he said cheerful-like: 'I'd be fatter if I'd had my breakfast!'

Whereat the ogre's wife laughed and bade Jack come in; for she was not, really, half as bad as she looked. But he had hardly finished the great bowl of porridge and milk she gave him when the whole house began to tremble and quake. It was the ogre coming home!

Thump!   Thump!!   THUMP!!!

'Into the oven with you, sharp!' cried the ogre's wife; and the iron oven door was just closed when the ogre strode in. Jack could see him through the little peephole slide at the top where the steam came out.

He was a big one for sure. He had three sheep strung to his belt, and these he threw down on the table. 'Here, wife,' he cried, 'roast me these snippets for breakfast; they are all I've been able to get this morning, worse luck! I hope the oven's hot?' And he went to touch the handle, while Jack burst out all of a sweat wondering what would happen next.

'Roast!' echoed the ogre's wife. 'Pooh! the little things would dry to cinders. Better boil them.'

So she set to work to boil them; but the ogre began sniffing about the room. 'They don't smell – mutton meat,' he growled. Then he frowned horribly and began the real ogre's rhyme:

> 'Fee-fi-fo-fum,
> I smell the blood of an Englishman.
> Be he alive, or be he dead,
> I'll grind his bones to make my bread.'

'Don't be silly!' said his wife. 'It's the bones of the little boy you had for supper that I'm boiling down for soup! Come, eat your breakfast, there's a good ogre!'

So the ogre ate his three sheep, and when he had done he went to a big oaken chest and took out three big bags of golden pieces. These he put on the table, and began to count their contents while his wife cleared away the breakfast things. And by and by his head began to nod, and at last he began to snore, and snored so loud that the whole house shook.

Then Jack nipped out of the oven and, seizing one of the bags of gold, crept away, and ran along the straight, wide, shining white road as fast as his legs would carry him till he came to the beanstalk. He couldn't climb down it with the bag of gold, it was so heavy, so he just flung his burden down first, and, helter-skelter, climbed after it.

And when he came to the bottom there was his mother picking up gold pieces out of the garden as fast as she could; for, of course, the bag had burst.

'Laws-a-mercy me!' she says. 'Wherever have you been? See! It's been rainin' gold!'

'No, it hasn't,' began Jack. 'I climbed up – ' Then he turned to look for the beanstalk; but lo, and behold! it wasn't there at all! So he knew, then, it was all real magic.

After that they lived happily on the gold pieces for a long time, and the bedridden father got all sorts of nice things to eat; but at last a day came when Jack's mother showed a doleful face as she put a big yellow sovereign into Jack's hand and bade him be careful marketing, because there was not one more in the coffer. After that they must starve.

That night Jack went supperless to bed of his own accord. If he couldn't make money, he thought, at any rate he could eat less money. It was a shame for a big boy to stuff himself and bring no grist to the mill.

He slept like a top, as boys do when they don't overeat themselves, and when he woke . . .

Hey, presto! the whole room showed greenish, and there was a curtain of leaves over the window! Another bean had grown in the night, and Jack was up it like a lamplighter before you could say knife.

This time he didn't take nearly so long climbing until he reached the straight, wide, white road, and in a trice he found himself before the tall white house, where on the wide white steps the ogre's wife was standing with the black porridge-pot in her hand.

And this time Jack was as bold as brass. 'Good-morning, 'm,' he said. 'I've come to ask you for breakfast, for I had no supper, and I'm as hungry as a hunter.'

'Go away, bad boy!' replied the ogre's wife. 'Last time I gave a boy breakfast my man missed a whole bag of gold. I believe you are the same boy.'

'Maybe I am, maybe I'm not,' said Jack, with a laugh. 'I'll tell you true when I've had my breakfast; but not till then.'

So the ogre's wife, who was dreadfully curious, gave him a big bowl full of porridge; but before he had half finished it he heard the ogre coming –

Thump!   Thump!!   THUMP!!!

'Into the oven with you,' shrieked the ogre's wife. 'You shall tell me when he has gone to sleep.'

This time Jack saw through the steam peephole that the ogre had three fat calves strung to his belt.

'Better luck today, wife!' he cried, and his voice shook the house. 'Quick! Roast these trifles for my breakfast! I hope the oven's hot?'

And he went to feel the handle of the door, but his wife cried out sharply: 'Roast! Why, you'd have to wait hours before they were done! I'll broil them – see how bright the fire is!'

'Umph!' growled the ogre. And then he began sniffing and calling out:

> 'Fee-fi-fo-fum,
> I smell the blood of an Englishman.
> Be he alive, or be he dead,
> I'll grind his bones to make my bread.'

'Twaddle!' said the ogre's wife. 'It's only the bones of the boy you had last week that I've put into the pig-bucket!'

'Umph!' said the ogre harshly; but he ate the broiled calves and then he said to his wife, 'Bring me my hen that lays the magic eggs. I want to see gold.'

So the ogre's wife brought him a great, big, black hen with a shiny red comb. She plumped it down on the table and took away the breakfast things.

Then the ogre said to the hen, 'Lay!' and it promptly laid – what do you think? – a beautiful, shiny, yellow golden egg!

'None so dusty, henny-penny,' laughed the ogre. 'I shan't have to beg as long as I've got you.' Then he said, 'Lay!' once more; and lo and behold! there was another beautiful, shiny, yellow, golden egg!

Jack could hardly believe his eyes, and made up his mind that he would have that hen, come what might. So, when the ogre began to doze, he just out like a flash from the oven, seized the hen, and ran for his life! But, you see, he reckoned without his prize; for hens, you know, always cackle when they leave their nests after laying an egg, and this one set up such a scrawing that it woke the ogre.

'Where's my hen?' he shouted, and his wife came rushing in, and they both rushed to the door; but Jack had got the better of them by a good start, and all they could see was a little figure right away down the wide white road, holding a big, scrawing, cackling, fluttering, black hen by the legs!

How Jack got down the beanstalk he never knew. It was all wings, and leaves, and feathers, and cacklings; but get down he did, and there was his mother wondering if the sky was going to fall!

But the very moment Jack touched ground he called out, 'Lay!' and the black hen ceased cackling and laid a great, big, shiny, yellow, golden egg.

So everyone was satisfied; and from that moment everybody had everything that money could buy. For, whenever they wanted anything, they just said, 'Lay!' and the black hen provided them with gold.

But Jack began to wonder if he couldn't find something else besides money in the sky. So one fine, moonlight, midsummer night he refused his supper, and before he went to bed stole out to the garden with a big watering can and watered the ground under his window; for, thought he, 'there must be two more beans somewhere, and perhaps it is too dry for them to grow.' Then he slept like a top.

And lo, and behold! when he woke, there was the green light shimmering through his room, and there he was in an instant on the beanstalk, climbing, climbing, climbing for all he was worth.

But this time he knew better than to ask for his breakfast; for the ogre's wife would be sure to recognise him. So he just hid in some bushes beside the great white house, till he saw her in the scullery, and then he slipped in and hid himself in the copper; for he knew she would be sure to look in the oven first thing.

And by and by he heard –

Thump!   THUMP!!   THUMP!!!

And peeping through a crack in the copper-lid he could see the ogre stalk in with three huge oxen strung at his belt. But this time, no sooner had the ogre got into the house than he begun shouting:

'Fee-fi-fo-fum,
I smell the blood of an Englishman.
But he alive, or be dead,
I'll grind his bones to make my bread.'

For, see you, the copper-lid didn't fit tight like the oven door, and ogres have noses like a dog's for scent.

'Well, I declare, so do I!' exclaimed the ogre's wife. 'It will be that horrid boy who stole the bag of gold and the hen. If so, he's hid in the oven!'

But when she opened the door, lo, and behold! Jack wasn't there! Only some joints of meat roasting and sizzling away. Then she laughed and said, 'You and me be fools for sure. Why, it's the boy you caught last night as I was getting ready for your breakfast. Yes, we be fools to take dead meat for live flesh! So eat your breakfast, there's a good ogre!'

But the ogre, though he enjoyed roast boy very much, wasn't satisfied, and every now and then he would burst out with '*Fee-fi-fo-fum*', and get up and search the cupboards, keeping Jack in a fever of fear lest he should think of the copper.

But he didn't. And when he had finished his breakfast he called out to his wife, 'Bring me my magic harp! I want to be amused.'

So she brought out a little harp and put it on the table. And the ogre leant back in his chair and said lazily:

'Sing!'

And lo, and behold! the harp began to sing. If you want to know what it sang about! Why! It sang about everything! And it sang so beautifully that Jack forgot to be frightened, and the ogre forgot to think of '*Fee-fi-fo-fum*', and fell asleep and

did

NOT

SNORE.

Then Jack stole out of the copper like a mouse and crept hands and knees to the table, raised himself up ever so softly and laid hold of the magic harp; for he was determined to have it.

But, no sooner had he touched it, than it cried out quite loud, 'Master! Master!' So the ogre woke, saw Jack making off, and rushed after him.

My goodness, it was a race! Jack was nimble, but the ogre's stride was twice as long. So, though Jack turned, and twisted, and doubled like a hare, yet at last, when he got to the beanstalk, the ogre was not a dozen yards behind him. There wasn't time to think, so Jack just flung himself on to the stalk and began to go down as fast as he could while the harp kept calling, 'Master!

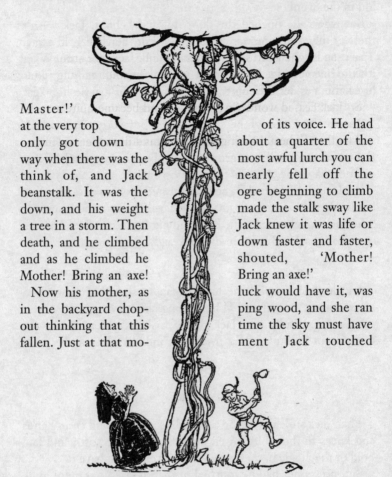

Master!'
at the very top
only got down
way when there was the
think of, and Jack
beanstalk. It was the
down, and his weight
a tree in a storm. Then
death, and he climbed
and as he climbed he
Mother! Bring an axe!
  Now his mother, as
in the backyard chop-
out thinking that this
fallen. Just at that mo-

of its voice. He had
about a quarter of the
most awful lurch you can
nearly fell off the
ogre beginning to climb
made the stalk sway like
Jack knew it was life or
down faster and faster,
shouted, 'Mother!
Bring an axe!'
luck would have it, was
ping wood, and she ran
time the sky must have
ment Jack touched

ground and he flung down the harp – which immediately began to sing of all sorts of beautiful things – and he seized the axe and gave a great chop at the beanstalk, which shook and swayed and bent like barley before a breeze.

'Have a care!' shouted the ogre, clinging on as hard as he could. But Jack *did* have a care, and he dealt that beanstalk such a shrewd blow that the whole of it, ogre and all, came toppling down, and, of course, the ogre broke his crown, so that he died on the spot.

After that everyone was quite happy. For they had gold and to spare, and if the bedridden father was dull, Jack just brought out the harp and said, 'Sing!' And lo, and behold! it sang about everything under the sun.

So Jack ceased wondering so much and became quite a useful person.

And the last bean hasn't grown yet. It is still in the garden.

I wonder if it will ever grow?

And what little child will climb its beanstalk into the sky?

And what will that child find?

Goody me!

The Black Bull of Norroway

Long ago in Norroway there lived a lady who had three daughters. Now they were all pretty, and one night they fell a-talking of whom they meant to marry.

And the eldest said, 'I will have no one lower than an earl.'

And the second said, 'I will have none lower than a lord.'

But the third, the prettiest and the merriest, tossed her head and said with a twinkle in her eye, 'Why so proud? As for me I would be content with the Black Bull of Norroway.'

At that the other sisters bade her be silent and not talk lightly of such a monster. For, see you, is it not written:

> 'To wilder measure now they turn
> The black black Bull of Norroway;
> Sudden the tapers cease to burn,
> The minstrels cease to play'?

So, no doubt, the Black Bull of Norroway was held to be a horrid monster.

But the youngest daughter would have her laugh, so she said three times that she would be content with the Black Bull of Norroway.

Well! It so happened that the very next morning a coach-and-six came swinging along the road, and in it sat an earl who had come to ask the hand of the eldest daughter in marriage. So there were great rejoicings over the wedding, and the bride and bridegroom drove away in the coach-and-six.

Then the next thing that happened was that a coach-and-four with a lord in it came swinging along the road; and he wanted to marry the second daughter. So they were wed, and there were great rejoicings, and the bride and bridegroom drove away in the coach-and-four.

Now after this there was only the youngest, the prettiest and the merriest of the sisters left, and she became the apple of her mother's eye. So you may imagine how the mother felt when one morning a terrible bellowing was heard at the door, and there was a great big Black Bull waiting for his bride.

She wept and she wailed, and at first the girl ran away and hid herself in the cellar for fear, but there the Bull stood waiting, and at last the girl came up and said: 'I promised I would be content with the Black Bull of Norroway, and I must keep my word. Farewell, mother, you will not see me again.'

Then she mounted on the Black Bull's back, and it walked away with her quite quietly. And ever it chose the smoothest paths and the easiest roads, so that at last the girl grew less afraid. But she became very hungry and was nigh to faint when the Black Bull said to her, in quite a soft voice that wasn't a bellow at all:

> 'Eat out of my left ear,
> > Drink out of my right,
> And set by what you leave
> > To serve the morrow's night.'

So she did as she was bid, and lo and behold, the left ear was full of delicious things to eat, and the right was full of the most delicious drinks, and there was plenty left over for several days.

Thus they journeyed on and they journeyed on through many dreadful forests and many lonely wastes, and the Black Bull never paused for bite or sup, but ever the girl he carried ate out of his left ear, and drank out of his right, and set by what she left to serve the morrow's night. And she slept soft and warm on his broad back.

Now at last they reached a noble castle where a large company of lords and ladies were assembled, and greatly the company wondered at the sight of these strange companions. And they invited the girl to supper, but the Black Bull they turned into the field, and left to spend the night after his kind.

But when the next morning came there he was ready for his burden again. Now, though the girl was loth to leave her pleasant companions, she remembered her promise, and mounted on his back, so they journeyed on and journeyed on and journeyed on through many tangled woods and over many high mountains. And ever the Black Bull chose the smoothest paths for her and set aside the briars and brambles, while she ate out of his left ear and drank out of his right.

So at last they came to a magnificent mansion where dukes and duchesses and earls and countesses were enjoying themselves. Now the company, though much surprised at the strange companions, asked the girl in to supper; and the Black Bull they would have turned into the park for the night, but that the girl, remembering how well he had cared for her, asked them to put him into the stable and give him a good feed.

So this was done, and the next morning he was waiting before the hall-door for his burden; and she, though somewhat loth at leaving the fine company, mounted him cheerfully enough, and they rode away, and they rode away, and they rode away, through thick briar brakes and up fearsome cliffs. But ever the Black Bull trod the brambles underfoot and chose the easiest paths, while she ate out of his left ear, and drank out of his right, and wanted for nothing, though he had neither bite nor sup. So it came to pass that he grew tired and was limping with one foot when just as the sun was setting they came to a beautiful palace where princes and princesses were disporting themselves with a ball on the green grass. Now, though the company greatly wondered at the strange companions, they asked the girl to join them, and ordered the grooms to lead away the Black Bull to a field.

But she, remembering all he had done for her said, 'Not so! He will stay with me!' Then seeing a large thorn in the foot with which he had been limping, she stooped down and pulled it out.

And lo and behold! in an instant, to everyone's surprise, there appeared, not a frightful monstrous bull, but one of the most beautiful princes ever beheld, who fell at his deliverer's feet, thanking her for having broken his cruel enchantment.

A wicked witch-woman who wanted to marry him had, he said, spelled him until a beautiful maiden of her own free will should do him a favour.

'But,' he said, 'the danger is not all over. You have broken the enchantment by night; that by day has yet to be overcome.'

So the next morning the prince had to resume the form of a bull, and they set out together; and they rode, and they rode, and they rode, till they came to a dark and ugsome glen. And here he bade her dismount, and sit on a great rock.

'Here you must stay,' he said, 'while I go yonder and fight the Old One. And mind! move neither hand nor foot whilst I am away, else I shall never find you again. If everything around you turns blue, I shall have beaten the Old One; but if everything turns red he will have conquered me.'

And with that, and a tremendous roaring bellow, he set off to find his foe.

Well! she sat as still as a mouse, moving neither hand nor foot, nor even her eyes, and waited, and waited, and waited. Then at last everything turned blue. But she was so overcome with joy to think that her lover was victorious that she forgot to keep still, and lifting one of her feet, crossed it over the other!

So she waited, and waited, and waited. Long she sat, and aye she wearied; and all the time he was seeking for her, but he never found her.

At last she rose and went she knew not whither, determined to seek for her lover through the whole wide world. So she journeyed on, and she journeyed on, and she journeyed on, until one day in a dark wood she came to a little hut where lived an old, old woman who gave her food and shelter, and bid her Godspeed on her errand, giving her three nuts, a walnut, a filbert and a hazelnut, with these words:

> 'When your heart is like to break,
>   And once again is like to break,
>   Crack a nut and in its shell
>   That will be that suits you well.'

After this she felt heartened, and wandered on till her road was blocked by a great hill of glass; and though she tried all she could to climb it, she could not, for aye she slipped back, and slipped back, and slipped back; for it was like ice.

Then she sought a passage elsewhere, and round and about the foot of the hill she went sobbing and wailing, but ne'er a foothold could she find. At last she came to a smithy; and the smith promised if she would serve him faithfully for seven years and seven days, that he would make her iron shoon wherewith to climb the hill of glass. So for seven long years and seven short days she toiled, and span, and swept, and washed in the smith's house. And for wage he gave her a pair of iron shoon, and with them she clomb the glassy hill and went on her way.

Now she had not gone far before a company of fine lords and ladies rode past her talking of all the grand doings that were to be done at the young Duke of Norroway's wedding. Then she passed a number of people carrying all sorts of good things which they told her were for the duke's wedding. And at last she came to a palace castle where the courtyards were full of cooks and bakers, some running this way, some running that, and all so busy that they did not know what to do first.

Then she heard the horns of hunters and cries of, 'Room! Room for the Duke of Norroway and his bride!'

And who should ride past but the beautiful prince she had but half unspelled, and by his side was the witch-woman who was determined to marry him that very day.

Well! at the sight she felt that her heart was indeed like to break, and over again was like to break, so that the time had come for her to crack one of the nuts. So she broke the walnut, as it was the biggest, and out of it came a wonderful, wee woman carding wool as fast as ever she could card.

Now when the witch-woman saw this wonderful thing she offered the girl her choice of anything in the castle for it.

'If you will put off your wedding with the duke for a day, and let me watch in his room tonight,' said the girl, 'you shall have it.'

Now, like all witch-women, the bride wanted everything her own way, and she was so sure she had her groom safe, that she consented; but before the duke went to rest she gave him, with her own hands, a posset so made that anyone who drank it would sleep till morning.

Thus though the girl was allowed alone into the duke's

chamber, and though she spent the livelong night sighing and singing:

> 'Far have I sought for thee,
> Long have I wrought for thee,
> Near am I brought to thee,
> Dear Duke o' Norroway,
> Wilt thou say naught to me – '

the duke never wakened, but slept on. So when day came the girl had to leave him without his ever knowing she had been there.

Then once again her heart was like to break, and over and over again like to break, and she cracked the filbert nut, because it was the next biggest. And out of it came a wonderful, wee, wee woman spinning away as fast as ever she could spin. Now when the witch-bride saw this wonderful thing she once again put off her wedding so that she might possess it. And once again the girl spent the livelong night in the duke's chamber sighing and singing:

> 'Far have I sought for thee,
> Long have I wrought for thee,
> Near am I brought to thee,
> Dear Duke o' Norroway,
> Wilt thou say naught to me?'

But the duke, who had drunk the sleeping-draught from the hands of his witch-bride, never stirred, and when dawn came the girl had to leave him without his ever knowing she had been there.

Then, indeed, the girl's heart was like to break, and over and over and over again, like to break, so she cracked the last nut – the hazelnut – and out of it came the most wonderful wee, wee, wee-est woman reeling away at yarn as fast as she could reel.

And this marvel so delighted the witch-bride that once again she consented to put off her wedding for a day, and allow the girl to watch in the duke's chamber the night through, in order to possess it.

Now it so happened that when the duke was dressing that

morning he heard his pages talking amongst themselves of the strange sighing and singing they had heard in the night; and he said to his faithful old valet, 'What do the pages mean?'

And the old valet, who hated the witch-bride, said: 'If the master will take no sleeping-draught tonight, mayhap he may also hear what for two nights has kept me awake.'

At this the duke marvelled greatly, and when the witch-bride brought him his evening posset, he made excuse it was not sweet enough, and while she went away to get honey to sweeten it withal, he poured away the posset and made believe he had swallowed it.

So that night when dark had come, and the girl stole in to his chamber with a heavy heart, thinking it would be the very last time she would ever see him, the duke was really broad awake. And when she sat down by his bedside and began to sing:

'Far have I sought for thee – '

he knew her voice at once, and clasped her in his arms.

Then he told her how he had been in the power of the witch-woman and had forgotten everything, but that now he remembered all and that the spell was broken for ever and aye.

So the wedding feast served for their marriage, since the witch-bride, seeing her power was gone, quickly fled the country and was never heard of again.

Catskin

Once upon a time there lived a gentleman who owned fine lands and houses, and he very much wanted to have a son to be heir to them. So when his wife brought him a daughter, though she was bonny as bonny could be, he cared nought for her, and said: 'Let me never see her face.'

So she grew up to be a beautiful maiden, though her father never set eyes on her till she was fifteen years old and was ready to be married.

Then her father said roughly, 'She shall marry the first that comes for her.' Now when this became known, who should come along and be first but a nasty, horrid, old man. So she didn't know what to do, and went to the hen-wife and asked her advice. And the hen-wife said, 'Say you will not take him unless they give you a robe of silver cloth.' Well, they gave her a robe of silver cloth, but she wouldn't take him for all that, but went again to the hen-wife, who said, 'Say you will not take him unless they give you a robe of beaten gold.' Well, they gave her a robe of beaten gold, but still she would not take the old man, but went again to the hen-wife, who said, 'Say you will not take him unless they give you a robe made of the feathers of all the birds of the air.' So they sent out a man with a great heap of peas; and the man cried to all the birds of the air, 'Each bird take a pea and put down a feather.' So each bird took a pea and put down one of its feathers: and they took all the feathers and made a robe of them and gave it to her; but still she would not take the nasty, horrid, old man, but asked the hen-wife once again what she was to do, and the hen-wife said, 'Say they must first make you a robe of catskin.' Then they made her a robe of catskin; and she put it on, and tied up her other robes into a bundle, and when it was night-time ran away with it into the woods.

Now she went along, and went along, and went along, till at the end of the wood she saw a fine castle. Then she hid her fine robes by a crystal waterfall and went up to the castle-gates and asked for work. The lady of the castle saw her, and told her, 'I'm sorry I have no better place, but if you like you may be our scullion.' So down she went into the kitchen, and they called her Catskin, because of her dress. But the cook was very cruel to her, and led her a sad life.

Well, soon after that it happened that the young lord of the castle came home, and there was to be a grand ball in honour of the occasion. And when they were speaking about it among the servants, 'Dear me, Mrs Cook,' said Catskin, 'how much I should like to go!'

'What! You dirty impudent slut,' said the cook, 'you go among all the fine lords and ladies with your filthy catskin? A fine figure you'd cut!' and with that she took a basin of water and dashed it into Catskin's face. But Catskin only shook her ears and said nothing.

Now when the day of the ball arrived, Catskin slipped out of the house and went to the edge of the forest where she had hidden her other robes. Then she bathed herself in a crystal waterfall, and put on her robe of silver cloth, and hastened away to the ball. As soon as she entered all were overcome by her beauty and grace, while the young lord at once lost his heart to her. He asked her to be his partner for the first dance; and he would dance with none other the livelong night.

When it came to parting time, the young lord said, 'Pray tell me, fair maid, where you live?'

But Catskin curtsied and said:

> 'Kind sir, if the truth I must tell,
> At the sign of the "Basin of Water" I dwell.'

Then she flew from the castle and donned her catskin robe again, and slipped into the scullery, unbeknown to the cook.

The young lord went the very next day and searched for the sign of the 'Basin of Water'; but he could not find it. So he went to his mother, the lady of the castle, and declared he would wed none other but the lady of the silver robe, and would never rest till he had found her. So another ball was soon arranged in hopes that the beautiful maid would appear again.

So Catskin said to the cook, 'Oh, how I should like to go!' Whereupon the cook screamed out in a rage, 'What, you, you dirty, impudent slut! You would cut a fine figure among all the fine lords and ladies.' And with that she up with a ladle and broke it across Catskin's back. But Catskin only shook her ears, and ran off to the forest, where, first of all, she bathed, and then she put on her robe of beaten gold, and off she went to the ballroom.

As soon as she entered all eyes were upon her; and the young lord at once recognised her as the lady of the 'Basin of Water', claimed her hand for the first dance, and did not leave her till the last. When that came, he again asked her where she lived. But all that she would say was:

> 'Kind sir, if the truth I must tell,
> At the sign of the "Broken Ladle" I dwell';

and with that she curtsied and flew from the ball, then off with her golden robe, on with her catskin, and into the scullery without the cook's knowing.

Next day, when the young lord could not find where the sign of the 'Broken Ladle' was, he begged his mother to have another grand ball, so that he might meet the beautiful maid once more.

Then Catskin said to the cook, 'Oh, how I wish I could go to the ball!' Whereupon the cook called out 'A fine figure you'd cut!' and broke the skimmer across her head. But Catskin only shook her ears, and went off to the forest, where she first bathed in the crystal spring, and then donned her coat of feathers, and so off to the ballroom.

When she entered everyone was surprised at so beautiful a face and form dressed in so rich and rare a robe, but the young lord at once recognised his beautiful sweetheart, and would dance with none but her the whole evening. When the ball came to an end he pressed her to tell him where she lived, but all she would answer was:

> 'Kind sir, if the truth I must tell
> At the sign of the "Broken Skimmer" I dwell';

and with that she curtsied, and was off to the forest. But this time the young lord followed her, and watched her change her fine dress of feathers for her catskin dress, and then he knew her for his own scullery-maid.

Next day he went to his mother, and told her that he wished to marry the scullery-maid, Catskin.

'Never,' said the lady of the castle, 'never so long as I live.'

Well, the young lord was so grieved, that he took to his bed and was very ill indeed. The doctor tried to cure him, but he would not take any medicine unless from the hands of Catskin. At last the doctor went to the mother, and said that her son would die if she did not consent to his marriage with Catskin; so she had to give way. Then she summoned Catskin to her, and Catskin put on her robe of beaten gold before she went to see the lady; and she, of course, was overcome at once, and was only too glad to wed her son to so beautiful a maid.

So they were married, and after a time a little son was born to them, and grew up a fine little lad. Now one day, when he was about four years old, a beggar woman came to the door, and Lady Catskin gave some money to the little lord and told him to go and give it to the beggar woman. So he went and gave it, putting it into the hand of the woman's baby child; and the child leant forward and kissed the little lord.

Now the wicked old cook (who had never been sent away, because Catskin was too kind-hearted) was looking on, and she said, 'See how beggars' brats take to one another!'

This insult hurt Catskin dreadfully: and she went to her husband, the young lord, and told him all about her father, and begged he would go and find out what had become of her parents. So they set out in the lord's grand coach, and travelled through the forest till they came to the house of Catskin's father. Then they put up at an inn near, and Catskin stopped there, while her husband went to see if her father would own she was his daughter.

Now her father had never had any other child, and his wife had died; so he was all alone in the world, and sat moping and miserable. When the young lord came in he hardly looked up, he was so miserable. Then Catskin's husband drew a chair close up to him, and asked him, 'Pray sir, had you not once a young daughter whom you would never see or own?'

And the miserable man said with tears, 'It is true; I am a hardened sinner. But I would give all my worldly goods if I could but see her once before I die.'

Then the young lord told him what had happened to Catskin, and took him to the inn, and afterwards brought his father-in-law to his own castle, where they lived happy ever afterwards.

The Three Little Pigs

Once upon a time there was an old sow who had three little pigs, and as she had not enough for them to eat, she said they had better go out into the world and seek their fortunes.

Now the eldest pig went first, and as he trotted along the road he met a man carrying a bundle of straw. So he said very politely: 'If you please, sir, could you give me that straw to build me a house?'

And the man, seeing what good manners the little pig had, gave him the straw, and the little pig set to work and built a beautiful house with it.

Now, when it was finished, a wolf happened to pass that way; and he saw the house, and *he smelt the pig inside*.

So he knocked at the door and said:

'*Little pig! Little pig! Let me in! Let me in!*'

But the little pig saw the wolf's big paws through the keyhole, so he answered back: '*No! No! No! by the hair of my chinny chin chin!*'

Then the wolf showed his teeth and said: '*Then I'll huff and I'll puff and I'll blow your house in.*'

So he huffed and he puffed and he blew the house in. Then he ate up the little piggy and went on his way.

Now, the next piggy, when he started, met a man carrying a bundle of furze, and, being very polite, he said to him: 'If you please, sir, could you give me that furze to build me a house?'

And the man, seeing what good manners the little pig had, gave him the furze, and the little pig set to work and built himself a beautiful house.

Now it so happened that when the house was finished the wolf passed that way; and he saw the house, and *he smelt the pig inside*.

So he knocked at the door and said: '*Little pig! Little pig! Let me in! Let me in!*'

But the little pig peeped through the keyhole and saw the wolf's great ears, so he answered back: '*No! No! No! by the hair of my chinny chin chin!*'

Then the wolf showed his teeth and said: '*Then I'll huff and I'll puff and I'll blow your house in!*'

So he huffed and he puffed and he blew the house in. Then he ate up little piggy and went on his way.

Now the third little piggy, when he started, met a man carrying a load of bricks, and, being very polite, he said: 'If you please, sir, could you give me those bricks to build me a house?'

And the man, seeing that he had been well brought up, gave him the bricks, and the little pig set to work and built himself a beautiful house.

And once again it happened that when it was finished the wolf chanced to come that way; and he saw the house, and *he smelt the pig inside*.

So he knocked at the door and said: '*Little pig! Little pig! Let me in! Let me in!*'

But the little pig peeped through the keyhole and saw the wolf's great eyes, so he answered: '*No! No! No! by the hair of my chinny chin chin!*'

'*Then I'll huff and I'll puff and I'll blow your house in!*' says the wolf, showing his teeth.

Well! He huffed and he puffed. He puffed and he huffed. And

he huffed, huffed, and he puffed, puffed; but he could *not* blow the house down. At last he was so out of breath that he couldn't huff and he couldn't puff any more. So he thought a bit. Then he said: 'Little pig! I know where there is ever such a nice field of turnips.'

'Do you,' says little piggy, 'and where may that be?'

'I'll show you,' says the wolf; 'if you will be ready at six o'clock tomorrow morning, I will call round for you, and we can go together to Farmer Smith's field and get turnips for dinner.'

'Thank you kindly,' says the little piggy, 'I will be ready at six o'clock sharp.'

But, you see, the little pig was not one to be taken in with chaff, so he got up at five, trotted off to Farmer Smith's field, rooted up the turnips, and was home eating them for breakfast when the wolf clattered at the door, and cried: 'Little pig! Little pig! Aren't you ready?'

'Ready?' says the little piggy. 'Why! what a sluggard you are! I've been to the field and come back again, and I'm having a nice potful of turnips for breakfast.'

Then the wolf grew red with rage; but he was determined to eat little piggy, so he said, as if he didn't care: 'I'm glad you like them; but I know of something better than turnips.'

'Indeed,' says little piggy, 'and what may that be?'

'A nice apple tree down in Merry Gardens with the juiciest, sweetest apples on it! So if you will be ready at five o'clock tomorrow morning I will come round for you and we can get the apples together.'

'Thank you kindly,' says little piggy. 'I will sure and be ready at five o'clock sharp.'

Now the next morning he bustled up ever so early, and it wasn't four o'clock when he started to get the apples; but, you see, the wolf had been taken in once and wasn't going to be taken in again, so he also started at four o'clock, and the little pig had just got his basket half full of apples when he saw the wolf coming down the road licking his lips.

'Hullo!' says the wolf, 'here already! You *are* an early bird! Are the apples nice?'

'Very nice,' says little piggy. 'I'll throw you down one to try.'

And he threw it so far away, that when the wolf had gone to pick it up, the little pig was able to jump down with his basket and run home.

Well, the wolf was fair angry; but he went next day to the little piggy's house and called through the door, as mild as milk: 'Little pig! Little pig! You are so clever, I should like to give you a fairing; so if you will come with me to the fair this afternoon you shall have one.'

'Thank you kindly,' says little piggy, 'what time shall we start?'

'At three o'clock sharp,' says the wolf, 'so be sure to be ready.'

'I'll be ready before three,' sniggered the little piggy. And he was! He started early in the morning and went to the fair. and rode in a swing, and enjoyed himself ever so much, and bought himself a butter-churn as a fairing, and trotted away towards home long before three o'clock. But just as he got to the top of the hill what should he see but the wolf coming up it, all panting and red with rage!

Well, there was no place to hide in but the butter-churn; so he crept into it, and was just pulling down the cover when the churn started to roll down the hill – *Bumpety, bumpety, bump!*

Of course piggy, inside, began to squeal, and when the wolf heard the noise, and saw the butter-churn rolling down on top of him – *Bumpety, bumpety, bump!* – he was so frightened that he turned tail and ran away. But he was still determined to get the little pig for his dinner; so he went next day to the house and told the little pig how sorry he was not to have been able to keep his promise of going to the fair, because of an awful, dreadful, terrible Thing that had rushed at him, making a fearsome noise.

'Dear me!' says the little piggy, 'that must have been me! I hid inside the butter-churn when I saw you coming, and it started to roll! I am sorry I frightened you!'

But this was too much. The wolf danced about with rage and swore he would come down the chimney and eat up the little pig for his supper. But while he was climbing on to the roof the little pig made up a blazing fire and put on a big pot full of water to boil. Then, just as the wolf was coming down the chimney, the little piggy off with the lid, and plump! in fell the wolf into the scalding water.

So the little piggy put on the cover again, boiled the wolf up, and ate *him* for supper.

Nix Naught Nothing

Once upon a time there lived a king and a queen who didn't differ much from all the other kings and queens who have lived since Time began. But they had no children, and this made them very sad indeed. Now it so happened that the king had to go and fight battles in a far country, and he was away for many long months. And lo and behold! while he was away the queen at long last bore him a little son. As you may imagine she was fair delighted, and thought how pleased the king would be when he came home and found that his dearest wish had been fulfilled. And all the courtiers were fine and pleased too, and set about at once to arrange a grand festival for the naming of the little prince. But the queen said, 'No! The child shall have no name till his father gives it to him. Till then we will call him "Nix! Naught! Nothing!" because his father knows nothing about him!'

So little Prince Nix Naught Nothing grew into a strong, hearty little lad; for his father did not come back for a long time, and did not even know that he had a son.

But at long last he turned his face homewards. Now, on the way, he came to a big, rushing river, which neither he nor his army could cross, for it was flood-time and the water was full of dangerous whirlpools, where nixies and water wraiths lived, always ready to drown men.

So they were stopped, until a huge giant appeared, who could take the river, whirlpool and all, in his stride; and he said kindly, 'I'll carry you all over, if you like.' Now, though the giant smiled and was very polite the king knew enough of the ways of giants to think it wiser to have a hard and fast bargain. So he said, quite curt, 'What's your pay?'

'Pay?' echoed the giant with a grin, 'what do you take me for?

Give me Nix Naught Nothing, and I'll do the job with a glad heart.'

Now the king felt just a trifle ashamed at the giant's generosity; so he said, 'Certainly, certainly. I'll give you nix naught nothing and my thanks into the bargain.'

So the giant carried them safely over the stream and past the whirlpools, and the king hastened homewards. If he was glad to see his dear wife, the queen, you may imagine how he felt when she showed him his young son, tall and strong for his age.

'And what's your name, young sir?' he asked of the child fast clasped in his arms.

'Nix Naught Nothing,' answered the boy; 'that's what they call me till my father gives me a name.'

Well! the king nearly dropped the child, he was so horrified. 'What have I done?' he cried. 'I promised to give nix naught nothing to the giant who carried us over the whirlpools where the nixies and water wraiths live.'

At this the queen wept and wailed; but being a clever woman she thought out a plan whereby to save her son. So she said to her husband the king, 'If the giant comes to claim his promise, we will give him the hen-wife's youngest boy. She has so many she will not mind if we give her a crown piece, and the giant will never know the difference.'

Now sure enough the very next morning the giant appeared to claim Nix Naught Nothing, and they dressed up the hen-wife's boy in the prince's clothes and wept and wailed when the giant, fine and satisfied, carried his prize off on his back. But after a while he came to a big stone and sat down to ease his shoulders. And he fell a-dozing. Now, when he woke, he started up in a fluster, and called out:

> 'Hodge, Hodge, on my shoulders! Say
> What d'ye make the time o' day?'

And the hen-wife's little boy replied:

> 'Time that my mother, the hen-wife, takes
> The eggs for the wise queen's breakfast cakes!'

Then the giant saw at once the trick that had been played on him, and he threw the hen-wife's boy on the ground, so that his head hit on the stone and he was killed.

Then the giant strode back to the palace in a tower of a temper, and demanded 'Nix Naught Nothing'. So this time they dressed up the gardener's boy, and wept and wailed when the giant, fine and satisfied, carried his prize off on his back. Then the same thing happened. The giant grew weary of his burden, and sat down on the big stone to rest. So he fell a-dozing, woke with a start, and called out:

> 'Hodge, Hodge, on my shoulders! Say
> What d'ye make the time o' day?'

And the gardener's boy replied:

> 'Time that my father, the gardener, took
> Greens for the wise queen's dinner to cook!'

So the giant saw at once that a second trick had been played on him and became quite mad with rage. He flung the boy from him so that he was killed, and then strode back to the palace, where he cried with fury: 'Give me what you promised to give, Nix Naught Nothing, or I will destroy you all, root and branch.'

So then they saw they must give up the dear little prince, and this time they really wept and wailed as the giant carried off the boy on his back. And this time, after the giant had had his rest at the big stone, and had woke up and called:

> 'Hodge, Hodge, on my shoulders! Say
> What d'ye make the time o' day?'

the little prince replied:

> 'Time for the king my father to call
> "Let supper be served in the banqueting hall." '

Then the giant laughed with glee and rubbed his hands saying, 'I've got the right one at last.' So he took Nix Naught Nothing to his own house under the whirlpools; for the giant was really a great magician who could take any form he chose. And the reason he wanted a little prince so badly was that he had lost his wife, and had only one little daughter who needed a playmate sorely. So Nix Naught Nothing and the magician's daughter grew up together and every year made them fonder and fonder of each other, until she promised to marry him.

Now the magician had no notion that his daughter should marry just an ordinary human prince, the like of whom he had eaten a thousand times, so he sought some way in which he could quietly get rid of Nix Naught Nothing. So he said one day, 'I have work for you, Nix Naught Nothing! There is a stable hard by which is seven miles long and seven miles broad and it has not been cleaned for seven years. By tomorrow evening you must have cleaned it, or I will have you for my supper.'

Well before dawn, Nix Naught Nothing set to work at his task; but, as fast as he cleared the muck it just fell back again. So by breakfast-time he was in a terrible sweat; yet not one whit nearer the end of his job was he. Now the magician's daughter, coming to bring him his breakfast, found him so distraught and distracted that he could scarce speak to her.

'We'll soon set that to rights,' she said. So she just clapped her hands and called:

> 'Beasts and birds o' each degree,
> Clean me this stable for love o' me.'

And lo and behold! in a minute the beasts of the fields came trooping, and the sky was just dark with the wings of birds, and they carried away the muck, and the stable was clean as a new pin before the evening.

Now when the magician saw this, he grew hot and angry, and he guessed it was his daughter's magic that had wrought the miracle. So he said: 'Shame on the wit that helped you; but I have a harder job for you tomorrow. Yonder is a lake seven miles long, seven miles broad and seven miles deep. Drain it by nightfall, so that not one drop remains, or, of a certainty, I eat you for supper.'

So once again Nix Naught Nothing rose before dawn, and began his task; but though he baled out the water without ceasing, it ever ran back, so that though he sweated and laboured, by breakfast-time he was no nearer the end of his job.

But when the magician's daughter came with his breakfast she only laughed and said, 'I'll soon mend that!' Then she clapped her hands and called:

> 'Oh! all ye fish of river and sea,
> Drink me this water for love of me!'

And lo and behold! the lake was thick with fishes. And they drank and drank, till not one drop remained.

Now when the magician returned in the morning and saw this he was as angry as angry. And he knew it was his daughter's magic, so he said: 'Double shame on the wit that helped you! Yet it betters you not, for I will give you a yet harder task than the last. If you do that, you may have my daughter. See you, yonder is a tree, seven miles high, and no branch to it till the top, and there on the fork is a nest with some eggs in it. Bring those eggs down without breaking one, or, sure as fate, I'll eat you for my supper.'

Then the magician's daughter was very sad; for with all her magic she could think of no way of helping her lover to fetch the eggs, and bring them down unbroken. So she sat with Nix Naught Nothing underneath the tree and thought and thought and thought, until an idea came to her, and she clapped her hands and cried:

> 'Fingers of mine, for love of me,
> Help my true lover to climb the tree.'

Then her fingers dropped off her hands one by one and ranged themselves like the steps of a ladder up the tree; but there were not quite enough of them to reach the top, so she cried again:

> 'Oh! toes of mine, for love o' me,
> Help my true lover to climb the tree.'

Then her toes began to drop off one by one and range themselves like the rungs of a ladder; but when the toes of one foot had gone to their places the ladder was tall enough. So Nix Naught Nothing climbed up it, reached the nest and got the seven eggs. Now, as he was coming down with the last, he was so overjoyed at having finished his task, that he turned to see if the magician's daughter was overjoyed too: and lo! the seventh egg slipped from his hand and fell

'Crash!'

'Quick! Quick!' cried the magician's daughter, who, as you will observe, always had her wits about her. 'There is nothing for it now but to fly at once. But first I must have my magic flask, or I shall be unable to help. It is in my room and the door is locked. Put your fingers, since I have none, in my pocket, take the key, unlock the door, get the flask, and follow me fast. I shall go slower than you for I have no toes on one foot!'

So Nix Naught Nothing did as he was bid, and soon caught up the magician's daughter. But alas! they could not run very fast, so ere long the magician, who had once again taken a giant's form in order to have a long stride, could be seen behind them. Nearer and nearer he came until he was just going to seize Nix Naught Nothing, when the magician's daughter cried: 'Put your fingers, since I have none, into my hair, take my comb and throw it down.' So Nix Naught Nothing did as he was bid, and lo and behold! out of every one of the comb-prongs there sprang up a prickly briar, which grew so fast that the magician found himself in the middle of a thorn hedge! You may guess how angry and scratched he was before he tore his way out. So Nix Naught Nothing and his sweetheart had time for a good start; but the magician's daughter could not run fast because she had lost her toes on one foot! Therefore the magician in giant form soon caught them up, and he was just about to grip Nix Naught Nothing when the magician's daughter cried: 'Put your fingers, since I have none, to my breast. Take out my veil-dagger and throw it down.'

So he did as he was bid, and in a moment the dagger had grown to thousands and thousands of sharp razors, crisscross on the ground, and the magician giant was howling with pain as he trod among them. You may guess how he danced and stumbled and how long it took for him to pick his way through as if he were walking on eggs!

So Nix Naught Nothing and his sweetheart were nearly out of sight ere the giant could start again; yet it wasn't long before he was like to catch them up; for the magician's daughter, you see, could not run fast because she had lost her toes on one foot! She did what she could, but it was no use.

So just as the giant was reaching out a hand to lay hold of Nix Naught Nothing she cried, breathlessly: 'There's nothing left but the magic flask. Take it out and sprinkle some of what it holds on the ground.'

And Nix Naught Nothing did as he was bid; but in his hurry he nearly emptied the flask altogether; and so the big, big wave of water which instantly welled up, swept him off his feet, and would have carried him away, had not the magician's daughter's loosened veil caught him and held him fast. But the wave grew, and grew, and grew behind them, until it reached the giant's waist; then it grew and grew until it reached his shoulders; and it grew and grew until it swept over his head: a great big sea-wave full of little fishes and crabs and sea-snails and all sorts of strange creatures.

So that was the last of the magician giant. But the poor little magician's daughter was so weary that, after a time, she couldn't move a step further, and she said to her lover, 'Yonder are lights burning. Go and see if you can find a night's lodging; I will climb this tree by the pool where I shall be safe, and by the time you return I shall be rested.'

Now, by chance it happened that the lights they saw were the lights of the castle where Nix Naught Nothing's father and mother, the king and queen, lived (though, of course, he did not know this); so, as he walked towards the castle he came upon the hen-wife's cottage and asked for a night's lodging.

'Who are you?' asked the hen-wife suspiciously.

'I am Nix Naught Nothing,' replied the young man.

Now the hen-wife still grieved over her boy who had been killed, so she instantly resolved to be revenged.

'I cannot give you a night's lodging,' she said. 'But you shall have a drink of milk, for you look weary. Then you can go on to the castle and beg for a bed there.'

So she gave him a cup of milk; but, being a witch-woman, she put a potion in it so that the very moment he saw his father and mother he should fall fast asleep, and none should be able to waken him. So he would be no use to anybody, and would not recognise his father and mother.

Now the king and queen had never ceased grieving for their lost son, so they were always very kind to wandering young men, and when they heard that one was begging a night's lodging, they went down to the hall to see him. And lo! the moment Nix Naught Nothing caught sight of his father and mother, there he was on the floor fast asleep, and none could waken him! And he did not recognise his father and mother and they did not recognise him.

But Prince Nix Naught Nothing had grown into a very handsome young man, so they pitied him very much, and when none, do what they would, could waken him, the king said, 'A maiden will likely take more trouble to waken him than others, seeing how handsome he is; so send forth a proclamation that if any maiden in my realm can waken this young man, she shall have him in marriage, and a handsome dowry to boot.'

So the proclamation was sent forth, and all the pretty maidens of the realm came to try their luck; but they had no success.

Now the gardener whose boy had been killed by the giant had a daughter who was very ugly indeed – so ugly that she thought it no use to try her luck, and went about her work as usual. So she took her pitcher to the pool to fill it. Now the magician's daughter was still hiding in the tree waiting for her lover to return. Thus it came to pass that the gardener's ugly daughter, bending down to fill her pitcher in the pool, saw a beautiful shadow in the water, and thought it was her own!

'If I am as pretty as that,' she cried, 'I'll draw water no longer!'

So she threw down her pitcher, and went straight to the castle to see if she hadn't a chance of the handsome stranger and the handsome dowry. But of course she hadn't; though at the sight of Nix Naught Nothing she fell so much in love with him that, knowing the hen-wife to be a witch, she went straight to her, and offered all her savings for a charm by which she could awaken the sleeper.

Now when the hen-wife witch heard her tale, she thought it would be a rare revenge to marry the king and queen's long-lost son to a gardener's ugly daughter; so she straightway took the girl's savings and gave her a charm by which she could unspell the prince or spell him again at her pleasure.

So away went the gardener's daughter to the castle, and sure enough, no sooner had she sung her charm, than Nix Naught Nothing awoke.

'I am going to marry you, my charmer,' she said coaxingly; but Nix Naught Nothing said he would prefer sleep. So she thought it wiser to put him to sleep again till the marriage feast was ready, and she had got her fine clothes. So she spelled him asleep again.

Now the gardener had, of course, to draw the water himself, since his daughter would not work. And he took the pitcher to the pool; and he also saw the magician's daughter's shadow in the water; but he did not think the face was his own, for, see you, he had a beard!

Then he looked up and saw the lady in the tree.

She, poor thing, was half dead with sorrow, and hunger, and fatigue, so, being a kind man, he took her to his house and gave her food. And he told her that that *very day* his daughter was to marry a handsome young stranger at the castle, and to get a handsome dowry to boot from the king and queen, in memory of their son, Nix Naught Nothing, who had been carried off by a giant when he was a little boy.

Then the magician's daughter felt sure that something had happened to her lover; so she went to the castle, and there she found him fast asleep in a chair.

But she could not waken him, for, see you, her magic had gone from her with the magic flask which Nix Naught Nothing had emptied.

So, though she put her fingerless hands on his and wept and sang:

> 'I cleaned the stable for love o' thee,
> I laved the lake and I clomb the tree,
> Wilt thou not waken for love o' me?'

he never stirred nor woke.

Now one of the old servants there, seeing how she wept, took pity on her and said, 'She that is to marry the young man will be back ere long, and unspell him for the wedding. Hide yourself and listen to her charm.'

So the magician's daughter hid herself, and, by and by, in comes the gardener's daughter in her fine wedding-dress, and begins to sing her charm. But the magician's daughter didn't wait for her to finish it; for the moment Nix Naught Nothing opened his eyes, she rushed out of her hiding-place, and put her fingerless hands in his.

Then Nix Naught Nothing remembered everything. He remembered the castle, he remembered his father and mother, he remembered the magician's daughter and all that she had done for him.

Then he drew out the magic flask and said, 'Surely, surely there must be enough magic in it to mend your hands.' And there was. There were just fourteen drops left, ten for the fingers and four for the toes; but there was not one for the little toe, so it could not be brought back. Of course after that there was great rejoicing, and Prince Nix Naught Nothing and the magician's daughter were married and lived happy ever after, even though she only had four toes on one foot. As for the hen-wife witch, she was burnt, and so the gardener's daughter got back her earnings; but she was not happy, because her shadow in the water was ugly again.

Mr and Mrs Vinegar

Mr and Mrs Vinegar, a worthy couple, lived in a glass pickle-jar. The house, though small, was snug, and so light that each speck of dust on the furniture showed like a molehill; so while Mr Vinegar tilled his garden with a pickle-fork and grew vegetables for pickling, Mrs Vinegar, who was a sharp, bustling, tidy woman, swept, brushed and dusted, brushed and dusted and swept to keep the house clean as a new pin. Now one day she lost her temper with a cobweb and swept so hard after it that bang! bang! the broom-handle went right through the glass, and crash! crash! clitter! clatter! there was the pickle-jar house about her ears all in splinters and bits.

She picked her way over these as best she might, and rushed into the garden.

'Oh, Vinegar, Vinegar!' she cried. 'We are clean ruined and done for! Quit these vegetables! they won't be wanted! What is the use of pickles if you haven't a pickle-jar to put them in, and – I've broken ours – into little bits!' And with that she fell to crying bitterly.

But Mr Vinegar was of different mettle; though a small man, he was a cheerful one, always looking at the best side of things, so he said, 'Accidents will happen, lovey! But there are as good pickle-bottles in the shop as ever came out of it. All we need is money to buy another. So let us go out into the world and seek our fortunes.'

'But what about the furniture,' sobbed Mrs Vinegar.

'I will take the door of the house with me, lovey,' quoth Mr Vinegar stoutly. 'Then no one will be able to open it, will they?'

Mrs Vinegar did not quite see how this fact would mend matters, but, being a good wife, she held her peace. So off they trudged into the world to seek their fortune, Mr Vinegar bearing the door on his back like a snail carries its house.

Well, they walked all day long, but not a brass farthing did they make, and when night fell, they found themselves in a dark, thick forest. Now Mrs Vinegar, for all she was a smart strong woman, was tired to death, and filled with fear of wild beasts, so she began once more to cry bitterly; but Mr Vinegar was cheerful as ever.

'Don't alarm yourself, lovey,' he said. 'I will climb into a tree, fix the door firmly in a fork, and you can sleep there as safe and comfortable as in your own bed.'

So he climbed the tree, fixed the door, and Mrs Vinegar lay down on it, and being dead tired was soon fast asleep. But her weight tilted the door sideways, so, after a time, Mr Vinegar, being afraid she might slip off, sat down on the other side to balance her and keep watch.

Now in the very middle of the night, just as he was beginning to nod, what should happen but that a band of robbers should meet beneath that very tree in order to divide their spoils. Mr Vinegar could hear every word said quite distinctly, and began to tremble like an aspen as he listened to the terrible deeds the thieves had done to gain their ends.

'Don't shake so!' murmured Mrs Vinegar, half asleep. 'You'll have me off the bed.'

'I'm not shaking, lovey,' whispered back Mr Vinegar in a quaking voice. 'It is only the wind in the trees.'

But for all his cheerfulness he was not really *very* brave *inside*, so he went on trembling and shaking and shaking and trembling, till, just as the robbers were beginning to parcel out the money, he actually shook the door right out of the tree-fork, and down it came – with Mrs Vinegar still asleep upon it – right on top of the robbers' heads!

As you may imagine, they thought the sky had fallen, and made off as fast as their legs would carry them, leaving their booty behind them. But Mr Vinegar, who had saved himself from the fall by clinging to a branch, was far too frightened to go down in the dark to see what had happened. So up in the tree he sat like a big bird until dawn came.

Then Mrs Vinegar woke, rubbed her eyes, yawned, and said,

'Where am I?'

'On the ground, lovey,' answered Mr Vinegar, scrambling down.

And when they lifted up the door what do you think they found?

One robber squashed flat as a pancake and forty golden guineas all scattered about!

My goodness! How Mr and Mrs Vinegar jumped for joy!

'Now, Vinegar!' said his wife when they had gathered up all the gold pieces, 'I will tell you what we must do. You must go to the next market-town and buy a cow; for, see you, money makes the mare to go, truly; but it also goes itself. Now a cow won't run away, but will give us milk and butter, which we can sell. So we shall live in comfort for the rest of our days.'

'What a head you have, lovey,' said Mr Vinegar admiringly, and started off on his errand.

'Mind you make a good bargain,' bawled his wife after him.

'I always do,' bawled back Mr Vinegar. 'I made a good bargain when I married such a clever wife, and I made a better one when I shook her down from the tree. I am the happiest man alive!'

So he trudged on, laughing and jingling the forty gold pieces in his pocket.

Now the first thing he saw in the market was an old red cow.

'I am in luck today,' he thought, 'that is the very beast for me. I shall be the happiest of men if I get that cow.' So he went up to the owner, jingling the gold in his pocket.

'What will you take for your cow?' he asked.

And the owner of the cow, seeing he was a simpleton, said 'What you've got in your pocket.'

'Done!' said Mr Vinegar, handed over the forty guineas and led off the cow, marching her up and down the market much against her will, to show off his bargain.

Now, as he drove it about, proud as Punch, he noticed a man who was playing the bagpipes. He was followed about by a crowd of children who danced to the music, and a perfect shower of pennies fell into his cap every time he held it out.

'Ho, ho!' thought Mr Vinegar. 'That is an easier way of

earning a livelihood than by driving about a beast of a cow! Then the feeding, and the milking, and the churning! Ah, I should be the happiest man alive if I had those bagpipes!'

So he went up to the musician and said, 'What will you take for your bagpipes?'

'Well,' replied the musician, seeing he was a simpleton, 'it is a beautiful instrument and I make so much money by it that I cannot take anything less than that red cow.'

'Done!' cried Mr Vinegar in a hurry, lest the man should repent of his offer.

So the musician walked off with the red cow, and Mr Vinegar tried to play the bagpipes. But, alas, and alack! Though he blew till he almost burst, not a sound could he make at first, and when he did at last, it was such a terrific squeal and screech that all the children ran away frightened, and the people stopped their ears.

But he went on and on, trying to play a tune, and never earning anything, save hootings and peltings, until his fingers were almost frozen with the cold, when of course the noise he made on the bagpipes was worse than ever.

Then he noticed a man who had on a pair of warm gloves, and he said to himself, 'Music is impossible when one's fingers are frozen. I believe I should be the happiest man alive if I had those gloves.'

So he went up to the owner and said, 'You seem, sir, to have a very good pair of gloves.' And the man replied, 'Truly, sir, my hands are as warm as toast this bitter November day.'

That quite decided Mr Vinegar and he asked at once what the owner would take for them; and the owner, seeing he was a simpleton, said, 'As your hands seem frozen, sir, I will, as a favour, let you have them for your bagpipes.'

'Done!' cried Mr Vinegar, delighted, and made the exchange.

Then he set off to find his wife, quite pleased with himself. 'Warm hands, warm heart!' he thought. 'I'm the happiest man alive!'

But as he trudged he grew very, very tired, and at last began to limp. Then he saw a man coming along the road with a stout stick.

'I should be the happiest man alive if I had that stick,' he thought. 'What is the use of warm hands if your feet ache!' So he said to the man with the stick, 'What will you take for your stick?' and the man, seeing he was a simpleton, replied: 'Well, I don't want to part with my stick, but as you are so pressing I'll oblige you, as a friend, for those warm gloves you are wearing.'

'Done for you!' cried Mr Vinegar delightedly; and trudged off with the stick, chuckling to himself over his good bargain.

But as he went along a magpie fluttered out of the hedge and sat on a branch in front of him, and chuckled and laughed as magpies do. 'What are you laughing at?' asked Mr Vinegar.

'At you, forsooth!' chuckled the magpie, fluttering just a little further. 'At *you*, Mr Vinegar, you foolish man – you simpleton – you blockhead! You bought a cow for forty guineas when she wasn't worth ten, you exchanged her for bagpipes you couldn't play – you changed the bagpipes for a pair of gloves, and the pair of gloves for a miserable stick. Ho, ho! Ha, ha! So you've nothing to show for your forty guineas save a stick you might have cut in any hedge. Ah, you fool! you simpleton! you blockhead!'

And the magpie chuckled, and chuckled, and chuckled in such guffaws, fluttering from branch to branch as Mr Vinegar trudged along, that at last he flew into a violent rage and flung his stick at the bird. And the stick stuck in a tree out of his reach; so he had to go back to his wife without anything at all.

But he was glad the stick had stuck in a tree, for Mrs Vinegar's hands were quite hard enough.

When it was all over Mr Vinegar said cheerfully, 'You are too violent, lovey. You broke the pickle-jar, and now you've nearly broken every bone in my body. I think we had better turn over a new leaf and begin afresh. I shall take service as a gardener, and you can go as a housemaid until we have enough money to buy a new pickle-jar. There are as good ones in the shop as ever came out of it.'

And that is the story of Mr and Mrs Vinegar.

The True History of Sir Thomas Thumb

At the court of great King Arthur, who lived, as all know, when knights were bold, and ladies were fair indeed, one of the most renowned of men was the wizard Merlin. Never before or since was there such another. All that was to be known of wizardry he knew, and his advice was ever good and kindly.

Now once, when he was travelling in the guise of a beggar, he chanced upon an honest ploughman and his wife who, giving him a hearty welcome, supplied him, cheerfully, with a big wooden bowl of fresh milk and some coarse brown bread on a wooden platter. Still, though both they and the little cottage where they dwelt were neat and tidy, Merlin noticed that neither the husband nor the wife seemed happy; and when he asked the cause they said it was because they had no children.

'Had I but a son, no matter if he were no bigger than my goodman's thumb,' said the poor woman, 'we should be quite content.'

Now this idea of a boy no bigger than a man's thumb, so tickled Wizard Merlin's fancy that he promised straight away that such a son should come in due time to bring the good couple content. This done he went off at once to pay a visit to the Queen of the Fairies, since he felt that the little people would best be able to carry out his promise. And, sure enough, the droll fancy of a mannikin no bigger than his father's thumb tickled the Fairy queen also, and she set about the task at once.

So behold the ploughman and his wife as happy as king and queen over the tiniest of tiny babies; and all the happier because the Fairy queen, anxious to see the little fellow, flew in at the window, bringing with her clothes fit for the wee mannikin to wear.

An oak-leaf hat he had for his crown;
His jacket was woven of thistledown.
His shirt was a web by spiders spun,
His breeches of softest feathers were done,
His stockings of red-apple rind were tyne,
With an eyelash plucked from his mother's eyne.
His shoes were made of a mouse's skin,
Tanned with the soft furry hair within.

Dressed in this guise he looked the prettiest little fellow ever seen, and the Fairy queen kissed him over and over again, and gave him the name of Tom Thumb.

Now as he grew older – though, mind you, he never grew bigger – he was so full of antics and tricks that he was for ever getting into trouble. Once his mother was making a batter pudding, and Tom, wanting to see how it was made, climbed up to the edge of the bowl. His mother was so busy beating the batter that she didn't notice him; and when his foot slipped, and he plumped head and ears into the bowl, she just went on beating until the batter was light enough. Then she put it into the pudding-cloth and set it on the fire to boil.

Now the batter had so filled poor Tom's mouth that he couldn't cry; but no sooner did he feel the hot water than he began to struggle and kick so much that the pudding bobbed up and down and jumped about in such strange fashion that the ploughman's wife thought it was bewitched, and in a great fright flung it out of the door.

Here a poor tinker passing by picked it up and put it in his wallet. But by this time Tom had got his mouth clear of the batter, and he began hollering, and making such a to-do, that the tinker, even more frightened than Tom's mother had been, threw the pudding in the road, and ran away as fast as he could run. Luckily for Tom, this second fall broke the pudding string and he was able to creep out all covered with half-cooked batter, and make his way home, where his mother, distressed to see her little dear in such a woeful state, put him into a teacup of water to clean him and then tucked him up in bed.

Another time Tom's mother went to milk her red cow in the meadow and took Tom with her, for she was ever afraid lest he should fall into mischief when left alone. Now the wind was high, and fearful lest he should be blown away, she tied him to a thistle-head with one of her own long hairs, and then began to milk. But the red cow, nosing about for something to do while she was being milked, as all cows will, spied Tom's oak-leaf hat, and thinking it looked good, curled its tongue round the thistle-stalk and –

There was Tom dodging the cow's teeth, and roaring as loud as he could –

'Mother! Mother! Help! Help!'

'Lawks-a-mercy-me,' cried his mother, 'where's the child got to now? Where are you, you bad boy?'

'Here!' roared Tom, 'in the red cow's mouth!'

With that his mother began to weep and wail, not knowing what else to do; and Tom, hearing her, roared louder than ever. Whereat the red cow, alarmed – and no wonder! – at the dreadful noise in her throat, opened her mouth, and Tom dropped out, luckily into his mother's apron; otherwise he would have been badly hurt falling so far.

Adventures like these were not Tom's fault. He could not help being so small, but he got into dreadful trouble once for which he was entirely to blame. This is what happened. He loved playing cherry-stones with the big boys, and when he had lost all his own he would creep unbeknownst into the other players' pockets or bags, and make off with cherry-stones enough and galore to carry on the game!

Now one day it so happened that one of the boys saw Master Tom on the point of coming out of a bag with a whole fistful of cherry-stones. So he just drew the string of the bag tight.

'Ha! Ha! Mr Thomas Thumb,' says he jeeringly, 'so you were going to pinch my cherry-stones, were you? Well! you shall have more of them than you like.' And with that he gave the cherry-stone bag such a hearty shake that all Tom's body and legs were sadly bruised black and blue; nor was he let out till he had promised never to steal cherry-stones again.

So the years passed, and when Tom was a lad, still no bigger than a thumb, his father thought he might begin to make himself useful. So he made him a whip out of a barley straw, and set him to drive the cattle home. But Tom, in trying to climb a furrow's ridge – which, to him, of course, was a steep hill – slipped down and lay half stunned, so that a raven, happening to fly over, thought he was a frog, and picked him up intending to eat him. Not relishing the morsel, however, the bird dropped him above the battlements of a big castle that stood close to the sea. Now the castle belonged to one Grumbo, an ill-tempered giant who happened to be taking the air on the roof of his tower. And when Tom dropped on his bald pate the giant put up his great hand to catch what he thought was an impudent fly, and finding something that smelt man's meat, he just swallowed the little fellow as he would have swallowed a pill!

He began, however, to repent very soon, for Tom kicked and struggled in the giant's inside as he had done in the red cow's throat until the giant felt quite squeamish, and finally got rid of Tom by being sick over the battlements into the sea.

And here, doubtless, would have been Tom Thumb's end by drowning, had not a big fish, thinking that he was a shrimp, rushed at him and gulped him down!

Now by good chance some fishermen were standing by with their nets, and when they drew them in, the fish that had swallowed Tom was one of the haul. Being a very fine fish it was sent to the court kitchen, where, when the fish was opened, out popped Tom on the dresser, as spry as spry, to the astonishment of the cook and the scullions! Never had such a mite of a man been seen, while his quips and pranks kept the whole buttery in roars of laughter. What is more he soon became the favourite of the whole court, and when the king went out a-riding Tom sat in the royal waistcoat pocket ready to amuse royalty and the Knights of the Round Table.

After a while, however, Tom wearied to see his parents again, so the king gave him leave to go home and take with him as much money as he could carry. Tom therefore chose a three-penny bit, and putting it into a purse made of a water bubble, lifted it with difficulty on to his back, and trudged away to his father's house, which was some half a mile distant.

It took him two days and two nights to cover the ground, and he was fair outwearied by his heavy burden ere he reached home. However, his mother put him to rest in a walnut shell by the fire and gave him a whole hazelnut to eat; which, sad to say, disagreed with him dreadfully. However, he recovered in some measure, but had grown so thin and light that to save him the trouble of walking back to the court, his mother tied him to a dandelion-clock, and as there was a high wind, away he went as if on wings. Unfortunately, however, just as he was flying low in order to alight, the court cook, an ill-natured fellow, was coming across the palace yard with a bowl of hot furmety for the king's supper. Now Tom was unskilled in the handling of dandelion horses, so what should happen but that he rode straight into the furmety, spilt the half of it, and splashed the other half, scalding hot, into the cook's face.

He was in a fine rage, and going straight to King Arthur said that Tom, at his old antics, had done it on purpose.

Now the king's favourite dish was hot furmety; so he also fell into a fine rage and ordered Tom to be tried for high treason. He was therefore imprisoned in a mousetrap, where he remained for several days tormented by a cat who, thinking him some new kind of mouse, spent its time in sparring at him through the bars. At the end of a week, however, King Arthur, having recovered from the loss of the furmety, sent for Tom and once more received him into favour. After this Tom's life was happy and successful. He became so renowned for his dexterity and wonderful activity, that he was knighted by the king under the name of Sir Thomas Thumb, and as his clothes, what with the batter and the furmety, to say nothing of the insides of giants and fishes, had become somewhat shabby, his majesty ordered him a new suit of clothes fit for a mounted knight to wear. He also gave him a beautiful prancing grey mouse as a charger.

It was certainly very diverting to see Tom dressed up to the nines, and as proud as Punch.

> Of butterflies' wings his shirt was made,
> His boots of chicken hide,
> And by a nimble fairy blade
> All learned in the tailoring trade,
> His coat was well supplied.
> A needle dangled at his side,
> And thus attired in stately pride
> A dapper mouse he used to ride.

In truth King Arthur and all the Knights of the Round Table were ready to expire with laughter at Tom on his fine curveting steed.

But one day, as the hunt was passing a farmhouse, a big cat, lurking about, made one spring and carried both Tom and the mouse up a tree. Nothing daunted Tom boldly drew his needle sword and attacked the enemy with such fierceness that she let her prey fall. Luckily one of the nobles caught the little fellow in his cap, otherwise he must have been killed by the fall. As it was he became very ill, and the doctor almost despaired of his life. However, his friend and guardian, the Queen of the Fairies, arrived in a chariot drawn by flying mice, and then and there carried Tom back with her to Fairyland where, amongst folk of his own size, he, after a time, recovered. But time runs swiftly in Fairyland, and when Tom Thumb returned to court he was surprised to find that his father and mother and nearly all his old friends were dead, and that King Thunstone reigned in King Arthur's place. So everyone was astonished at his size, and carried him as a curiosity to the Audience Hall.

'Who art thou, mannikin?' asked King Thunstone; 'whence dost come? And where dost live?'

To which Tom replied with a bow –

> 'My name is well known.
> From the Fairies I come.
> When King Arthur shone,
> This court was my home.
> By him I was knighted,
> In me he delighted
> – Your servant – Sir Thomas Thumb.'

This address so pleased his majesty that he ordered a little golden chair to be made, so that Tom might sit beside him at table. Also a little palace of gold, but a span high, with doors a bare inch wide, in which the little fellow might take his ease.

Now King Thunstone's queen was a very jealous woman, and could not bear to see such honours showered on the little fellow; so she up and told the king all sorts of bad tales about his favourite; amongst others that he had been saucy and rude to her.

Whereupon the king sent for Tom; but forewarned is forearmed, and knowing by bitter experience the danger of royal displeasure, Tom hid himself in an empty snail-shell, where he lay till he was nigh starved. Then seeing a fine large butterfly on a dandelion close by, he climbed up and managed to get astride it. No sooner had he gained his seat than the butterfly was off, hovering from tree to tree, from flower to flower.

At last the royal gardener saw it and gave chase, then the nobles joined in the hunt, even the king himself, and finally the queen, who forgot her anger in the merriment. Hither and thither they ran trying in vain to catch the pair, and almost expiring with laughter, until poor Tom, dizzy with so much fluttering, and doubling, and flittering, fell from his seat into a watering-pot, where he was nearly drowned.

So they all agreed he must be forgiven, because he had afforded them so much amusement.

Thus Tom was once more in favour; but he did not live long to enjoy his good luck, for a spider one day attacked him, and though he fought well, the creature's poisonous breath proved too much for him; he fell dead on the ground where he stood, and the spider soon sucked every drop of his blood.

Thus ended Sir Thomas Thumb; but the king and the court were so sorry at the loss of their little favourite that they went into mourning for him. And they put a fine white marble monument over his grave whereon was carven the following epitaph:

Here lyes Tom Thumb, King Arthur's knight,
Who died by a spider's fell despite.
He was well known in Arthur's court,
Where he afforded gallant sport.
He rode at tilt and tournament
And on a mouse a-hunting went.
Alive he filled the court with mirth,
His death to sadness must give birth.
So wipe your eyes and shake your head,
And say, 'Alas, Tom Thumb is dead!'

Henny-Penny

One day Henny-penny was picking up corn in the rickyard when – whack! – an acorn hit her upon the head. 'Goodness gracious me!' said Henny-penny; 'the sky's a-going to fall, I must go and tell the king.'

So she went along, and she went along, and she went along till she met Cocky-locky. 'Where are you going, Henny-penny?' says Cocky-locky. 'Oh! I'm going to tell the king the sky's a-falling,' says Henny-penny. 'May I come with you?' says Cocky-locky. 'Certainly,' says Henny-penny. So Henny-penny and Cocky-locky went to tell the king the sky was falling.

They went along, and they went along, and they went along, till they met Ducky-daddles. 'Where are you going to, Henny-penny and Cocky-locky?' says Ducky-daddles. 'Oh! we're going to tell the king the sky's a-falling,' said Henny-penny and Cocky-locky. 'May I come with you?' says Ducky-daddles. 'Certainly,' said Henny-penny and Cocky-locky. So Henny-penny, Cocky-locky, and Ducky-daddles went to tell the king the sky was a-falling.

So they went along, and they went along, and they went along, till they met Goosey-poosey. 'Where are you going to, Henny-penny, Cocky-locky and Ducky-daddles?' said Goosey-poosey. 'Oh! we're going to tell the king the sky's a-falling,' said Henny-penny and Cocky-locky and Ducky-daddles. 'May I come with you?' said Goosey-poosey. 'Certainly,' said Henny-penny, Cocky-locky and Ducky-daddles. So Henny-penny, Cocky-locky, Ducky-daddles and Goosey-poosey went to tell the king the sky was a-falling.

So they went along, and they went along, and they went along, till they met Turkey-lurkey. 'Where are you going, Henny-penny, Cocky-locky, Ducky-daddles and Goosey-poosey?' says

Turkey-lurkey. 'Oh! we're going to tell the king the sky's a-falling,' said Henny-penny, Cocky-locky, Ducky-daddles and Goosey-poosey. 'May I come with you, Henny-penny, Cocky-locky, Ducky-daddles and Goosey-poosey?' said Turkey-lurkey. 'Oh, certainly, Turkey-lurkey,' said Henny-penny, Cocky-locky, Ducky-daddles and Goosey-poosey. So Henny-penny, Cocky-locky, Ducky-daddles, Goosey-poosey and Turkey-lurkey all went to tell the king the sky was a-falling.

So they went along and they went along, and they went along, till they met Foxy-woxy, and Foxy-woxy said to Henny-penny, Cocky-locky, Ducky-daddles, Goosey-poosey and Turkey-lurkey: 'Where are you going, Henny-penny, Cocky-locky, Ducky-daddles Goosey-poosey and Turkey-lurkey?' And Henny-penny, Cocky-locky, Ducky-daddles, Goosey-poosey and Turkey-lurkey said to Foxy-woxy, 'We're going to tell the king the sky's a-falling.'

'Oh! but this is not the way to the king, Henny-penny, Cocky-locky, Ducky-daddles, Goosey-poosey and Turkey-lurkey,' says Foxy-woxy; 'I know the proper way; shall I show it you?' 'Oh, certainly, Foxy-woxy,' said Henny-penny, Cocky-locky, Ducky-daddles, Goosey-poosey and Turkey-lurkey. So Henny-penny, Cocky-locky, Ducky-daddles, Goosey-poosey, Turkey-lurkey and Foxy-woxy all went to tell the king the sky was a-falling. So they

went along, and they went along, and they went along, till they came to a narrow and dark hole. Now this was the door of Foxy-woxy's burrow. But Foxy-woxy said to Henny-penny, Cocky-locky, Ducky-daddles, Goosey-poosey and Turkey-lurkey, 'This is the short cut to the king's palace: you'll soon get there if you follow me. I will go first and you come after, Henny-penny, Cocky-locky, Ducky-daddles, Goosey-poosey and Turkey-lurkey.' 'Why of course, certainly, without doubt, why not?' said Henny-penny, Cocky-locky, Ducky-daddles, Goosey-poosey and Turkey-lurkey.

So Foxy-woxy went into his burrow, and he didn't go very far but turned round to wait for Henny-penny, Cocky-locky, Ducky-daddles, Goosey-poosey and Turkey-lurkey. Now Turkey-lurkey was the first to go through the dark hole into the burrow. He hadn't got far when –

'Hrumph!'

Foxy-woxy snapped off Turkey-lurkey's head and threw his body over his left shoulder. Then Goosey-poosey went in, and –

'Hrumph!'

Off went her head and Goosey-poosey was thrown beside Turkey-lurkey. Then Ducky-daddles waddled down, and –

'Hrumph!'

Foxy-woxy had snapped off Ducky-daddles' head and Ducky-daddles was thrown alongside Turkey-lurkey and Goosey-poosey. Then Cocky-locky strutted down into the burrow and he hadn't gone far when –

'Hrumph!'

But Cocky-locky *will* always crow whether you want him to do so or not, and so he had just time for one 'Cock-a-doo-dle-d – ' before he went to join Turkey-lurkey, Goosey-poosey and Ducky-daddles over Foxy-woxy's shoulders.

Now when Henny-penny, who had just got into the dark burrow, heard Cocky-locky crow, she said to herself: 'My goodness! it must be dawn. Time for me to lay my egg.'

So she turned round and bustled off to her nest; so she escaped – and she never told the king the sky was falling!

The Three Heads of the Well

Once upon a time there reigned a king in Colchester, valiant, strong wise, famous as a good ruler.

But in the midst of his glory his dear queen died, leaving him with a daughter just touching woman's estate; and this maiden was renowned, far and wide, for beauty, kindness and grace. Now strange things happen, and the King of Colchester, hearing of a lady who had immense riches, had a mind to marry her, though she was old, ugly, hook-nosed and ill-tempered; and though she was, furthermore, possessed of a daughter as ugly as herself. None could give the reason why, but only a few weeks after the death of his dear queen, the king brought this loathly bride to court, and married her with great pomp and festivities. Now the very first thing she did was to poison the king's mind against his own beautiful, kind, gracious daughter, of whom, naturally, the ugly queen and her ugly daughter were dreadfully jealous.

Now when the young princess found that even her father had turned against her, she grew weary of court life, and longed to get away from it; so, one day, happening to meet the king alone in the garden, she went down on her knees, and begged and prayed him to give her some help, and let her go out into the world to seek her fortune. To this the king agreed, and told his consort to fit the girl out for her enterprise in proper fashion. But the jealous woman only gave her a canvas bag of brown bread and hard cheese, with a bottle of small-beer.

Though this was but a pitiful dowry for a king's daughter, the princess was too proud to complain; so she took it, returned her thanks, and set off on her journey through woods and forests, by rivers and lakes, over mountain and valley.

At last she came to a cave at the mouth of which, on a stone, sat an old, old man with a white beard.

'Good morrow, fair damsel,' he said, 'whither away so fast?'

'Reverend father,' replies she, 'I go to seek my fortune.'

'And what hast thou for dowry, fair damsel?' said he, 'in thy bag and bottle?'

'Bread and cheese and small-beer, father,' says she, smiling. 'Will it please you to partake of either?'

'With all my heart,' says he, and when she pulled out her provisions he ate them nearly all. But once again she made no complaint, but bade him eat what he needed, and welcome.

Now, when he had finished he gave her many thanks, and said: 'For your beauty, and your kindness, and your grace, take this wand. There is a thick thorny hedge before you which seems impassable. But strike it thrice with this wand, saying each time, "Please, hedge, let me through," and it will open a pathway for you. Then, when you come to a well, sit down on the brink of it, do not be surprised at anything you may see, but, whatever you are asked to do, that do!'

So saying the old man went into the cave and she went on her way. After a while she came to a high, thick thorny hedge; but when she struck it three times with the wand, saying, 'Please, hedge, let me through,' it opened a wide pathway for her. So she came to the well, on the brink of which she sat down, and no sooner had she done so, than a golden head without any body came up through the water, singing as it came:

> 'Wash me and comb me, lay me on the bank to dry
> Softly and prettily to watch the passers-by.'

'Certainly,' she said, pulling out her silver comb. Then, placing the head on her lap, she began to comb the golden hair. When she had combed it, she lifted the golden head softly, and laid it on a primrose bank to dry. No sooner had she done this than another golden head appeared, singing as it came:

> 'Wash me and comb me, lay me on the bank to dry
> Softly and prettily to watch the passers-by.'

'Certainly,' says she, and after combing the golden hair, placed the golden head softly on the primrose bank, beside the first one.

Then came a third head out of the well, and it said the same thing:

> 'Wash me and comb me, lay me on the bank to dry
> Softly and prettily to watch the passers-by.'

'With all my heart,' says she, graciously, and after taking the head on her lap, and combing its golden hair with her silver comb, there were the three golden heads in a row on the primrose bank. And she sat down to rest herself and looked at them, they were so quaint and pretty; and as she rested she cheerfully ate and drank the meagre portion of the brown bread, hard cheese and small-beer which the old man had left to her; for, though she was a king's daughter, she was too proud to complain.

Then the first head spoke. 'Brothers, what shall we weird for this damsel who has been so gracious unto us? I weird her to be so beautiful that she shall charm everyone she meets.'

'And I,' said the second head, 'weird her a voice that shall exceed the nightingale's in sweetness.'

'And I,' said the third head, 'weird her to be so fortunate that she shall marry the greatest king that reigns.'

'Thank you with all my heart,' says she; 'but don't you think I had better put you back in the well before I go on? Remember you are golden, and the passers-by might steal you.'

To this they agreed; so she put them back. And when they had thanked her for her kind thought and said goodbye, she went on her journey.

Now she had not travelled far before she came to a forest where the king of the country was hunting with his nobles, and as the gay cavalcade passed down the glade she stood back to avoid them; but the king caught sight of her and drew up his horse, fairly amazed at her beauty.

'Fair maid,' he said, 'who art thou, and whither goest thou through the forest thus alone?'

'I am the King of Colchester's daughter, and I go to seek my fortune,' says she, and her voice was sweeter than the nightingale's.

Then the king jumped from his horse, being so struck by her that he felt it would be impossible to live without her, and falling on his knee begged and prayed her to marry him without delay.

And he begged and prayed so well that at last she consented. So, with all courtesy, he mounted her on his horse behind him, and commanding the hunt to follow, he returned to his palace, where the wedding festivities took place with all possible pomp and merriment. Then, ordering out the royal chariot, the happy pair started to pay the King of Colchester a bridal visit: and you may imagine the surprise and delight with which, after so short an absence, the people of Colchester saw their beloved, beautiful, kind and gracious princess return in a chariot all gemmed with gold, as the bride of the most powerful king in the world. The bells rang out, flags flew, drums beat, the people huzzaed, and all was gladness, save for the ugly queen and her ugly daughter, who were ready to burst with envy and malice; for, see you, the despised maiden was now above them both, and went before them at every court ceremonial.

So, after the visit was ended, and the young king and his bride had gone back to their own country, there to live happily ever after, the ugly ill-natured princess said to her mother, the ugly queen: 'I also will go into the world and seek my fortune. If that drab of a girl with her mincing ways got so much, what may I not get?'

So her mother agreed, and furnished her forth with silken dresses and furs, and gave her as provisions, sugar, almonds and sweetmeats of every variety, besides a large flagon of Malaga sack. Altogether a right royal dowry.

Armed with these she set forth, following the same road as her stepsister. Thus she soon came upon the old man with a white beard, who was seated on a stone by the mouth of a cave.

'Good morrow,' says he. 'Whither away so fast?'

'What's that to you, old man?' she replied rudely.

'And what hast thou for dowry in bag and bottle?' he asked quietly.

'Good things with which you shall not be troubled,' she answered pertly.

'Wilt thou not spare an old man something?' he said.

Then she laughed. 'Not a bite, not a sup, lest they should choke you: though that would be small matter to me,' she replied with a toss of her head.

'Then ill luck go with thee,' remarked the old man as he rose and went into the cave.

So she went on her way, and after a time came to the thick thorny hedge, and seeing what she thought was a gap in it, she tried to pass through; but no sooner had she got well into the middle of the hedge than the thorns closed in around her so that she was all scratched and torn before she went her way. Thus, streaming with blood, she went on to the well, and seeing water, sat on the brink intending to cleanse herself. But just as she dipped her hands, up came a golden head singing as it came:

> 'Wash me and comb me, lay me on the bank to dry
> Softly and prettily to watch the passers-by.'

'A likely story,' says she. 'I'm going to wash myself.' And with that she gave the head such a bang with her bottle that it bobbed below the water. But it came up again, and so did a second head, singing as it came:

'Wash me and comb me, lay me on the bank to dry
Softly and prettily to watch the passers-by.'

'Not I,' scoffs she. 'I'm going to wash *my* hands and face and have my dinner.' So she fetches the second head a cruel bang with the bottle and both heads ducked down in the water.

But when they came up again all draggled and dripping, the third head came also, singing as it came:

'Wash me and comb me, lay me on the bank to dry
Softly and prettily to watch the passers-by.'

By this time the ugly princess had cleansed herself, and seated on the primrose bank had her mouth full of sugar and almonds.

'Not I,' says she as well as she could. 'I'm not a washerwoman nor a barber. So take that for your washing and combing.'

And with that, having finished the Malaga sack, she flung the empty bottle at the three heads.

But this time they didn't duck. They looked at each other and said. 'How shall we weird this rude girl for her bad manners?' Then the first head said: 'I weird that to her ugliness shall be added blotches on her face.'

And the second head said: 'I weird that she shall ever be hoarse as a crow and speak as if she had her mouth full.'

Then the third head said: 'And I weird that she shall be glad to marry a cobbler.'

Then the three heads sank into the well and were no more seen, and the ugly princess went on her way. But lo and behold! when she came to a town, the children ran from her ugly blotched face screaming with fright, and when she tried to tell them she was the King of Colchester's daughter, her voice squeaked like a corn-crake's, was hoarse as a crow's, and folk could not understand a word she said, because she spoke as if her mouth was full!

Now in the town there happened to be a cobbler who not long before had mended the shoes of a poor old hermit; and the latter, having no money, had paid for the job by the gift of a wonderful ointment which would cure blotches on the face, and a bottle of medicine that would banish any hoarseness.

So, seeing the miserable, ugly princess in great distress, he went up to her and gave her a few drops out of his bottle; and then understanding from her rich attire and clearer speech that she was indeed a king's daughter, he craftily said that if she would take him for a husband, he would undertake to cure her.

'Anything! Anything!' sobbed the miserable princess.

So they were married, and the cobbler straightway set off with his bride to visit the King of Colchester. But the bells did not ring, the drums did not beat, and the people, instead of huzzaing, burst into loud guffaws at the cobbler in leather, and his wife in silks and satins.

As for the ugly queen, she was so enraged and disappointed that she went mad, and hanged herself in wrath. Whereupon the king, really pleased at getting rid of her so soon, gave the cobbler a hundred pounds and bade him go about his business with his ugly bride.

Which he did quite contentedly, for a hundred pounds means much to a poor cobbler. So they went to a remote part of the kingdom and lived unhappily for many years, he cobbling shoes, and she spinning the thread for him.

Mr Fox

Lady Mary was young and Lady Mary was fair, and she had more lovers than she could count on the fingers of both hands.

She lived with her two brothers who were very proud and very fond of their beautiful sister, and very anxious that she should choose well amongst her many suitors.

Now amongst them there was a certain Mr Fox, handsome and young and rich; and though nobody quite knew who he was, he was so gallant and so gay that everyone liked him. And he wooed Lady Mary so well that at last she promised to marry him. But though he talked much of the beautiful home to which he would take her, and described the castle and all the wonderful things that furnished it, he never offered to show it to her, neither did he invite Lady Mary's brothers to see it.

Now this seemed to her very strange indeed; and, being a lass of spirit, she made up her mind to see the castle if she could.

So one day, just before the wedding, when she knew Mr Fox would be away seeing the lawyers with her brothers, she just kilted up her skirts and set out unbeknownst – for, see you, the whole household was busy preparing for the marriage feastings – to see for herself what Mr Fox's beautiful castle was like.

After many searchings, and much travelling, she found it at last: and a fine strong building it was, with high walls and a deep moat to it. A bit frowning and gloomy, but when she came up to the wide gateway she saw these words carven over the arch:

BE BOLD – BE BOLD.

So she plucked up courage, and the gate being open went through it and found herself in a wide, empty, open courtyard. At the end of this was a smaller door, and over this was carven:

BE BOLD, BE BOLD; BUT NOT TOO BOLD.

So she went through it to a wide, empty hall, and up the wide empty staircase. Now at the top of the staircase there was a wide, empty gallery at one end of which were wide windows with the sunlight streaming through them from a beautiful garden, and at the other end a narrow door, over the archway of which was carven:

BE BOLD, BE BOLD; BUT NOT TOO BOLD,
LEST THAT YOUR HEART'S BLOOD SHOULD RUN COLD.

Now Lady Mary was a lass of spirit, and so, of course, she turned her back on the sunshine, and opened the narrow, dark door. And there she was in a narrow, dark passage. But at the end there was a chink of light. So she went forward and put her eye to the chink – and what do you think she saw?

Why! a wide saloon lit with many candles, and all round it, some hanging by their necks, some seated on chairs, some lying on the floor, were the skeletons and bodies of numbers of beautiful young maidens in their wedding-dresses that were all stained with blood.

Now Lady Mary, for all she was a lass of spirit, and brave as brave, could not look for long on such a horrid sight, so she turned and fled. Down the dark narrow passage, through the dark narrow door (which she did not forget to close behind her) and along the wide gallery she fled like a hare, and was just going down the wide stairs into the wide hall when, what did she see, through the window, but Mr Fox dragging a beautiful young lady across the wide courtyard. There was nothing for it, Lady Mary decided, but to hide herself as quickly, and as best she might, so she fled faster down the wide stairs, and hid herself behind a big wine-butt that stood in a corner of the wide hall. She was only just in time, for, there at the wide door, was Mr Fox dragging the poor young maiden along by the hair; and he dragged her across the wide hall and up the wide stairs. And when she clutched at the bannisters to stop herself, Mr Fox cursed and swore dreadfully; and at last he drew his sword and brought it down so hard on the poor young lady's wrist that the hand, cut off, jumped up into the air so that the diamond ring on the finger flashed in the sunlight as it fell, of all places in the world, into Lady Mary's very lap as she crouched behind the wine-butt!

Then she was fair frightened, thinking Mr Fox would be sure to find her; but after looking about a little while in vain (for, of course, he coveted the diamond ring), he continued his dreadful task of dragging the poor beautiful young maiden upstairs to the horrid chamber, intending, doubtless, to return when he had finished his loathly work, and seek for the hand.

But by that time Lady Mary had fled; for no sooner did she hear the awful, dragging noise pass into the gallery, than she upped and ran for dear life. Through the wide door with

BE BOLD, BE BOLD, BUT NOT TOO BOLD

engraven over the arch, across the wide courtyard past the wide gate with

BE BOLD — BE BOLD

engraven over it, never stopping, never thinking till she reached her own chamber. And all the while the hand with the diamond ring lay in her kilted lap.

Now the very next day, when Mr Fox and Lady Mary's brothers returned from the lawyers, the marriage-contract had to be signed. And all the neighbourhood was asked to witness it and partake of a splendid breakfast. And there was Lady Mary in bridal array, and there was Mr Fox, looking so gay and so gallant. He was seated at the table just opposite Lady Mary, and he looked at her and said: 'How pale you are this morning, dear heart.'

Then Lady Mary looked at him quietly and said, 'Yes, dear sir! I had a bad night's rest, for I had horrible dreams.'

Then Mr Fox smiled and said, 'Dreams go by contraries, dear heart; but tell me your dream, and your sweet voice will speed the time till I can call you mine.'

'I dreamed,' said Lady Mary, with a quiet smile, and her eyes were clear, 'that I went yesterday to seek the castle that is to be my home, and I found it in the woods with high walls and a deep dark moat. And over the gateway were carven these words:

BE BOLD – BE BOLD.'

Then Mr Fox spoke in a hurry, 'But it is not so – nor was it ever so.'

'Then I crossed the wide courtyard and went through a wide door over which was carven:

BE BOLD, BE BOLD, BUT NOT TOO BOLD,'

went on Lady Mary, still smiling, though her voice was cold; 'but, of course, it is not so and it was not so.'

And Mr Fox said nothing; he sat like a stone.

'Then I dreamed,' continued Lady Mary, still smiling, though her eyes were stern, 'that I passed through a wide hall and up a wide stair and along a wide gallery until I came to a dark narrow door, and over it was carven:

BE BOLD, BE BOLD, BUT NOT TOO BOLD,
LEST THAT YOUR HEART'S BLOOD SHOULD RUN COLD.

But it is not so, of course, and it was not so.'

And Mr Fox said nothing; he sat frozen.

'Then I dreamed that I opened the door and went down a dark narrow passage,' said Lady Mary, still smiling, though her voice was ice. 'And at the end of the passage there was a door, and the door had a chink in it. And through the chink I saw a wide saloon lit with many candles, and all round it were the bones and bodies of poor dead maidens, their clothes all stained with blood; but of course it is not so, and it was not so.'

By this time all the neighbours were looking Mr Fox-wards with all their eyes, while he sat silent.

But Lady Mary went on and her smiling lips were set.

'Then I dreamed that I ran downstairs and had just time to hide myself when you, Mr Fox, came in dragging a young lady by the hair. And the sunlight glittered on her diamond ring as she clutched the stair-rail, and you out with your sword, and cut off the poor lady's hand.'

Then Mr Fox rose in his seat stonily and glared about him as if to escape, and his eyeteeth showed like a fox beset by the dogs, and he grew pale.

And he said, trying to smile, though his whispering voice could scarcely be heard: 'But it is not so, dear heart, and it was not so, and God forbid it should be so!'

Then Lady Mary rose in her seat also, and the smile left her face, and her voice rang as she cried:

> 'But it is so, and it was so,
> Here's hand and ring I have to show.'

And with that she pulled out the poor dead hand with the glittering ring from her bosom and pointed it straight at Mr Fox.

At this all the company rose, and drawing their swords cut Mr Fox to pieces.

And served him very well right.

Dick Whittington and His Cat

More than five hundred years ago there was a little boy named Dick Whittington, and this is true. His father and mother died when he was too young to work, and so poor little Dick was very badly off. He was quite glad to get the parings of the potatoes to eat and a dry crust of bread now and then, and more than that he did not often get, for the village where he lived was a very poor one and the neighbours were not able to spare him much.

Now the country folk in those days thought that the people of London were all fine ladies and gentlemen, and that there was singing and dancing all the day long, and so rich were they there that even the streets, they said, were paved with gold. Dick used to sit by and listen while all these strange tales of the wealth of London were told, and it made him long to go and live there and have plenty to eat and fine clothes to wear instead of the rags and hard fare that fell to his lot in the country.

So one day when a great wagon with eight horses stopped on its way through the village, Dick made friends with the wagoner and begged to be taken with him to London. The man felt sorry for poor little Dick when he heard that he had no father or mother to take care of him, and saw how ragged and how badly in need of help he was. So he agreed to take him, and off they set.

How far it was and how many days they took over the journey I do not know, but in due time Dick found himself in the wonderful city which he had heard so much of and pictured to himself so grandly. But oh! how disappointed he was when he got there. How dirty it was! And the people, how unlike the gay company, with music and singing, that he had dreamt of! He wandered up and down the streets, one after another, until he was tired out, but not one did he find that was paved with gold.

Dirt in plenty he could see, but none of the gold that he thought to have put in his pockets as fast as he chose to pick it up.

Little Dick ran about till he was tired and it was growing dark. And at last he sat himself down in a corner and fell asleep. When morning came he was very cold and hungry, and though he asked everyone he met to help him, only one or two gave him a halfpenny to buy some bread. For two or three days he lived in the streets in this way, only just able to keep himself alive; then he managed to get some work to do in a hayfield, and that kept him for a short time longer, till the haymaking was over.

After this he was as badly off as ever, and did not know where to turn. One day in his wanderings he lay down to rest in the doorway of the house of a rich merchant whose name was Fitzwarren. But here he was soon seen by the cook-maid who was an unkind, bad-tempered woman, and she cried out to him to be off. 'Lazy rogue,' she called him; and she said she'd precious quick throw some dirty dishwater over him, boiling hot, if he didn't go. However, just then Mr Fitzwarren himself came home to dinner, and when he saw what was happening, he asked Dick why he was lying there. 'You're old enough to be at work, my boy,' he said. 'I'm afraid you have a mind to be lazy.'

'Indeed, sir,' said Dick to him, 'indeed that is not so;' and he told him how hard he had tried to get work to do, and how ill he was for want of food. Dick, poor fellow was now so weak that though he tried to stand he had to lie down again, for it was more than three days since he had had anything to eat at all. The kind merchant gave orders for him to be taken into the house and gave him a good dinner, and then he said that he was to be kept, to do what work he could to help the cook.

And now Dick would have been happy enough in this good family if it had not been for the ill-natured cook, who did her best to make life a burden to him. Night and morning she was forever scolding him. Nothing he did was good enough. It was 'Look sharp here,' and 'Hurry up there,' and there was no pleasing her. And many's the beating he had from the broomstick or the ladle, or whatever else she had in her hand.

At last it came to the ears of Miss Alice, Mr Fitzwarren's

daughter, how badly the cook was treating poor Dick. And she told the cook that she would quickly lose her place if she didn't treat him more kindly, for Dick had become quite a favourite with the family.

After that the cook's behaviour was a little better, but Dick still had another hardship that he bore with difficulty. For he slept in a garret where were so many holes in the walls and the floor, that every night as he lay in bed the room was overrun with rats and mice, and sometimes he could hardly sleep a wink. One day when he had earned a penny for cleaning a gentleman's shoes, he met a little girl with a cat in her arms and asked whether she would not sell it to him. Yes, she would, she said, though the cat was such a good mouser that she was sorry to part with her. This just suited Dick,  who kept pussy up in his garret, feeding her on scraps of his own dinner that he saved for her every day. In a little while he had no more bother with the rats and mice. Puss soon saw to that, and he slept sound every night.

Soon after this Mr Fitzwarren had a ship ready to sail; and as it was his custom that all his servants should be given a chance of good fortune as well as himself, he called them all into the counting-house and asked them what they would send out.

They all had something that they were willing to venture except poor Dick, who had neither money nor goods, and so could send nothing. For this reason he did not come into the room with the rest. But Miss Alice guessed what was the matter, and ordered him to be called in. She then said, 'I will lay down some money for him out of my own purse'; but her father told her that would not do, for it must be something of his own.

When Dick heard this he said, 'I have nothing whatever but a cat, which I bought for a penny some time ago.'

'Go, my boy, fetch your cat then,' said his master, and let her go.'

Dick went upstairs and fetched poor puss, but there were tears in his eyes when he gave her to the captain. 'For,' he said, 'I shall now be kept awake all night by the rats and mice.' All the company laughed at Dick's odd venture and Miss Alice, who felt sorry for him, gave him some money to buy another cat.

Now this, and other marks of kindness shown him by Miss Alice, made the ill-tempered cook jealous of poor Dick and she began to use him more cruelly than ever, and was always making game of him for sending his cat to sea. 'What do you think your cat will sell for?' she'd ask. 'As much money as would buy a stick to beat you with?'

At last poor Dick could not bear this usage any longer, and he thought he would run away. So he made a bundle of his things – he hadn't many – and started very early in the morning, on All-hallows Day, the first of November. He walked as far as Holloway, and there he sat down to rest on a stone, which to this day, they say, is called 'Whittington's Stone', and began to wonder to himself which road he should take.

While he was thinking what he should do the Bells of Bow Church in Cheapside began to chime, and as they rang he fancied that they were singing over and over again:

> 'Turn again, Whittington,
> Lord Mayor of London.'

'Lord Mayor of London!' said he to himself. 'Why, to be sure, wouldn't I put up with almost anything now to be Lord Mayor of London, and ride in a fine coach, when I grow to be a man! Well, I'll go back, and think nothing of the cuffing and scolding of the cross old cook if I am be Lord Mayor of London at last.'

So back he went, and he was lucky enough to get into the house, and set about his work before the cook came down.

But now you must hear what befell Mrs Puss all this while. The ship *Unicorn* that she was on was a long time at sea, and the cat made herself useful, as she would, among the unwelcome rats that lived on board too. At last the ship put into harbour on the coast of Barbary, where the only people are the Moors. They had never before seen a ship from England, and flocked in numbers to see the sailors, whose different colour and foreign dress were a great wonder to them. They were soon eager to buy the goods with which the ship was laden, and patterns were sent ashore for the King of Barbary to see. He was so much pleased with them that he sent for the captain to come to the palace, and honoured him with an invitation to dinner. But no sooner were they seated, as is the custom there, on the fine rugs and carpets that covered the floor, than great numbers of rats and mice came scampering in, swarming over all the dishes, and helping themselves from all the good things there were to eat. The captain was amazed, and wondered whether they didn't find such a pest most unpleasant.

'Oh yes,' said they, 'indeed we do, and the king would give half his treasure to be freed of them, for they not only spoil his dinner, but they even attack him in his bed at night, so that a watch has to be kept while he is sleeping, for fear of them.'

The captain was overjoyed; he thought at once of poor Dick Whittington and his cat, and said he had a creature on board ship that would soon do for all these vermin if she were there. Of course, when the king heard this he was eager to possess this wonderful animal.

'Bring it to me at once,' he said; 'for the vermin are dreadful, and if only it will do what you say, I will load your ship with gold and jewels in exchange for it.'

The captain who knew his business, took care not to underrate the value of Dick's cat. He told his majesty how inconvenient it would be to part with her, as when she was gone the rats might destroy the goods in the ship; however, to oblige the king, he would fetch her.

'Oh, make haste, do!' cried the queen, 'I, too, am all impatience to see this dear creature.'

Off went the captain, while another dinner was got ready. He took Puss under his arm and got back to the palace just in time to see the carpet covered with rats and mice once again. When Puss saw them, she didn't wait to be told, but jumped out of the captain's arms, and in no time almost all the rats and mice were dead at her feet, while the rest of them had scuttled off to their holes in fright.

The king was delighted to get rid so easily of such an intolerable plague, and the queen desired that the animal who had done them such a service might be brought to her. Upon which the captain called out, 'Puss, puss, puss,' and she came running to him. Then he presented her to the queen, who was rather afraid at first to touch a creature who had wreaked such havoc with her claws. However, when the captain called her, 'Pussy, pussy,' and began to stroke her, the queen also ventured to touch her and cried, 'Putty, putty,' in imitation of the captain, for she hadn't learned to speak English. He then put her on to the queen's lap where she purred and played with her majesty's hand and was soon asleep.

The king having seen what Mrs Puss could do and learning that her kittens would soon stock the whole country, and keep it free from rats, after bargaining with the captain for the whole ship's cargo, then gave him ten times as much for the cat as all the rest amounted to.

The captain then said farewell to the court of Barbary, and after a fair voyage reached London again with his precious load of gold and jewels safe and sound.

One morning early Mr Fitzwarren had just come to his counting-house and settled himself at the desk to count the cash, when there came a knock at the door. 'Who's there?' said he. 'A friend,' replied a voice. 'I come with good news of your ship the *Unicorn*.' The merchant in haste opened the door, and who were there but the ship's captain and the mate, bearing a chest of jewels and a bill of lading. When he had looked this over he lifted his eyes and thanked heaven for sending him such a prosperous voyage.

The honest captain next told him all about the cat, and showed him the rich present the king had sent for her to poor Dick. Rejoicing on behalf of Dick as much as he had done over his own good fortune, he called out to his servants to come and to bring up Dick:

> 'Go fetch him, and we'll tell him of his fame;
> Pray call him Mr Whittington by name.'

The servants, some of them, hesitated at this, and said so great a treasure was too much for a lad like Dick; but Mr Fitzwarren now showed himself the good man that he was and refused to deprive him of the value of a single penny. 'God forbid!' he cried. 'It's all his own, and he shall have it, to a farthing.'

He then sent for Dick, who at the moment was scouring pots for the cook and was black with dirt. He tried to excuse himself from coming into the room in such a plight, but the merchant made him come, and had a chair set for him. And he then began to think they must be making game of him, so he begged them not to play tricks on a poor simple boy, but to let him go downstairs again back to his work in the scullery.

'Indeed, Mr Whittington,' said the merchant, 'we are all quite in earnest with you, and I most heartily rejoice at the news that these gentlemen have brought. For the captain has sold your cat to the King of Barbary, and brings you in return for her more riches than I possess in the whole world; and may you long enjoy them!'

Mr Fitzwarren then told the men to open the great treasure they had brought with them, saying, 'There is nothing more now for Mr Whittington to do but to put it in some place of safety.'

Poor Dick hardly knew how to behave himself for joy. He begged his master to take what part of it he pleased since he owed it all to his kindness. 'No, no,' answered Mr Fitzwarren, 'this all belongs to you; and I have no doubt that you will use it well.'

Dick next begged his mistress, and then Miss Alice, to accept a part of his good fortune, but they would not, and at the same time told him what great joy they felt at his great success. But he was far too kind-hearted to keep it all to himself; so he made a present to the captain, the mate, and the rest of Mr Fitzwarren's servants; and even to his old enemy, the cross cook.

After this Mr Fitzwarren advised him to send for a tailor and get himself dressed like a gentleman, and told him he was welcome to live in his house till he could provide himself with a better.

When Whittington's face was washed, his hair curled, and he was dressed in a smart suit of clothes he was just as handsome and fine a young man as any who visited at Mr Fitzwarren's, and so thought fair Alice Fitzwarren, who had once been so kind to him and looked upon him with pity. And now she felt he was quite fit to be her sweetheart, and none the less, no doubt, because Whittington was always thinking what he could do to please her, and making her the prettiest presents that could be.

Mr Fitzwarren soon saw which way the wind blew, and ere long proposed to join them in marriage, and to this they both readily agreed. A day for the wedding was soon fixed; and they were attended to church by the Lord Mayor, the court of aldermen, the sheriffs, and a great number of the richest merchants in London, whom they afterwards treated with a magnificent feast.

History tells us that Mr Whittington and his lady lived in great splendour, and were very happy. They had several children. He was Sheriff and thrice Lord Mayor of London, and received the honour of knighthood from Henry V.

After the king's conquest of France, Sir Richard Whittington entertained him and the queen at dinner at the Mansion House in so sumptuous a manner that the king said, 'Never had prince such a subject!' To which Sir Richard replied, 'Never had subject such a prince.'

The Old Woman and Her Pig

An old woman was sweeping her house, and she found a little crooked sixpence. 'What,' said she, 'shall I do with this little sixpence? I will go to market, and buy a little pig.'

So she bought a little pig; but as she was coming home, she came to a stile, and the piggy would not go over the stile.

She went a little further, and she met a dog. So she said to him, 'Dog! dog! bite pig; piggy won't go over the stile; and I shan't get home till midnight.' But the dog wouldn't.

She went a little further, and she met a stick. So she said, 'Stick! stick! beat dog; dog won't bite pig; piggy won't get over the stile; and I shan't get home till midnight.' But the stick wouldn't.

She went a little further, and she met a fire. So she said, 'Fire! fire! burn stick; stick won't beat dog; dog won't bite pig; pig won't get over the stile; and I shan't get home till midnight.' But the fire wouldn't.

She went a little further, and she met some water. So she said, 'Water! water! quench fire; fire won't burn stick; stick won't beat dog; dog won't bite pig; pig won't get over the stile, and I shan't get home till midnight.' But the water wouldn't.

She went a little further, and she met an ox. So she said, 'Ox! ox! drink water; water won't quench fire; fire won't burn stick; stick won't beat dog; dog won't bite pig; pig won't get over the stile; and I shan't get home till midnight.' But the ox wouldn't.

She went a little further, and she met a butcher. So she said, 'Butcher! butcher! kill ox; ox won't drink water; water won't quench fire; fire won't burn stick; stick won't beat dog; dog won't bite pig; pig won't get over the stile; and I shan't get home till midnight.' But the butcher wouldn't.

She went a little further, and she met a rope. So she said, 'Rope! rope! hang butcher; butcher won't kill ox; ox won't drink water; water won't quench fire; fire won't burn stick; stick won't beat dog; dog won't bite pig; pig won't get over the stile; and I shan't get home till midnight.' But the rope wouldn't.

She went a little further, and she met a rat. So she said, 'Rat! rat! gnaw rope; rope won't hang butcher; butcher won't kill ox; ox won't drink water; water won't quench fire; fire won't burn stick; stick won't beat dog; dog won't bite pig; pig won't get over the stile; and I shan't get home till midnight.' But the rat wouldn't.

She went a little further, and she met a cat. So she said, 'Cat! cat! kill rat; rat won't gnaw rope; rope won't hang butcher; butcher won't kill ox; ox won't drink water; water won't quench fire; fire won't burn stick; stick won't beat dog; dog won't bite pig; pig won't get over the stile; and I shan't get home till midnight.' But the cat said to her, 'If you will go to yonder cow, and fetch me a saucer of milk, I will kill the rat.' So away went the old woman to the cow.

But the cow said to her, 'If you will go to yonder haystack, and fetch me a handful of hay, I'll give you the milk.' So away went the old woman to the haystack; and she brought the hay to the cow.

As soon as the cow had eaten the hay, she gave the old woman the milk; and away she went with it in a saucer to the cat.

As soon as the cat had lapped up the milk, the cat began to kill the rat; the rat began to gnaw the rope; the rope began to hang the butcher; the butcher began to kill the ox; the ox began to drink the water; the water began to quench the fire; the fire began to burn the stick; the stick began to beat the dog; the dog began to bite the pig; the little pig squealed and jumped over the stile; and so the old woman got home before midnight.

The Wee Bannock

Once upon a time there was an old man and his old wife who lived in a wee cottage beside a wee burnie. They had two cows, five hens and a cock, a cat and two kittens. Now the old man looked after the cows, the cock looked after the hens, the cat looked after a mouse in the cupboard, and the two kittens looked after the old wife's spindle as it twirled and tussled about on the hearthstone. But though the old wife should have looked after the kittens, the more she said, 'Sho! Sho! Go away, kitty!' the more they looked after the spindle!

So, one day, when she was quite tired out with saying 'Sho! Sho!' the old wife felt hungry and thought she could take a wee bite of something. So she up and baked two wee oatmeal bannocks and set them to toast before the fire. Now just as they were toasting away, smelling so fresh and tasty, in came the old man, and seeing them look so crisp and nice takes up one of them and snaps a piece out of it. On this the other bannock thought it high time to be off, so up it jumps and away it trundles as fast as ever it could. And away ran the old wife after it as fast as she could run with her spindle in one hand, and her distaff in the other. But the wee bannock trundled faster than she could run, so it was soon out of sight, and the old wife was obliged to go back and tussle with the kittens again.

The wee bannock meanwhile trundled gaily down the hill till it came to a big thatched house, and it ran boldly in at the door and sat itself down by the fireside quite comfortably. Now there were three tailors in the room working away on a big bench, and being tailors they were, of course, dreadfully afraid, and jumped up to hide behind the goodwife who was carding wool by the fire.

'Hout-tout!' she cried. 'What are ye a-feared of? 'Tis naught but a wee bit bannock. Just grip hold o' it, and I'll give ye a sup o' milk to drink with it.'

So up she gets with the carders in her hands and the tailor had his iron goose and the apprentices, one with the big scissors and the other with the ironing-board, and they all made for the wee bannock; but it was too clever for them, and dodged about the fireside until one apprentice, thinking to snap it with the big scissors, fell into the hot ashes and got badly burnt. Then the tailor cast the goose at it, and the other apprentice the ironing-board; but it wouldn't do. The wee bannock got out at the doorway where the goodwife flung the carders at it; but it dodged them and trundled away gaily till it came to a small house by the roadside. So in it ran bold as bold and sat itself down by the hearth where the wife was winding a clue of yarn for her husband, the weaver, who was click-clacking away at his loom.

'Tibby!' quoth the weaver. 'Whatever's that?'

'Naught but a wee bannock,' quoth she.

'Well, come and welcome,' says he, 'for the porridge was thin the morn; so grip it, woman! grip it!'

'Aye,' says she, and reaches out her hand to it. But the wee bannock just dodged.

'Man!' says she, 'yon's a clever wee bannockie! Catch it, man! Catch it if you can.'

But the wee bannock just dodged. 'Cast the clue at it, woman!' shouted the weaver.

But the wee bannock was out at the door, trundling away over the hill like a new tarred sheep or a mad cow!

And it trundled away till it came to a cowherd's house where the goodwife was churning her butter.

'Come in by,' cried the goodwife when she saw the wee bannock all crisp and fresh and tasty, 'I've plenty cream to eat with you.'

But at this the wee bannock began dodging about, and it dodged so craftily that the goodwife overset the churn in trying to grip it, and before she set it straight again the wee bannock was off, trundling away down the hill till it came to a mill-house where the miller was sifting meal. So in it ran and sat down by the trough.

'Ho, ho!' says the miller. 'It's a sign o' plenty when the likes of you run about the countryside with none to look after you. But come in by. I like bannock and cheese for supper, so I'll give ye a night's quarters.' And with that he tapped his fat stomach.

At this the wee bannock turned and ran; it wasn't going to trust itself with the miller and his cheese; and the miller, having nothing but the meal to fling after it, just stood and stared; so the wee bannock trundled quietly along the level till it came to the smithy where the smith was welding horsenails.

'Hullo!' says he, 'you're a well-toasted bannock. You'll do fine with a glass of ale! So come in by and I'll give you a lodging inside.' And with that he laughed, and tapped his fat stomach.

But the wee bannock thought the ale was as bad as the cheese, so it up and away, with the smith after it. And when he couldn't come up with it, he just cast his hammer at it. But the hammer missed and the wee bannock was out of sight in a crack, and trundled and trundled till it came to a farmhouse where the goodman and his wife were beating out flax and combing it. So it ran into the fireside and began to toast itself again.

'Janet,' says the goodman, 'yon is a well-toasted wee bannock. I'll have the half of it.'

'And I'll take the t'other half,' says the goodwife, and reached out a hand to grip it. But the wee bannock played dodgings again.

'My certy,' says the wife, 'but you're spirity!' And with that she cast the flax comb at it. But it was too clever for her, so out it trundled through the door and away was it down the road, till it came to another house where the goodwife was stirring the scalding soup and the goodman was plaiting a thorn collar for the calf. So it trundled in, and sat down by the fire.

'Ho, Jock!' quoth the goodwife, 'you're always crying on a well-toasted bannock. Here's one! Come and eat it!'

Then the wee bannock tried dodgings again, and the goodwife cried on the goodman to help her grip it.

'Aye, mother!' says he, 'but where's it gone?'

'Over there!' cries she. 'Quick! run to t'other side o' yon chair.' And the chair upset, and down came the goodman among the thorns. And the goodwife she flung the soup spoon at it, and the scalding soup fell on the goodman and scalded him, so the wee bannock ran out in a crack and was away to the next house where the folk were just sitting down to their supper and the goodwife was scraping the pot.

'Look!' cries she, 'here's a wee well-toasted bannock for him as catches it!'

'Let's shut the door first,' says the cautious goodman, 'afore we try to get a grip on it.'

Now when the wee bannock heard this it judged it was time to be off; so away it trundled and they after it helter-skelter. But though they threw their spoons at it, and the goodman cast his best hat, the wee bannock was too clever for them, and was out of sight in a crack.

Then away it trundled till it came to a house where the folk were just away to their beds. The goodwife she was raking out the fire, and the goodman had taken off his breeches.

'What's yon?' says he, for it was nigh dark.

'It will just be a wee bannock,' says she.

'I could eat the half of it,' says he.

'And I could eat the t'other,' quoth she.

Then they tried to grip it; but the wee bannock tried dodging. And the goodman and the goodwife tumbled against each other in the dark and grew angry.

'Cast your breeches at it, man!' cries the goodwife at last. 'What's the use of standing staring like a stuck pig?'

So the goodman cast his breeches at it and thought he had smothered it sure enough; but somehow it wriggled out, and away it was, the goodman after it without his breeches. You never saw such a race – a real clean chase over the park and through the whins, and round by the bramble patch. But there the goodman lost sight of it and had to go back all scratched and tired and shivering.

The wee bannock, however, trundled on till it was too dark even for a wee bannock to see.

Then it came to a fox's hole in the side of a big whin-bush and trundled in to spend the night there; but the fox had had no meat for three whole days, so he just said, 'You're welcome, friend! I wish there were two of you!'

And there were two! For he snapped the wee bannock into halves with one bite. So that was an end of it!

How Jack Went Out to Seek His Fortune

Once on a time there was a boy named Jack, and one morning he started to go and seek his fortune. He hadn't gone very far before he met a cat.

'Where are you going, Jack?' said the cat.

'I am going to seek my fortune.'

'May I go with you?'

'Yes,' said Jack, 'the more the merrier.'

So on they went, Jack and the cat. Jiggelty-jolt, jiggelty-jolt, jiggelty-jolt!

They went a little farther and they met a dog.

'Where are you going, Jack?' said the dog.

'I am going to seek my fortune.'

'May I go with you?'

'Yes,' said Jack, 'the more the merrier.'

So on they went, Jack, the cat and the dog! Jiggelty-jolt, jiggelty-jolt, jiggelty-jolt!

They went a little farther and they met a goat.

'Where are you going, Jack?' said the goat.

'I am going to seek my fortune.'

'May I go with you?'

'Yes,' said Jack, 'the more the merrier.'

So on they went, Jack, the cat, the dog and the goat. Jiggelty-jolt, jiggelty-jolt, jiggelty-jolt!

They went a little farther and they met a bull.

'Where are you going, Jack?' said the bull.

'I am going to seek my fortune.'

'May I go with you?'

'Yes,' said Jack, 'the more the merrier.'

So on they went, Jack, the cat, the dog, the goat and the bull. Jiggelty-jolt, jiggelty-jolt, jiggelty-jolt!

They went a little farther and they met a rooster.

'Where are you going, Jack?' said the rooster.

'I am going to seek my fortune.'

'May I go with you?'

'Yes,' said Jack, 'the more the merrier.'

So on they went, Jack, the cat, the dog, the goat, the bull and the rooster. Jiggelty-jolt, jiggelty-jolt, jiggelty-jolt!

And they went on jiggelty-jolting till it was about dark, and it was time to think of some place where they could spend the night. Now, after a bit, they came in sight of a house, and Jack told his companions to keep still while he went up and looked in through the window to see if all was safe. And what did he see through the window but a band of robbers seated at a table counting over great bags of gold!

'That gold shall be mine,' quoth Jack to himself. 'I have found my fortune already.'

Then he went back and told his companions to wait till he gave the word, and then to make all the noise they possibly could in their own fashion. So when they were all ready Jack gave the word, and the cat mewed, and the dog barked, and the goat bleated, and the bull bellowed, and the rooster crowed, and all together they made such a terrific hubbub that the robbers jumped up in a fright and ran away, leaving their gold on the table. So, after a good laugh, Jack and his companions went in and took possession of the house and the gold.

Now Jack was a wise boy, and he knew that the robbers would come back in the dead of the night to get their gold, and so when it came time to go to bed he put the cat in the rocking-chair, and he put the dog under the table, and he put the goat upstairs, and he put the bull in the cellar, and bade the rooster fly up on to the roof.

Then he went to bed.

Now sure enough, in the dead of the night, the robbers sent one man back to the house to look after their money. But before long he came back in a great fright and told them a fearsome tale!

'I went back to the house,' said he, 'and went in and tried to sit down in the rocking-chair, and there was an old woman knitting there, and she – oh my! stuck her knitting-needles into me.'

(*That was the cat, you know.*)

'Then I went to the table to look after the money, but there was a shoemaker under the table, and my! how he stuck his awl into me.'

(*That was the dog, you know.*)

'So I started to go upstairs, but there was a man up there threshing, and goody! how he knocked me down with his flail!'

(*That was the goat, you know.*)

'Then I started to go down to the cellar, but – oh dear me! there was a man down there chopping wood, and he knocked me up and he knocked me down just terrible with his axe.'

(*That was the bull, you know.*)

'But I shouldn't have minded all that if it hadn't been for an awful little fellow on the top of the house by the kitchen chimney, who kept a-hollering and hollering, "Cook him in a stew! Cook him in a stew! Cook him in a stew!"'

(*And that, of course, was the cock-a-doodle-do.*)

Then the robbers agreed that they would rather lose their gold than meet with such a fate; so they made off, and Jack next morning went gaily home with his booty. And each of the animals carried a portion of it. The cat hung a bag on its tail (a cat when it walks always carries its tail stiff), the dog on his collar, the goat and the bull on their horns, but Jack made the rooster carry a golden guinea in its beak to prevent it from calling all the time:

> 'Cock-a-doodle-do,
> Cook him in a stew!'

The Bogey-Beast

There was once a woman who was very, very cheerful, though she had little to make her so; for she was old, and poor, and lonely. She lived in a little bit of a cottage and earned a scant living by running errands for her neighbours, getting a bite here, a sup there, as reward for her services. So she made shift to get on, and always looked as spry and cheery as if she had not a want in the world.

Now one summer evening, as she was trotting, full of smiles as ever, along the high road to her hovel, what should she see but a big black pot lying in the ditch!

'Goodness me!' she cried, 'that would be just the very thing for me if I only had something to put in it! But I haven't! Now who could have left it in the ditch?'

And she looked about her expecting the owner would not be far off; but she could see nobody.

'Maybe there is a hole in it,' she went on, 'and that's why it has been cast away. But it would do fine to put a flower in for my window; so I'll just take it home with me.'

And with that she lifted the lid and looked inside. 'Mercy me!' she cried, fair amazed. 'If it isn't full of gold pieces. Here's luck!'

And so it was, brimful of great gold coins. Well, at first she simply stood stock-still, wondering if she was standing on her head or her heels. Then she began saying: 'Lawks! But I *do* feel rich. I feel awful rich!'

After she had said this many times, she began to wonder how she was to get her treasure home. It was too heavy for her to carry, and she could see no better way than to tie the end of her shawl to it and drag it behind her like a go-cart.

'It will soon be dark,' she said to herself as she trotted along. 'So much the better! The neighbours will not see what I'm bringing home, and I shall have all the night to myself, and be able to think what I'll do! Mayhap I'll buy a grand house and just sit by the fire with a cup o' tea and do no work at all like a queen. Or maybe I'll bury it at the garden-foot and just keep a bit in the old china teapot on the chimney-piece. Or maybe – Goody! Goody! I feel that grand I don't know myself.'

By this time she was a bit tired of dragging such a heavy weight, and, stopping to rest a while, turned to look at her treasure.

And lo! it wasn't a pot of gold at all! It was nothing but a lump of silver.

She stared at it and rubbed her eyes and stared at it again.

'Well! I never,' she said at last. 'And me thinking it was a pot of gold! I must have been dreaming. But this is luck! Silver is far less trouble – easier to mind, and not so easy stolen. Them gold pieces would have been the death o' me, and with this great lump of silver – '

So she went off again planning what she would do, and feeling as rich as rich, until becoming a bit tired again she stopped to rest and gave a look round to see if her treasure was safe; and she saw nothing but a great lump of iron!

'Well! I never!' says she again. 'And I mistaking it for silver! I must have been dreaming. But this is luck! It's real convenient. I can get penny pieces for old iron, and penny pieces are a deal handier for me than your gold and silver. Why! I should never have slept a wink for fear of being robbed. But a penny piece comes in useful, and I shall sell that iron for a lot and be real rich – rolling rich.'

So on she trotted full of plans as to how she would spend her penny pieces, till once more she stopped to rest and looked round to see if her treasure was safe. And this time she saw nothing but a big stone.

'Well! I never!' she cried, full of smiles. 'And to think I mistook it for iron. I must have been dreaming. But here's luck indeed, and me wanting a stone terrible bad to stick open the gate. Eh my! but it's a change for the better! It's a fine thing to have good luck.'

So, all in a hurry to see how the stone would keep the gate open she trotted off down the hill till she came to her own cottage. She unlatched the gate and then turned to unfasten her shawl from the stone which lay on the path behind her. Aye! it was a stone sure enough. There was plenty light to see it lying there, douce and peaceable as a stone should.

So she bent over it to unfasten the shawl end, when –

'Oh my!'

All of a sudden it gave a jump, a squeal, and in one moment was as big as a haystack. Then it let down four great lanky legs and threw out two long ears, flourished a great long tail and romped off, kicking and squealing and whinnying and laughing like a naughty mischievous boy!

The old woman stared after it till it was fairly out of sight, then she burst out laughing too.

'Well!' she chuckled, 'I am in luck! Quite the luckiest body hereabouts. Fancy my seeing the Bogey-Beast all to myself; and making myself so free with it too! My goodness! I do feel that uplifted – that *GRAND*!'

So she went into her cottage and spent the evening chuckling over her good luck.

Little Red Riding Hood

Once upon a time there was a little girl who was called little Red Riding Hood, because she was quite small and because she always wore a red cloak with a big red hood to it, which her grandmother had made for her.

Now one day her mother, who had been churning and baking cakes, said to her: 'My dear, put on your red cloak with the hood to it, and take this cake, and this pot of butter to your Grannie, and ask how she is, for I hear she is ailing.'

Now little Red Riding Hood was very fond of her grandmother who made her so many nice things, so she put on her cloak joyfully and started on her errand. But her grandmother lived some way off, and to reach the cottage little Red Riding Hood had to pass through a vast lonely forest. However, some woodcutters were at work in it, so little Red Riding Hood was not so very much alarmed when she saw a great big wolf coming towards her, because she knew that wolves were cowardly things.

And sure enough the wolf, though but for the woodcutters he would surely have eaten little Red Riding Hood, only stopped and asked her politely where she was going.

'I am going to see Grannie, take her this cake and this pot of butter and ask how she is,' says little Red Riding Hood.

'Does she live a very long way off?' asks the wolf craftily.

'Not so very far if you go by the straight road,' replied little Red Riding Hood. 'You only have to pass the mill and the first cottage on the right is Grannie's; but I am going by the wood-path because there are such a lot of nuts and flowers and butterflies.'

'I wish you good luck,' says the wolf politely. 'Give my respects to your grandmother and tell her I hope she is quite well.'

And with that he trotted off. But instead of going his ways he turned back, took the straight road to the old woman's cottage, and knocked at the door.

Rap! Rap! Rap!

'Who's there?' asked the old woman, who was in bed.

'Little Red Riding Hood,' sings out the wolf, making his voice as shrill as he could. 'I've come to bring dear Grannie a pot of butter and a cake from Mother, and to ask how you are.'

'Pull the bobbin, and the latch will go up,' says the old woman, well satisfied.

So the wolf pulled the bobbin, the latch went up, and oh my! It wasn't a minute before he had gobbled up old Grannie, for he had had nothing to eat for a week.

Then he shut the door, put on Grannie's nightcap, and getting into bed rolled himself well up in the clothes.

By and by along comes little Red Riding Hood, who had been amusing herself by gathering nuts, running after butterflies, and picking flowers.

So she knocked at the door.

Rap! Rap! Rap!

'Who's there?' says the wolf, making his voice as soft as he could.

Now little Red Riding Hood heard the voice was very gruff, but she thought her grandmother had a cold; so she said: 'Little Red Riding Hood with a pot of butter and a cake from Mother to ask how you are.'

'Pull the bobbin, and the latch will go up.'

So little Red Riding Hood pulled the bobbin, the latch went up, and there, she thought, was her grandmother in the bed; for the cottage was so dark one could not see well. Besides, the crafty wolf turned his face to the wall at first. And he made his voice as soft as he could, when he said: 'Come and kiss me, my dear.'

Then little Red Riding Hood took off her cloak and went to the bed.

'Oh, Grandmamma, Grandmamma,' says she, 'what big arms you've got!'

'All the better to hug you with,' says he.

'But Grandmamma, Grandmamma, what big legs you have!'

'All the better to run with, my dear.'

'Oh, Grandmamma, Grandmamma, what big ears you've got!'

'All the better to hear with, my dear.'

'But Grandmamma, Grandmamma, what big eyes you've got!'

'All the better to see you with, my dear!'

'Oh, Grandmamma, Grandmamma, what big teeth you've got!'

'All the better to eat you with, my dear!' says that wicked, wicked wolf, and with that he gobbled up little Red Riding Hood.

Childe Rowland

> Childe Rowland and his brothers twain
> Were playing at the ball.
> Their sister, Burd Helen, she played
> In the midst among them all.

For Burd Helen loved her brothers and they loved her exceedingly. At play she was ever their companion and they cared for her as brothers should. And one day when they were at ball close to the churchyard –

> Childe Rowland kicked it with his foot
> And caught it on his knee.
> At last as he plunged among them all
> O'er the church he made it flee.

Now Childe Rowland was Burd Helen's youngest, dearest brother, and there was ever a loving rivalry between them as to which should win. So with a laugh –

> Burd Helen round about the aisle
> To seek the ball is gone.

Now the ball had trundled to the right of the church; so, as Burd Helen ran the nearest way to get it, she ran contrary to the sun's course, and the light, shining full on her face, sent her shadow behind her. Thus that happened which will happen at times when folk forget and run widershins, that is against the light, so that their shadows are out of sight and cannot be taken care of properly.

Now what happened you will learn by and by; meanwhile, Burd Helen's three brothers waited for her return.

> But long they waited, and longer still,
> And she came not back again.

Then they grew alarmed, and –

> They sought her east, they sought her west,
> They sought her up and down.
> And woe were the hearts of her brethren,
> Since she was not to be found.

Not to be found anywhere – she had disappeared like dew on a May morning.

So at last her eldest brother went to Great Merlin the magician, who could tell and foretell, see and foresee all things under the sun and beyond it, and asked him where Burd Helen could have gone.

'Fair Burd Helen,' said the magician, 'must have been carried off with her shadow by the fairies when she was running round the church widershins; for fairies have power when folk go against the light. She will now be in the Dark Tower of the King of Elfland, and none but the boldest knight in Christendom will be able to bring her back.'

'If it be possible to bring her back,' said the eldest brother, 'I will do it, or perish in the attempt.'

'Possible it is,' quoth Merlin the magician gravely. 'But woe be to the man or mother's son who attempts the task if he be not well taught beforehand what he is to do.'

Now the eldest brother of fair Burd Helen was brave indeed, danger did not dismay him, so he begged the magician to tell him exactly what he should do, and what he should not do, as he was determined to go and seek his sister. And the great magician told him, and schooled him, and after he had learnt his lesson right well, he girt on his sword, said goodbye to his brothers and his mother, and set out for the Dark Tower of Elfland to bring Burd Helen back.

> But long they waited, and longer still,
> With doubt and muckle pain.
> But woe were the hearts of his brethren,
> For he came not back again.

So after a time Burd Helen's second brother went to Merlin the magician and said: 'School me also, for I go to find my brother and sister in the Dark Tower of the King of Elfland and bring them back.' For he also was brave indeed, danger did not dismay him.

Then when he had been well schooled and had learnt his lesson, he said goodbye to Childe Rowland, his brother, and to his mother the good queen, girt on his sword and set out for the Dark Tower of Elfland to bring back Burd Helen and her brother.

> But long they waited, and longer still,
> With muckle doubt and pain.
> And woe were his mother's and brother's hearts,
> For he came not back again.

Now when they had waited and waited a long, long time, and none had come back from the Dark Tower of Elfland, Childe Rowland, the youngest, the best beloved of Burd Helen's brothers, besought his mother to let him also go on the quest; for he was the bravest of them all, and neither death nor danger could dismay him. But at first his mother the queen said: 'Not so! You are the last of my children; if you are lost, all is lost indeed!'

But he begged so hard that at length the good queen his mother bade him Godspeed, and girt about his waist his father's sword, the brand that never struck in vain, and as she girt it on she chanted the spell that gives victory.

So Childe Rowland bade her goodbye and went to the cave of the great magician Merlin.

'Yet once more, master,' said the youth, 'and but once more, tell how man or mother's son may find fair Burd Helen and her brothers twain in the Dark Tower of Elfland.'

'My son,' replied the wizard Merlin, 'there be things twain; simple they seem to say, but hard are they to perform. One thing is to do, and one thing is not to do. Now the first thing you have to do is this: After you have once entered the Land of Faery, *whoever speaks to you*, you must out with your father's brand and cut off their head. In this you must not fail. And the second thing you have not to do is this: after you have entered the Land of

Faery, bite no bite, sup no drop; for if in Elfland you sup one drop or bite one bite, never again will you see Middle Earth.'

Then Childe Rowland said these two lessons over and over until he knew them by heart; so, well schooled, he thanked the great master and went on his way to seek the Dark Tower of Elfland.

And he journeyed far, and he journeyed fast, until at last on a wide moorland he came upon a horse-herd feeding his horses: and the horses were wild, and their eyes were like coals of fire.

Then he knew they must be the horses of the King of Elfland, and that at last he must be in the Land of Faery.

So Childe Rowland said to the horse-herd, 'Canst tell me where lies the Dark Tower of the Elfland king?'

And the horse-herd answered, 'Nay, that is beyond my ken; but go a little farther and thou wilt come to a cow-herd who mayhap can tell thee.'

Then at once Childe Rowland drew his father's sword that never struck in vain, and smote off the horse-herd's head, so that it rolled on the wide moorland and frightened the King of Elfland's horses. And he journeyed further till he came to a wide pasture where a cow-herd was herding cows. And the cows looked at him with fiery eyes, so he knew that they must be the King of Elfland's cows, and that he was still in the Land of Faery. Then he said to the cow-herd: 'Canst tell me where lies the Dark Tower of the Elfland king?'

And the cow-herd answered, 'Nay, that is beyond my ken; but go a little farther and thou wilt come to a hen-wife who, mayhap, can tell thee.'

So at once Childe Rowland, remembering his lesson, out with his father's good sword that never struck in vain, and off went the cow-herd's head spinning amongst the grasses and frightening the King of Elfland's cows.

Then he journeyed further, till he came to an orchard where an old woman in a grey cloak was feeding fowls. And the fowls' little eyes were like little coals of fire, so he knew that they were the King of Elfland's fowls, and that he was still in the Land of Faery.

And he said to the hen-wife, 'Canst tell me where lies the Dark Tower of the King of Elfland?'

Now the hen-wife looked at him and smiled. 'Surely I can tell you,' said she; 'go on a little farther. There you will find a low green hill; green and low against the sky. And the hill will have three terrace-rings upon it from bottom to top. Go round the first terrace saying:

> "Open from within;
> Let me in! Let me in!"

Then go round the second terrace and say:

> "Open wide, open wide.
> Let me inside."

Then go round the third terrace and say:

> "Open fast, open fast,
> Let me in at last."

Then a door will open and let you in to the Dark Tower of the King of Elfland. Only remember to go round widershins. If you go round with the sun the door will not open. So good luck to you!'

Now the hen-wife spoke so fair, and smiled so frank that Childe Rowland forgot for a moment what he had to do. Therefore he thanked the old woman for her courtesy and was just going on, when, all of a sudden, he remembered his lesson. And he out with his father's sword that never yet struck in vain and smote off the hen-wife's head, so that it rolled among the corn and frightened the fiery-eyed fowls of the King of Elfland.

After that he went on and on, till, against the blue sky, he saw a round green hill set with three terraces from top to bottom.

Then he did as the hen-wife had told him, not forgetting to go round widershins, so that the sun was always on his face.

Now when he had gone round the third terrace saying:

> 'Open fast, open fast,
> Let me in at last,'

what should happen but that he should see a door in the hillside. And it opened and let him in. Then it closed behind him with a click, and Childe Rowland was left in the dark; for he had gotten at last to the Dark Tower of the King of Elfland.

It was very dark at first, perhaps because the sun had part blinded his eyes; for after a while it became twilight, though where the light came from none could tell, unless through the walls and the roof; for there were neither windows nor candles. But in the gloaming light he could see a long passage of rough arches made of rock that was transparent and all encrusted with silver, rock-spar and many bright stones. And the air was warm as it ever is in Elfland. So he went on and on in the twilight that came from nowhere, till he found himself before two wide doors all barred with iron. But they flew open at his touch and he saw a wonderful large and spacious hall that seemed to him to be as long and as broad as the green hill itself. The roof was supported by pillars wide and lofty beyond the pillars of a cathedral; and they were of gold and silver, fretted into foliage, and between and around them were woven wreaths of flowers. And the flowers were of diamonds, and rubies, and topaz, and the leaves of emerald. And the arches met in the middle of the roof where hung, by a golden chain, an immense lamp made of a hollowed pearl, white and translucent. And in the middle of this lamp was a mighty carbuncle, blood-red, that kept spinning round and round, shedding its light to the very ends of the huge hall, which thus seemed to be filled with the shining of the setting sun.

Now at one end of the hall was a marvellous, wondrous, glorious couch of velvet, and silk, and gold; and on it sat fair Burd Helen combing her beautiful golden hair with a golden comb. But her face was all set and wan, as if it were made of stone. And when she saw Childe Rowland she never moved, and her voice came like the voice of the dead as she said:

> 'God pity you, poor luckless fool!
> What have you here to do?'

Now at first Childe Rowland felt he must clasp this semblance of his dear sister in his arms; but he remembered the lesson which the great magician Merlin had taught him, and drawing his father's brand which had never yet been drawn in vain, and turning his eyes from the horrid sight, he struck with all his force at the enchanted form of fair Burd Helen.

And lo! when he turned to look in fear and trembling, there she was her own self, her joy fighting with her fears. And she clasped him in her arms and cried:

> 'Oh, hear you this, my youngest brother,
> Why didn't you bide at home?
> Had you a hundred thousand lives,
> Ye couldn't spare ne'er a one!
>
> But sit you down, my dearest dear,
> Oh! woe that ye were born,
> For, come the King of Elfland in
> Your fortune is forlorn.'

So with tears and smiles she seated him beside her on the wondrous couch, and they told each other what they each had suffered and done. He told her how he had come to Elfland, and she told him how she had been carried off, shadow and all, because she ran round a church widershins, and how her brothers had been enchanted, and lay intombed as if dead, as she had been, because they had not had courage to obey the great magician's lesson to the letter, and cut off her head.

Now after a time Childe Rowland, who had travelled far and travelled fast, became very hungry, and forgetting all about the second lesson of the magician Merlin, asked his sister for some food. And she, being still under the spell of Elfland could not warn him of his danger; she could only look at him sadly as she rose up and brought him a golden basin full of bread and milk.

Now in those days it was manners before taking food from anyone to say thank you with your eyes, and so just as Childe Rowland was about to put the golden bowl to his lips, he raised his eyes to his sister's.

And in an instant he remembered what the great magician had said: 'Bite no bite, sup no drop, for if in Elfland you sup one drop or bite one bite, never again will you see Middle Earth.'

So he dashed the bowl to the ground, and standing square and fair, lithe, and young, and strong, he cried like a challenge: 'Not a sup will I swallow, not a bite will I bite till fair Burd Helen is set free.'

Then immediately there was a loud noise like thunder, and a voice was heard saying:

> 'Fee, fo, fi, fum,
> I smell the blood of a Christian man.
> Be he alive or dead, my brand
> Shall dash his brains from his brain-pan.'

Then the folding-doors of the vast hall burst open and the King of Elfland entered like a storm of wind. What he was really like Childe Rowland had not time to see, for with a bold cry: 'Strike, Bogle! thy hardest if thou dar'st!' he rushed to meet the foe, his good sword, that never yet did fail, in his hand.

And Childe Rowland and the King of Elfland fought, and fought, and fought, while Burd Helen with her hands clasped, watched them in fear and hope.

So they fought, and fought, and fought, until at last Childe Rowland beat the King of Elfland to his knees. Whereupon he cried, 'I yield me. Thou hast beaten me in fair fight.'

Then Childe Rowland said, 'I grant thee mercy if thou wilt release my sister and my brothers from all spells and enchantments, and let us go back to Middle Earth.'

So that was agreed; and the Elfin king went to a golden chest whence he took a phial that was filled with a blood-red liquor. And with this liquor he anointed the ears and the eyelids, the nostrils, the lips and the fingertips of the bodies of Burd Helen's two brothers that lay as dead in two golden coffers.

And immediately they sprang to life and declared that their souls only had been away, but had now returned.

After this the Elfin king said a charm which took away the very last bit of enchantment, and adown the huge hall that showed as if it were lit by the setting sun, and through the long passage of rough arches made of rock that was transparent and all encrusted with silver, rock-spar and many bright stones, where twilight reigned, the three brothers and their sister passed. Then the door opened in the green hill, it clicked behind them, and they left the Dark Tower of the King of Elfland never to return.

For, no sooner were they in the light of day, than they found themselves at home.

But fair Burd Helen took care never to go widershins round a church again.

The Wise Men of Gotham

Of Buying Sheep

There were two men of Gotham, and one of them was going to market in Nottingham to buy sheep, and the other came from the market, and they both met together upon Nottingham bridge.

'Where are you going?' said the one who came from Nottingham.

'Marry,' said he that was going to Nottingham, 'I am going to buy sheep.'

'Buy sheep?' said the other, 'and which way will you bring them home?'

'Marry,' said the other, 'I will bring them over this bridge.'

'By Robin Hood,' said he that came from Nottingham, 'but thou shalt not.'

'By Maid Marion,' said he that was going thither, 'but I will.'

'You will not,' said the one.

'I will.'

Then they beat their staves against the ground, one against the other, as if there had been a hundred sheep between them.

'Hold in,' said one; 'beware lest my sheep leap over the bridge.'

'I care not,' said the other; 'they shall not come this way.'

'But they shall,' said the other.

Then the other said, 'If that thou make much to do, I will put my fingers in thy mouth.'

'Will you?' said the other.

Now, as they were at their contention, another man of Gotham came from the market with a sack of meal upon a horse, and seeing and hearing his neighbours at strife about sheep, though there were none between them, said: 'Ah, fools! will you ever learn wisdom? Help me, and lay my sack upon my shoulders.'

They did so, and he went to the side of the bridge, unloosened the mouth of the sack, and shook all his meal out into the river.

'Now, neighbours,' he said, 'how much meal is there in my sack?'

'Marry,' said they, 'there is none at all.'

'Now, by my faith,' said he, 'even as much wit as is in your two heads to stir up strife about a thing you have not.'

Which was the wisest of these three persons, judge yourself.

Of Hedging a Cuckoo

Once upon a time the men of Gotham would have kept the cuckoo so that she might sing all the year, and in the midst of their town they made a hedge round in compass and they got a cuckoo, and put her into it, and said, 'Sing there all through the year, or thou shalt have neither meat nor water.' The cuckoo, as soon as she perceived herself within the hedge, flew away. 'A vengeance on her!' said they. 'We did not make our hedge high enough.'

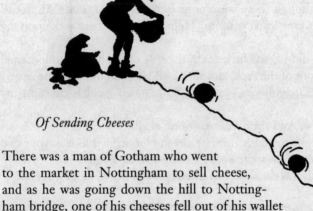

Of Sending Cheeses

There was a man of Gotham who went to the market in Nottingham to sell cheese, and as he was going down the hill to Nottingham bridge, one of his cheeses fell out of his wallet and rolled down the hill. 'Ah, gaffer,' said the fellow, 'can you run to market alone? I will send one after another after you.' Then he laid down his wallet and took out the cheeses, and rolled them down the hill. Some went into one bush, and some went into another.

'I charge you all to meet me near the marketplace,' cried he; and when the fellow came to the market to meet his cheeses, he stayed there till the market was nearly done. Then he went about to enquire of his friends and neighbours, and other men, if they did see his cheeses come to the market.

'Who should bring them?' said one of the market men.

'Marry, themselves,' said the fellow; 'they know the way well enough.' He sighed, 'A vengeance on them all. I did fear, to see them run so fast, that they would run beyond the market. I am now fully persuaded that they must be now almost at York.' Whereupon he forthwith hired a horse to ride to York, to seek his cheeses where they were not; but to this day no man can tell him of his cheeses.

Of Drowing Eels

When Good Friday came the men of Gotham cast their heads together what to do with their white herrings, their red herrings, their sprats and other salt fish. One consulted with the other, and agreed that such fish should be cast into their pond (which was in the middle of the town), that they might breed against the next year, and every man that had salt fish left cast them into the pool.

'I have many white herrings,' said one.

'I have many sprats,' said another.

'I have many red herrings,' said the other.

'I have much salt fish. Let all go into the pond or pool, and we shall fare like lords next year.'

At the beginning of next year following the men drew near the pond to have their fish, and there was nothing but a great eel. 'Ah,' said they all, 'a mischief on this eel, for he has eaten up all our fish.'

'What shall we do to him?' said one to the other.

'Kill him,' said one.

'Chop him into pieces,' said another.

'Not so,' said another; 'let us drown him.'

'Be it so,' said all. And they went to another pond, and cast the eel into the pond. 'Lie there and shift for yourself, for no help thou shalt have from us;' and they left the eel to drown.

Of Sending Rent

Once on a time the men of Gotham had forgotten to pay their landlord. One said to the other, 'Tomorrow is our pay-day, and what shall we find to send our money to our landlord?'

The one said, 'This day I have caught a hare, and he shall carry it, for he is light of foot.'

'Be it so,' said all; 'he shall have a letter and a purse to put our money in, and we shall direct him the right way.' So when the letters were written and the money put in a purse, they tied it round the hare's neck, saying, 'First you go to Lancaster, then you must go to Loughborough, and in Newark is our landlord; commend us to him, and there are his dues.'

The hare, as soon as he was out of their hands, ran on along the country way. Some cried, 'Thou must go to Lancaster first.'

'Let the hare alone,' said another; 'he can tell a nearer way than the best of us all. Let him go.'

Another said, 'It is a subtle hare, let her alone; she will not keep the highway for fear of dogs.'

Of Counting

On a certain time there were twelve men of Gotham who went fishing, and some went into the water and some on dry ground; and, as they were coming back, one of them said, 'We have ventured much this day wading; I pray God that none of us that did come from home be drowned.'

'Marry,' said one, 'let us see about that. Twelve of us came out.' And every man did count eleven, and the twelfth man did never count himself.

'Alas!' said one to another, 'one of us is drowned.' They went back to the brook where they had been fishing, and looked up and down for him that was drowned, and made great lamentation. A courtier came riding by, and he did ask what they were seeking, and why they were so sorrowful. 'Oh,' said they, 'this day we came to fish in this brook, and there were twelve of us, and one is drowned.'

'Why,' said the courtier, 'count me how many of you there be,' and one counted eleven and did not count himself. 'Well,' said the courtier, 'what will you give me if I find the twelfth man?'

'Sir,' said they, 'all the money we have.'

'Give me the money,' said the courtier; and he began with the first, and gave him a whack over the shoulders that he groaned, and said, 'There is one, and he served all of them that they groaned; but when he came to the last he gave him a good blow, saying, 'Here is the twelfth man.'

'God bless you on your heart,' said all the company, 'you have found our neighbour.'

Caporushes

Once upon a time, a long, long while ago, when all the world was young and all sorts of strange things happened, there lived a very rich gentleman whose wife had died leaving him three lovely daughters. They were as the apple of his eye, and he loved them exceedingly.

Now one day he wanted to find out if they loved him in return, so he said to the eldest, 'How much do you love me, my dear?'

And she answered as pat as may be, 'As I love my life.'

'Very good, my dear,' said he, and gave her a kiss. Then he said to the second girl, 'How much do you love me, my dear?'

And she answered as swift as thought, 'Better than all the world beside.'

'Good!' he replied, and patted her on the cheek. Then he turned to the youngest, who was also the prettiest.

'And how much do *you* love me, my dearest?'

Now the youngest daughter was not only pretty, she was clever. So she thought a moment, then she said slowly: 'I love you as fresh meat loves salt!'

Now when her father heard this he was very angry, because he really loved her more than the others.

'What!' he said. 'If that is all you give me in return for all I've given you, out of my house you go.' So there and then he turned her out of the home where she had been born and bred, and shut the door in her face.

Not knowing where to go, she wandered on and she wandered on, till she came to a big fen where the reeds grew ever so tall and the rushes swayed in the wind like a field of corn. There she sat down and plaited herself an overall of rushes and a cap to match, so as to hide her fine clothes, and her beautiful golden hair that was all set with milk-white pearls. For she was a wise girl, and thought that in such lonely country, mayhap, some robber might fall in with her and kill her to get her fine clothes and jewels.

It took a long time to plait the dress and cap, and while she plaited she sang a little song:

> 'Hide my hair, O cap o' rushes,
> Hide my heart, O robe o' rushes.
> Sure! my answer had no fault,
> I love him more than he loves salt.'

And the fen birds sat and listened and sang back to her:

> 'Cap o' rushes, shed no tear,
> Robe o' rushes, have no fear;
> With these words if fault he'd find,
> Sure your father must be blind.'

When her task was finished she put on her robe of rushes and it hid all her fine clothes, and she put on the cap and it hid all her beautiful hair, so that she looked quite a common country girl. But the fen birds flew away, singing as they flew:

> 'Cap-o-rushes! we can see,
> Robe o' rushes! what you be,
> Fair and clean, and fine and tidy,
> So you'll be what ere betide ye.'

By this time she was very, very hungry, so she wandered on, and she wandered on; but ne'er a cottage or a hamlet did she see, till just at sun-setting, she came on a great house on the edge of the fen. It had a fine front door to it; but mindful of her dress of rushes she went round to the back. And there she saw a strapping fat scullion washing pots and pans with a very sulky face. So, being a clever girl, she guessed what the maid was wanting and said: 'If I may have a night's lodging, I will scrub the pots and pans for you.'

'Why! Here's luck,' replied the scullery-maid, ever so pleased. 'I was just wanting badly to go a-walking with my sweetheart. So if you will do my work you shall share my bed and have a bite of my supper. Only mind you scrub the pots clean or cook will be at me.'

Now next morning the pots were scraped so clean that they looked like new, and the saucepans were polished like silver, and the cook said to the scullion, 'Who cleaned these pots – not you, I'll swear.' So the maid had to up and out with the truth. Then the cook would have turned away the old maid and put on the new, but the latter would not hear of it.

'The maid was kind to me and gave me a night's lodging,' she said. 'So now I will stay without wage and do the dirty work for her.'

So Caporushes – for so they called her since she would give no other name – stayed on and cleaned the pots and scraped the saucepans.

Now it so happened that her master's son came of age, and to celebrate the occasion a ball was given to the neighbourhood, for the young man was a grand dancer, and loved nothing so well as a country measure. It was a very fine party, and after supper was served, the servants were allowed to go and watch the quality from the gallery of the ballroom.

But Caporushes refused to go, for she also was a grand dancer, and she was afraid that when she heard the fiddles starting a merry jig, she might start dancing. So she excused herself by saying she was too tired with scraping pots and washing saucepans; and when the others went off, she crept up to her bed.

But alas! and alack a-day! The door had been left open, and as she lay in her bed she could hear the fiddlers fiddling away and the tramp of dancing feet.

Then she upped and off with her cap and robe of rushes, and there she was ever so fine and tidy. She was in the ballroom in a trice joining in the jig, and none was more beautiful or better dressed than she. While as for her dancing . . . !

Her master's son singled her out at once, and with the finest of bows engaged her as his partner for the rest of the night. So she danced away to her heart's content, while the whole room was agog, trying to find out who the beautiful young stranger could be. But she kept her own counsel and, making some excuse, slipped away before the ball finished; so when her fellow-servants came to bed, there she was in hers in her cap and robe of rushes, pretending to be fast asleep.

Next morning, however, the maids could talk of nothing but the beautiful stranger.

'You should ha' seen her,' they said. 'She was the loveliest young lady as ever you did see, not a bit like the likes o' we. Her golden hair was all silvered wi' pearls, and her dress – law! You wouldn't believe how she was dressed. Young master never took his eyes off her.'

And Caporushes only smiled and said with a twinkle in her eye, 'I should like to see her, but I don't think I ever shall.'

'Oh yes, you will,' they replied, 'for young master has ordered another ball tonight in hopes she will come to dance again.'

But that evening Caporushes refused once more to go to the gallery, saying she was too tired with cleaning pots and scraping saucepans. And once more when she heard the fiddlers fiddling she said to herself, 'I must have one dance – just one with the young master: he dances so beautifully.' For she felt certain he would dance with her.

And sure enough, when she had upped and offed with her cap and robe of rushes, there he was at the door waiting for her to come; for he had determined to dance with no one else.

So he took her by the hand, and they danced down the ballroom. It was a sight of all sights! Never were such dancers! So young, so handsome, so fine, so gay!

But once again Caporushes kept her own counsel and just slipped away on some excuse in time, so that when her fellow-servants came to their beds they found her in hers, pretending to be fast asleep; but her cheeks were all flushed and her breath came fast. So they said, 'She is dreaming. We hope her dreams are happy.'

But next morning they were full of what she had missed. Never was such a beautiful young gentleman as young master! Never was such a beautiful young lady! Never was such beautiful dancing! Everyone else had stopped theirs to look on.

And Caporushes with a twinkle in her eyes said, 'I should like to see her; but I'm *sure* I never shall!'

'Oh yes!' they replied. 'If you come tonight you're sure to see her; for young master has ordered another ball in hopes the beautiful stranger will come again; for it's easy to see he is madly in love with her.'

Then Caporushes told herself she would not dance again, since it was not fit for a gay young master to be in love with his scullery-maid; but, alas! the moment she heard the fiddlers fiddling, she just upped and offed with her rushes, and there she was fine and tidy as ever! She didn't even have to brush her beautiful golden hair! And once again she was in the ballroom in a trice, dancing away with young master who never took his eyes off her, and implored her to tell him who she was. But she kept her own counsel and only told him that she never, never, never would come to dance any more, and that he must say goodbye. And he held her hand so fast that she had a job to get away, and lo and behold! his ring came off his finger, and as she ran up to her bed there it was in her hand! She had just time to put on her cap and robe of rushes, when her fellow-servants came trooping in and found her awake.

'It was the noise you made coming upstairs,' she made excuse; but they said, 'Not we! It is the whole place that is in an uproar searching for the beautiful stranger. Young master he tried to detain her: but she slipped from him like an eel. But he declares he will find her for if he doesn't he will die of love for her.'

Then Caporushes laughed. 'Young men don't die of love,' says she. 'He will find someone else.'

But he didn't. He spent his whole time looking for his beautiful dancer, but go where he might, and ask whom he would, he never heard anything about her. And day by day he grew thinner and thinner, and paler and paler, until at last he took to his bed.

And the housekeeper came to the cook and said, 'Cook the nicest dinner you can cook, for young master eats nothing.'

Then the cook prepared soups, and jellies, and creams, and roast chicken, and bread sauce; but the young man would have none of them.

And Caporushes cleaned the pots and scraped the saucepans and said nothing.

Then the housekeeper came crying and said to the cook, 'Prepare some gruel for young master. Mayhap he'd take that. If not he will die for love of the beautiful dancer. If she could see him now she would have pity on him.'

So the cook began to make the gruel, and Caporushes left scraping saucepans and watched her.

'Let me stir it,' she said, 'while you fetch a cup from the pantry-room.'

So Caporushes stirred the gruel, and what did she do but slip young master's ring into it before the cook came back!

Then the butler took the cup upstairs on a silver salver. But when the young master saw it he waved it away, till the butler with tears begged him just to taste it.

So the young master took a silver spoon and stirred the gruel; and he felt something hard at the bottom of the cup. And when he fished it up, lo! it was his own ring! Then he sat up in bed and said quite loud, 'Send for the cook!'

And when she came he asked her who made the gruel.

'I did,' she said, for she was half-pleased and half-frightened.

Then he looked at her all over and said, 'No, you didn't! You're too stout! Tell me who made it and you shan't be harmed!'

Then the cook began to cry. 'If you please, sir, I *did* make it; but Caporushes stirred it.'

'And who is Caporushes?' asked the young man.

'If you please, sir, Caporushes is the scullion,' whimpered the cook.

Then the young man sighed and fell back on his pillow. 'Send Caporushes here,' he said in a faint voice; for he really was very near dying.

And when Caporushes came he just looked at her cap and her robe of rushes and turned his face to the wall; but he asked her in a weak little voice, 'From whom did you get that ring?'

Now when Caporushes saw the poor young man so weak and worn with love for her, her heart melted, and she replied softly: 'From him that gave it me,' quoth she, and offed with her cap and robe of rushes, and there she was as fine and tidy as ever, with her beautiful golden hair all silvered over with pearls.

And the young man caught sight of her with the tail of his eye, and sat up in bed as strong as may be, and drew her to him and gave her a great big kiss.

So, of course, they were to be married in spite of her being only a scullery-maid, for she told no one who she was. Now everyone far and near was asked to the wedding. Amongst the invited guests was Caporushes' father, who from grief at losing his favourite daughter, had lost his sight, and was very dull and miserable. However, as a friend of the family, he had to come to the young master's wedding.

Now the marriage feast was to be the finest ever seen; but Caporushes went to her friend the cook and said: 'Dress every dish without one mite of salt.'

'That'll be rare and nasty,' replied the cook; but because she prided herself on having let Caporushes stir the gruel and so saved the young master's life, she did as she was asked, and dressed every dish for the wedding breakfast without one mite of salt.

Now when the company sat down to table their faces were full of smiles and content, for all the dishes looked so nice and tasty; but no sooner had the guests begun to eat than their faces fell; for nothing can be tasty without salt.

Then Caporushes' blind father, whom his daughter had seated next to her, burst out crying.

'What is the matter?' she asked.

Then the old man sobbed, 'I had a daughter whom I loved dearly, dearly. And I asked her how much she loved me, and she replied, "As fresh meat loves salt." And I was angry with her and turned her out of house and home, for I thought she didn't love me at all. But now I see she loved me best of all.'

And as he said the words his eyes were opened, and there beside him was his daughter lovelier than ever.

And she gave him one hand, and her husband, the young master, the other, and laughed saying, 'I love you both as fresh meat loves salt.' And after that they were all happy for evermore.

The Babes in the Wood

Now ponder well, you parents dear,
    These words which I shall write;
A doleful story you shall hear,
    In time brought forth to light.
A gentleman of good account,
    In Norfolk dwelt of late,
Who did in honour far surmount
    Most men of his estate.

Sore sick he was and like to die,
    No help his life could save;
His wife by him as sick did lie,
    And both possest one grave.
No love between these two was lost,
    Each was to other kind;
In love they lived, in love they died,
    And left two babes behind.

The one a fine and pretty boy
    Not passing three years old,
The other a girl more young than he,
    And framed in beauty's mould.
The father left his little son,
    As plainly did appear,
When he to perfect age should come,
    Three hundred pounds a year;

And to his little daughter Jane
    Five hundred pounds in gold,
To be paid down on marriage-day,
    Which might not be controlled.

But if the children chanced to die
    Ere they to age should come,
Their uncle should possess their wealth;
    For so the will did run.

'Now, brother,' said the dying man,
    'Look to my children dear;
Be good unto my boy and girl,
    No friends else have they here;
To God and you I recommend
    My children dear this day;
But little while be sure we have
    Within this world to stay.

'You must be father and mother both,
    And uncle, all in one;
God knows what will become of them
    When I am dead and gone.'
With that bespake their mother dear:
    'O brother kind,' quoth she,
'You are the man must bring our babes
    To wealth or misery.

'And if you keep them carefully,
    Then God will you reward;
But if you otherwise should deal,
    God will your deeds regard.'
With lips as cold as any stone,
They kissed their children small:
'God bless you both, my children dear!'
    With that the tears did fall.

These speeches then their brother spoke
    To this sick couple there:
'The keeping of your little ones,
    Sweet sister, do not fear;
God never prosper me nor mine,
    Nor aught else that I have,

If I do wrong your children dear
    When you are laid in grave!'

The parents being dead and gone,
    The children home he takes,
And brings them straight unto his house
    Where much of them he makes.
He had not kept these pretty babes
    A twelvemonth and a day,
But, for their wealth, he did devise
    To make them both away.

He bargained with two ruffians strong,
    Which were of furious mood,
That they should take these children young,
    And slay them in a wood.
He told his wife an artful tale
    He would the children send
To be brought up in London town
    With one that was his friend.

Away then went those pretty babes,
    Rejoicing at that tide,
Rejoicing with a merry mind
    They should on cock-horse ride.
They prate and prattle pleasantly,
    As they ride on the way,
To those that should their butchers be
    And work their lives' decay:

So that the pretty speech they had
    Made Murder's heart relent;
And they that undertook the deed
    Full sore now did repent.
Yet one of them, more hard of heart,
    Did vow to do his charge,
Because the wretch that hired him
    Had paid him very large.

The other won't agree thereto,
    So there they fall to strife;
With one another they did fight
    About the children's life;
And he that was of mildest mood
    Did slay the other there,
Within an unfrequented wood;
    The babes did quake for fear!

He took the children by the hand,
    Tears standing in their eye,
And bade them straightway follow him,
    And look they did not cry;
And two long miles he led them on,
    While they for food complain:
'Stay here,' quoth he, 'I'll bring you bread,
    When I come back again.'

These pretty babes, with hand in hand,
    Went wandering up and down;
But never more could see the man
    Approaching from the town.
Their pretty lips with blackberries
    Were all besmeared and dyed;
And when they saw the darksome night,
    They sat them down and cried.

Thus wandered these poor innocents,
    Till death did end their grief;
In one another's arms they died,
    As wanting due relief:
No burial this pretty pair
    From any man receives,
Till Robin Redbreast piously
      Did cover them with leaves.

And now the heavy wrath of God
    Upon their uncle fell;
Yea, fearful fiends did haunt his house,
    His conscience felt an hell:

His barns were fired, his goods consumed,
    His lands were barren made,
His cattle died within the field,
    And nothing with him stayed.

And in a voyage to Portugal
    Two of his sons did die;
And to conclude, himself was brought
    To want and misery;
He pawned and mortgaged all his land
    Ere seven years came about.
And now at last this wicked act
    Did by this means come out:

The fellow that did take in hand
    These children for to kill,
Being for a robbery judged to die,
    Such was God's blessed will,
He did confess the very truth,
    As here hath been displayed,
The uncle having died in jail,
    Where he for debt was laid.

You that executors be made,
    And overseers eke,
Of children that be fatherless,
    And infants mild and meek,
Take you example by this thing,
    And yield to each his right,
Lest God with suchlike misery
    Your wicked minds requite.

The Red Ettin

There was once a widow that lived on a small bit of ground, which she rented from a farmer. And she had two sons; and by and by it was time for the wife to send them away to seek their fortune. So she told her elder son one day to take a can and bring her water from the well, that she might bake a cake for him; and however much or however little water he might bring, the cake would be great or small accordingly, and that cake was to be all that she could give him when he went on his travels.

The lad went away with the can to the well, and filled it with water, and then came away home again; but the can being broken, the most part of the water had run out before he got back. So his cake was very small; yet small as it was, his mother asked him if he was willing to take the half of it with her blessing, telling him that, if he chose rather to take the whole, he would only get it with her curse. The young man, thinking he might have to travel a fair way, and not knowing when or how he might get other provisions, said he would like to have the whole cake, come of his mother's malison what might; so she gave him the whole cake, and her malison along with it. Then he took his brother aside and gave him a knife to keep till he should come back, desiring him to look at it every morning, and as long as it continued to be clear, then he might he sure that the owner of it was well; but if it grew dim and rusty, then for certain some ill had befallen him.

So the young man went to seek his fortune. And he went all that day, and all the next day; and on the third day, in the afternoon, he came up to where a shepherd was sitting with a flock of sheep. And he went up to the shepherd and asked him to whom the sheep belonged; and he answered:

'To the Red Ettin of Ireland
  Who lives in Ballygan,
He stole King Malcolm's daughter,
  The King of fair Scotland.
He beats her, he binds her,
  He lays her on a band;
And every day he strikes her
  With a bright silver wand.
'Tis said there's one predestinate
  To be his mortal foe;
But sure that man is yet unborn,
  And long may it be so!'

After this the shepherd told him to beware of the beasts he should next meet, for they were of a very different kind from any he had yet seen.

So the young man went on, and by and by he saw a multitude of very dreadful, terrible, horrible beasts, with two heads, and on every head four horns! And he was sore frightened, and ran away from them as fast as he could; and glad was he when he came to a castle that stood on a hillock, with the door standing wide open in the wall. And he went into the castle for shelter, and there he saw an old wife sitting beside the kitchen fire. He asked the wife if he might stay for the night, as he was tired with a long journey; and the wife said he might, but it was not a good place for him to be in, as it belonged to the Red Ettin, who was a very terrible monster with three heads, who spared no living man it could get hold of. The young man would have gone away, but he was afraid of the two-headed four-horned beasts outside; so he beseeched the old woman to hide him as best she could, and not tell the Ettin he was there. He thought, if he could put up for the night, he might get away in the morning, without meeting with the dreadful, terrible, horrible beasts, and so escape.

But he had not been long in his hiding-hole, before the awful Ettin came in; and no sooner was he in, than he was heard crying:

'Snouk but! and snouk ben!
I find the smell of an earthly man,
Be he living, or be he dead,
His heart this night shall kitchen my bread.'

Well, the monster began to search about, and he soon found the poor young man, and pulled him from his hiding-place. And when he had got him out, he told him that if he could answer him three questions his life should be spared.

So the first head asked: 'A thing without an end, what's that?'

But the young man knew not.

Then the second head said: 'The smaller, the more dangerous, what's that?'

But the young man knew not.

And then the third head asked: 'The dead carrying the living? Riddle me that.'

But the young man knew not.

So the lad not being able to answer one of these questions, the Red Ettin took a mallet from behind the door, knocked him on the head, and turned him into a pillar of stone.

Now on the morning after this happened the younger brother took out the knife to look at it, and he was grieved to find it all brown with rust. So he told his mother that the time was now come for him to go away upon his travels also. At first she refused to let him go; but at last she requested him to take the can to the well for water, that she might make a cake for him. So he went, but as he was bringing home the water, a raven over his head cried to him to look, and he would see that the water was running out. Now being a young man of sense, and seeing the water running out, he took some clay and patched up the holes, so that he brought home enough water to bake a large cake. And when his mother put it to him to take the half cake with her blessing, he took it instead of having the whole with her malison.

So he went away on his journey with his mother's blessing. Now after he had travelled a long way, he met with an old woman who asked him if he would give her a bit of his cake. And he said, 'I will gladly do that;' so he gave her a piece of the cake.

Then the old woman, who was a fairy, gave him a magic wand, that might yet be of service to him, if he took care to use it rightly; and she told him a great deal that would happen to him, and what he ought to do in all circumstances; and after that, she vanished in an instant, out of his sight. Then he went on his way until he came up to the old man who was herding the sheep; and when he asked to whom these sheep belonged, the answer was:

> 'To the Red Ettin of Ireland
>   Who lives in Ballygan,
> He stole King Malcolm's daughter,
>   The king of fair Scotland.
> He beats her, he binds her,
>   He lays her on a band;
> And every day he strikes her
>   With a bright silver wand.
> But now I fear his end is near,
>   And death is close at hand;
> For you're to be, I plainly see,
>   The heir of all his land.'

So the younger brother went on his way; but when he came to the place where the dreadful, terrible, horrible beasts were standing, he did not stop nor run away, but went boldly through amongst them. One came up roaring with open mouth to devour him, but he struck it with his wand, and laid it in an instant dead at his feet. He soon came to the Ettin's castle, where he found the door shut, but he knocked boldly, and was admitted. Then the old woman who sat by the fire warned him of the terrible Ettin, and what had been the fate of his brother; but he was not to be daunted, and would not even hide.

Then by and by the monster came in, crying as before:

> 'Snouk but! and snouk ben!
> I find the smell of an earthly man;
> Be he living, or be he dead,
> His heart this night shall kitchen my bread.'

Well, he quickly espied the young man, and bade him stand

forth on the floor and told him that if he could answer three questions his life would be spared.

So the first head asked 'What's the thing without an end?'

Now the younger brother had been told by the fairy to whom he had given a piece of his cake, what he ought to say; so he answered:

'A bowl.'

Then the first head frowned, but the second head asked: 'The smaller the more dangerous; what's that?'

'A bridge,' says the younger brother, quite fast.

Then the first and the second heads frowned, but the third head asked: 'When does the dead carry the living? Riddle me that.'

At this the young man answered up at once and said: 'When a ship sails on the sea with men inside her.'

When the Red Ettin found all his riddles answered, he knew that his power was gone, so he tried to escape, but the young man took up an axe and hewed off the monster's three heads. Then he asked the old woman to show him where the king's daughter lay; and the old woman took him upstairs, and opened a great many doors, and out of every door came a beautiful lady who had been imprisoned there by the Red Ettin; and last of all the ladies was the king's daughter. Then the old woman took him down into a low room, and there stood a stone pillar; but he had only to touch it with his wand, and his brother started into life.

So the whole of the prisoners were overjoyed at their deliverance, for which they thanked the younger brother again and again. Next day they all set out for the king's court, and a gallant company they made. Then the king married his daughter to the young man who had delivered her, and gave a noble's daughter to his brother.

So they all lived happily all the rest of their days.

The Fish and the Ring

Once upon a time there lived a baron who was a great magician, and could tell by his arts and charms everything that was going to happen at any time.

Now this great lord had a little son born to him as heir to all his castles and lands. So, when the little lad was about four years old, wishing to know what his fortune would be, the baron looked in his *Book of Fate* to see what it foretold.

And lo and behold! it was written that this much-loved, much-prized heir to all the great lands and castles was to marry a low-born maiden. So the baron was dismayed, and set to work by more arts and charms to discover if this maiden were already born, and if so, where she lived.

And he found out that she had just been born in a very poor house, where the poor parents were already burdened with five children.

So he called for his horse and rode away, and away, until he came to the poor man's house, and there he found the poor man sitting at his doorstep very sad and doleful.

'What is the matter, my friend?' asked he, and the poor man replied: 'May it please your honour, a little lass has just been born to our house; and we have five children already, and where the bread is to come from to fill the sixth mouth, we know not.'

'If that be all your trouble,' quoth the baron readily, 'mayhap I can help you, so don't be downhearted. I am looking for just such a little lass to companion my son, so if you will, I will give you ten crowns for her.'

Well! the man he nigh jumped for joy, since he was to get good money, and his daughter, so he thought, a good home. Therefore he brought out the child then and there and the baron, wrapping the babe in his cloak, rode away. But when he got to the river he flung the little thing into the swollen stream and said to himself as he galloped back to his castle: 'There goes fate!'

But, you see, he was just sore mistaken. For the little lass didn't sink. The stream was very swift, and her long clothes kept her up till she caught in a snag just opposite a fisherman, who was mending his nets.

Now the fisherman and his wife had no children, and they were just longing for a baby; so when the good man saw the little lass he was overcome with joy, and took her home to his wife, who received her with open arms.

And there she grew up, the apple of their eyes, into the most beautiful maiden that ever was seen.

Now when she was about fifteen years of age it so happened that the baron and his friends went a-hunting along the banks of the river and stopped to get a drink of water at the fisherman's hut. And who should bring the water out but, as they thought, the fisherman's daughter.

Now the young men of the party noticed her beauty, and one of them said to the baron, 'She should marry well; read us her fate since you are so learned in the art.'

Then the baron, scarce looking at her, said carelessly: 'I could guess her fate! Some wretched yokel or other. But to please you, I will cast her horoscope by the stars; so tell me, girl, what day were you born?'

'That I cannot tell, sir,' replied the girl, 'for I was picked up in the river about fifteen years ago.'

Then the baron grew pale, for he guessed at once that she was the little lass he had flung into the stream, and that fate had been stronger than he was. But he kept his own counsel and said nothing at the time. Afterwards, however, he thought out a plan, so he rode back and gave the girl a letter.

'See you!' he said. 'I will make your fortune. Take this letter to my brother, who needs a good girl, and you will be settled for life.'

Now the fisherman and his wife were growing old and needed help; so the girl said she would go, and took the letter.

And the baron rode back to his castle saying to himself once more: 'There goes fate!'

For what he had written in the letter was this:

DEAR BROTHER – Take the bearer and put her to death immediately.

But once again he was sore mistaken; since on the way to the town where his brother lived, the girl had to stop the night in a little inn. And it so happened that that very night a gang of thieves broke into the inn, and not content with carrying off all that the innkeeper possessed they searched the pockets of the guests, and found the letter which the girl carried. And when they read it, they agreed that it was a mean trick and a shame. So their captain sat down, and taking pen and paper wrote instead:

DEAR BROTHER – Take the bearer and marry her to my son without delay.

Then, after putting the note into an envelope and sealing it up, they gave it to the girl and bade her go on her way. So when she arrived at the brother's castle, though rather surprised, he gave orders for a wedding feast to be prepared. And the baron's son, who was staying with his uncle, seeing the girl's great beauty, was nothing loth, so they were fast wedded.

Well! when the news was brought to the baron, he was nigh beside himself; but he was determined not to be done by fate. So he rode post-haste to his brother's and pretended to be quite pleased. And then one day, when no one was nigh, he asked the young bride to come for a walk with him, and when they were close to some cliffs, seized hold of her, and was for throwing her over into the sea. But she begged hard for her life.

'It is not my fault,' she said. 'I have done nothing. It is fate. But if you will spare my life I promise that I will fight against fate also. I will never see you or your son again until you desire it. That will be safer for you; since, see you, the sea may preserve me, as the river did.'

Well! the baron agreed to this. So he took off his gold ring from his finger and flung it over the cliffs into the sea and said: 'Never dare to show me your face again till you can show me that ring likewise.'

And with that he let her go.

Well! the girl wandered on and she wandered on, until she came to a nobleman's castle; and there, as they needed a kitchen girl, she engaged as a scullion, since she had been used to such work in the fisherman's hut.

Now one day as she was cleaning a big fish, she looked out of the kitchen window and who should she see driving up to dinner but the baron and his young son, her husband. At first, she thought that, to keep her promise, she must run away; but afterwards she remembered they would not see her in the kitchen, so she went on with her cleaning of the big fish.

And lo and behold! she saw something shine in its inside, and there, sure enough, was the baron's ring! She was glad enough to see it, I can tell you; so she slipped it on to her thumb. But she went on with her work, and dressed the fish as nicely as ever she could, and served it up as pretty as may be, with parsley sauce and butter.

Well! when it came to table the guests liked it so well that they asked the host who cooked it? And he called to his servants, 'Send up the cook who cooked that fine fish, that she may get her reward.'

Well! when the girl heard she was wanted she made herself ready, and with the gold ring on her thumb, went boldly into the dining-hall. And all the guests when they saw her were struck dumb by her wonderful beauty. And the young husband started up gladly; but the baron, recognising her, jumped up angrily and looked as if he would kill her. So, without one word, the girl held up her hand before his face and the gold ring shone and glittered on it; and she went straight up to the baron, and laid her hand with the ring on it before him on the table.

Then the baron understood that fate had been too strong for him; so he took her by the hand, and, placing her beside him, turned to the guests and said: 'This is my son's wife. Let us drink a toast in her honour.'

And after dinner he took her and his son home to his castle, where they all lived as happy as could be for ever afterwards.

Lawkamercyme

There was an old woman, as I've heard tell,
She went to the market her eggs for to sell;
She went to the market, all on a market-day,
And she fell asleep on the king's highway.

There came by a pedlar, whose name it was Stout,
He cut all her petticoats all round about;
He cut her petticoats up to the knees,
Which made the old woman to shiver and freeze.

When this old woman first did awake,
She 'gan to shiver, she 'gan to shake;
She 'gan to wonder, she 'gan to cry –
'Lawkamercyme! this is none of I!'

'But if it be I, as I do hope it be,
I've a little dog at home, and sure he'll know me;
If it be I, he'll wag his little tail,
And if it be not I, then he'll bark and wail.'

Home went the old woman, all in the dark;
Up got the little dog, and he began to bark,
He began to bark, and she began to cry –
'Lawkamercyme! this is none of I!'

Master of All Masters

A girl once went to the fair to hire herself for servant. At last a funny-looking old gentleman engaged her, and took her home to his house. When she got there, he told her that he had something to teach her, for that in his house he had his own names for things.

He said to her, 'What will you call me?'

'Master or mister, or whatever you please, sir,' says she.

He said, 'You must call me "master of all masters". And what would you call this?' pointing to his bed.

'Bed or couch, or whatever you please, sir.'

'No that's my "barnacle". And what do you call these?' said he, pointing to his pantaloons.

'Breeches or trousers, or whatever you please, sir.'

'You must call them "squibs and crackers". And what would you call her?' pointing to the cat.

'Cat or kit, or whatever you please, sir.'

'You must call her "white-faced simminy". And this now,' showing the fire, 'what would you call this?'

'Fire or flame, or whatever you please, sir.'

'You must call it "hot cockalorum", and what this?' he went on, pointing to the water.

'Water or wet, or whatever you please, sir.'

'No, "pondalorum" is its name. And what do you call all this?' asked he, as he pointed to the house.

'House or cottage, or whatever you please, sir.'

'You must call it "high topper mountain".'

That very night the servant woke her master up in a fright and said, 'Master of all masters, get out of your barnacle and put on your squibs and crackers. For white-faced simminy has got a spark of hot cockalorum on its tail, and unless you get some pondalorum high topper mountain will be all on hot cockalorum.' . . .

That's all!!

Molly Whuppie and the Double-Faced Giant

Once upon a time there was a man and his wife who were not over rich. And they had so many children that they couldn't find meat for them; so, as the three youngest were girls, they just took them out to the forest one day, and left them there to fend for themselves as best they might.

Now the two eldest were just ordinary girls, so they cried a bit and felt afraid; but the youngest, whose name was Molly Whuppie, was bold, so she counselled her sisters not to despair, but to try and find some house where they might get a night's lodging. So they set off through the forest, and journeyed, and journeyed, and journeyed, but never a house did they see. It began to grow dark, her sisters were faint with hunger, and even Molly Whuppie began to think of supper. At last in the distance they saw a great big light, and made for it. Now when they drew near they saw that it came from a huge window in a huge house.

'It will be a giant's house,' said the two elder girls, trembling with fright.

'If there were two giants in it, I still mean to have my supper,' quoth Molly Whuppie, and knocked at a huge door, as bold as brass. It was opened by the giant's wife, who shook her head when Molly Whuppie asked for victuals and a night's lodging.

'You wouldn't thank me for it,' she said, 'for my man is a giant, and when he comes home he will kill you of a certainty.'

'But if you give us supper at once,' says Molly craftily, 'we shall have finished it before the giant comes home; for we are very sharp-set.'

Now, the giant's wife was not unkindly; besides her three daughters, who were just of an age with Molly and her sisters, tugged at her skirts well pleased; so she took the girls in, set them by the fire, and gave them each a bowl of bread and milk.

But they had hardly begun to gobble it up before the door burst open, and a fearful giant strode in saying:

> 'Fee-fi-fo-fum,
> I smell the smell of some earthly one.'

'Don't put yourself about, my dear,' said the giant's wife trying to make the best of it. 'See for yourself. They are only three poor little girlies like our girlies. They were cold and hungry so I gave them some supper; but they have promised to go away as soon as they have finished. Now be a good giant and don't touch them. They've eaten of our salt, so don't *you* be at fault!'

Now this giant was not at all a straightforward giant. He was a double-faced giant. So he only said,

> 'Umph!'

and remarked that as they had come, they had better stay all night, since they could easily sleep with his three daughters. And after he had had his supper he made himself quite pleasant, and plaited chains of straw for the little strangers to wear round their necks, to match the gold chains his daughters wore. Then he wished them all pleasant dreams and sent them to bed.

Dear me! He *was* a double-faced giant!

But Molly Whuppie, the youngest of the three girls, was not only bold, she was clever. So when she was in bed, instead of going to sleep like the others, she lay awake and thought, and thought, and thought; until at last she up ever so softly, took off her own and her sisters' straw chains, put them round the necks of the ogre's daughters, and placed their gold chains round her own and her sisters' necks.

And even then she did not go to sleep; but lay still and waited to see if she was wise; and she was! For in the very middle of the night, when everybody else was dead asleep, and it was pitch dark, in comes the giant, all stealthy, feels for the straw chains, twists them tight round the wearers' necks, half strangles his daughters, drags them on to the floor, and beats them till they are quite dead. Then, all stealthy and satisfied, he goes back to his own bed, thinking he has been very clever.

But he was no match you see for Molly Whuppie; for she at once roused her sisters, bade them be quiet, and follow her. Then they slipped out of the giant's house and ran, and ran, and ran until the dawn broke and they found themselves before another great house. It was surrounded by a wide deep moat, which was spanned by a drawbridge. But the drawbridge was up. However, beside it, hung a single-hair rope over which anyone very light-footed could cross.

Now Molly's sisters were feared to try it; besides they said that for aught they knew the house might be another giant's house, and they had best keep away.

'Taste and try,' says Molly Whuppie, laughing, and was over the Bridge of a Single Hair before you could say knife. And, after all, it was not a giant's house but a king's castle. Now it so happened that the very giant whom Molly had tricked was the terror of the whole countryside, and it was to gain safety from him that the drawbridge was kept up, and the Bridge of a Single Hair had been made.

So when the sentry heard Molly Whuppie's tale, he took her to the king and said: 'My lord! Here is a girlie who has tricked the giant!'

Then the king when he had heard the story said, 'You are a clever girl, Molly Whuppie, and you managed very well; but if you could manage still better and steal the giant's sword in which part of his strength lies, I will give your eldest sister in marriage to my eldest son.'

Well! Molly Whuppie thought this would be a very good downsitting for her sister, so she said she would try.

So that evening, all alone, she ran across the Bridge of a Single Hair, and ran and ran till she came to the giant's house. The sun was just setting and shone on it so beautifully that Molly Whuppie thought it looked like a castle in Spain, and could hardly believe that such a dreadful, double-faced giant lived within. However she knew he did; so she slipped into the house unbeknownst, stole up to the giant's room and crept in behind the bed. By and by the giant came home, ate a huge supper, and came crashing up the stairs to his bed. But Molly kept very still and held her breath. After a time he fell asleep, and soon he began to snore. Then Molly crept out from under the bed, ever so softly, and crept up the bedclothes, and crept past his great snoring face, and laid hold of the sword that hung above it. But alas! as she jumped from the bed in a hurry, the sword rattled in the scabbard. The noise woke the giant, and up he jumped and ran after Molly, who ran as she had never run before, carrying the sword over her shoulder. And he ran, and she ran, and they both ran, until they came to the Bridge of a Single Hair. Then she fled over it light-footed, balancing the sword, but he couldn't. So he stopped, foaming at the mouth with rage and called after her: 'Woe worth you, Molly Whuppie! Never you dare to come again!'

And she, turning her head about as she sped over the one-hair bridge, laughed lightly: 'Twice yet, gaffer, will I come to the castle in Spain!'

So Molly gave the sword to the king, and, as he had promised, his eldest son wedded her eldest sister.

But after the marriage festivities were over the king says again to Molly Whuppie: 'You're a main clever girl, Molly, and you have managed very well, but if you could manage still better and steal the giant's purse in which part of his strength lies, I will marry my second son to your second sister. But you need to be careful, for the giant sleeps with the purse under his pillow!'

Well! Molly Whuppie thought this would be a very good downsitting, indeed, for her second sister, so she said she would try her luck.

So that evening, just at sunsetting, she ran over the one-hair bridge, and ran, and ran, and ran until she came to the giant's house, looking for all the world like a castle in the air, all ruddy and golden and glinting. She could scarce believe such a dreadful double-faced giant lived within. However she *knew* he did; so she slipped into the house unbeknownst, stole up to the giant's room, and crept in below the giant's bed. By and by the giant came home, ate a hearty supper, and then came crashing upstairs, and soon fell a-snoring. Then Molly Whuppie slipped from under the bed, and slipped up the bedclothes, and reaching out her hand slipped it under the pillow, and got hold of the purse. But the giant's head was so heavy on it she had to tug and tug away. At last out it came, she fell backward over the bedside, the purse opened, and some of the money fell out with a crash. The noise wakened the giant, and she had only time to grab the money off the floor, when he was after her. How they ran, and ran, and ran, and ran! At last she reached the Bridge of a Single Hair and, with the purse in one hand and the money in the other, she sped across it while the giant shook his fist at her, and cried: 'Woe worth you, Molly Whuppie! Never you dare to come again!'

And she turning her head laughed lightly: 'Yet once more, gaffer, will I come to the castle in Spain.'

So she took the purse to the king, and he ordered a splendid marriage feast for his second son, and her second sister.

But after the wedding was over the king says to her, says he: 'Molly! You are the most main clever girl in the world; but if you would do better yet, and steal me from his finger the giant's ring in which all his strength lies, I will give you my dearest, youngest, handsomest son for yourself.'

Now Molly thought the king's son was the nicest young prince she had ever seen, so she said she would try, and that evening, all alone, she sped across the Bridge of a Single Hair as light as a feather, and ran, and ran, and ran, until she came to the giant's house all lit up with the red setting sun like any castle in the air. And she slipped inside, stole upstairs and crept under the bed in no time. And the giant came in, and supped, and crashed up to bed, and snored. Oh! he snored louder than ever!

But you know, he was a double-faced giant; so perhaps he snored louder on purpose. For no sooner had Molly Whuppie began to tug at his ring than . . . My! . . .

He had her fast between his finger and thumb. And he sat up in bed, and shook his head at her and said, 'Molly Whuppie, you are a main clever girl! Now, if I had done as much ill to you as you have done to me, what would you do to me?'

Then Molly thought for a moment and she said, 'I'd put you in a sack, and I'd put the cat inside with you, and I'd put the dog inside with you, and I'd put a needle and thread and a pair of shears inside with you, and I'd hang you up on a nail, and I'd go to the wood and cut the thickest stick I could get, and come home and take you down and bang you, and bang, and bang, and bang you till you were dead!'

'Right you are!' cried the giant gleefully, 'and that's just what I'll do to you!'

So he got a sack and put Molly into it with the dog and the cat and the needle and thread and the shears, and hung her on a nail in the wall, and went out to the wood to choose a stick.

Then Molly Whuppie began to laugh like anything, and the dog joined in with barks, and the cat with mews.

Now the giant's wife was sitting in the next room, and when she heard the commotion she went in to see what was up.

'Whatever is the matter?' quoth she.

'Nothing, 'm,' quoth Molly Whuppie from inside the sack, laughing like anything. 'Ho, ho! Ha, ha! If you saw what we see you'd laugh too. Ho, ho! Ha, ha!'

And no matter how the giant's wife begged to know what she saw, there never was any answer but, 'Ho, ho! Ha, ha! Could ye but see what I see!!!'

At last the giant's wife begged Molly to let her see, so Molly took the shears, cut a hole in the sack, jumped out, helped the giant's wife in, and sewed up the hole! For of course she hadn't forgotten to take out the needle and thread with her.

Now, just at that very moment, the giant burst in, and Molly had barely time to hide behind the door before he rushed at the sack, tore it down, and began to batter it with a huge tree he had cut in the wood.

'Stop! stop!' cried his wife. 'It's me! It's me!'

But he couldn't hear, for, see you, the dog and the cat had tumbled one on the top of the other, and such a growling and spitting, and yelling and caterwauling you never heard! It was fair deafening, and the giant would have gone on battering till his wife was dead had he not caught sight of Molly Whuppie escaping with the ring which he had left on the table.

Well, he threw down the tree and ran after her. Never was

such a race. They ran, and they ran, and they ran, and they ran, until they came to the Bridge of a Single Hair. And then balancing herself with the ring like a hoop, Molly Whuppie sped over the bridge light as a feather, but the giant had to stand on the other side, and shake his fist at her, and cry louder than ever: 'Woe worth you, Molly Whuppie! Never you dare to come again!'

And she, turning her head back as she sped, laughed gaily: 'Never more, gaffer, will I come to the castle in the air!'

So she took the ring to the king, and she and the handsome young prince were married, and no one ever saw the double-faced giant again.

The Ass, the Table and the Stick

A lad named Jack was once so unhappy at home through his father's ill-treatment, that he made up his mind to run away and seek his fortune in the wide world.

He ran, and he ran, till he could run no longer, and then he ran right up against a little old woman who was gathering sticks. He was too much out of breath to beg pardon, but the woman was good-natured, and she said he seemed to be a likely lad, so she would take him to be her servant, and would pay him well. He agreed, for he was very hungry! and she brought him to her house in the wood, where he served her for a twelvemonths and a day. When the year had passed, she called him to her, and said she had good wages for him. So she presented him with an ass out of the stable, and he had but to pull Neddy's ears to make him begin at once to hee-haw! And when he brayed there dropped from his mouth silver sixpences and half-crowns and golden guineas.

The lad was well pleased with the wage he had received, and away he rode till he reached an inn. There he ordered the best of everything, and when the innkeeper refused to serve him without being paid beforehand, the boy went off to the stable, pulled the ass's ears, and obtained his pocket full of money. The host had watched all this through a crack in the door, and when night came on he substituted an ass of his own for the precious Neddy belonging to the youth. So Jack, without knowing that any change had been made, rode away next morning to his father's house.

Now, I must tell you that near his home dwelt a poor widow with an only daughter. The lad and the maiden were fast friends and trueloves. So when Jack returned he asked his father's leave to marry the girl.

'Never till you have the money to keep her,' was the reply.

'I have that, father,' said the lad, and going to the ass he pulled its long ears; well, he pulled, and he pulled, till one of them came off in his hands, but Neddy, though he hee-hawed and he hee-hawed, let fall no half-crowns or guineas. Then the father picked up a hayfork and beat his son out of the house.

I promise you he ran; he ran and ran till he came bang against a door, and burst it open, and there he was in a joiner's shop 'You're a likely lad,' said the joiner; 'serve me for a twelvemonths and a day and I will pay you well.' So he agreed, and served the carpenter for a year and a day. 'Now,' said the master, 'I will give you your wage;' and he presented him with a table, telling him he had but to say, 'Table, be covered,' and at once it would be spread with lots to eat and drink.

Jack hitched the table on his back, and away he went with it till he came to the inn. 'Well, host,' shouted he, putting down the table, 'my dinner today, and that of the best.'

'Very sorry, sir,' says the host, 'but there is nothing in the house but ham and eggs.'

'No ham and eggs for me!' exclaimed Jack. 'I can do better than that. Come, my table, be covered!'

So at once the table was spread with turkey and sausages, roast mutton, potatoes and greens. The innkeeper opened his eyes, but he said nothing, not he! But that night he fetched down from his attic a table very like the magic one, and exchanged the two, and Jack, none the wiser, next morning hitched the worthless table on to his back and carried it home.

'Now, father, may I marry my lass?' he asked.

'Not unless you can keep her,' replied the father.

'Look here!' exclaimed Jack. 'Father, I have a table which does all my bidding.'

'Let me see it,' said the old man.

The lad set it in the middle of the room, and bade it be covered; but all in vain; the table remained bare. Then in a rage, the father caught the warming-pan down from the wall and warmed his son's back with it so that the boy fled howling from the house, and ran and ran till he came to a river and tumbled in.

A man picked him out and bade him help in making a bridge over the river by casting a tree across. Then Jack climbed up to the top of the tree and threw his weight on it, so that when the man had rooted the tree up, Jack and the tree-head dropped on the farther bank.

'Thank you,' said the man; 'and now for what you have done I will pay you;' so saying, he tore a branch from the tree, and fettled it up into a club with his knife. 'There,' exclaimed he; 'take this stick, and when you say to it, "Up, stick, and bang him," it will knock anyone down who angers you.'

The lad was overjoyed to get this stick, for he had begun to see he had been tricked by the innkeeper, so away he went with it to the inn, and as soon as the man appeared he cried: 'Up, stick, and bang him!'

At the word the cudgel flew from his hand and battered the old fellow on the back, rapped his head, bruised his arms, tickled his ribs, till he fell groaning on the floor; and still the stick belaboured the prostrate man, nor would Jack call it off till he had got back the stolen ass and table. Then he galloped home on the ass, with the table on his shoulders, and the stick in his hand. When he arrived there he found his father was dead, so he brought his ass into the stable, and pulled its ears till he had filled the manger with money.

It was soon known through the town that Jack had returned rolling in wealth, and accordingly all the girls in the place set their caps at him.

'Now,' said Jack, 'I shall marry the richest lass in the place; so tomorrow do you all come in front of my house with your money in your aprons.'

Next morning the street was full of girls with aprons held out, and gold and silver in them; but Jack's own sweetheart was among them, and she had neither gold nor silver; nought but two copper pennies, that was all she had.

'Stand aside, lass,' said Jack to her, speaking roughly. 'Thou hast no silver nor gold – stand off from the rest.' She obeyed, and the tears ran down her cheeks, and filled her apron with diamonds.

'Up, stick, and bang them!' exclaimed Jack; whereupon the cudgel leaped up, and running along the line of girls, knocked them all on the heads and left them senseless on the pavement. Jack took all their money and poured it into his truelove's lap. 'Now, lass,' he exclaimed, 'thou art the richest, and I shall marry thee.'

The Well of the World's End

Once upon a time, and a very good time it was, though it wasn't in my time, nor in your time, nor anyone else's time, there was a girl whose mother had died, and her father had married again. And her stepmother hated her because she was more beautiful than she was. And she was very cruel to her; she used to make her do all the servants' work, and never let her have any peace.

At last, one day, the stepmother thought to get rid of her altogether; so she handed her a sieve and said to her: 'Go, fill it at the Well of the World's End and bring it home to me full, or woe betide you.' For she thought she would never be able to find the Well of the World's End and, if she did, how could she bring home a sieve full of water?

Well, the girl started off, and asked everyone she met to tell her where was the Well of the World's End. But nobody knew, and she didn't know what to do, when a queer little old woman, all bent double, told her where it was, and how she could get to it. So she did what the old woman told her, and at last arrived at the Well of the World's End. But when she dipped the sieve in the cold cold water, it all ran out again. She tried and she tried again, but every time it was the same; and at last she sat down and cried as if her heart would break.

Suddenly she heard a croaking voice, and she looked up and saw a great frog with goggle eyes looking at her and speaking to her.

'What's the matter, dearie?' it said.

'Oh dear! oh dear!' she said, 'my stepmother has sent me all this long way to fill this sieve with water from the Well of the World's End, and I can't fill it no how at all.'

'Well,' said the frog, 'if you promise me to do whatever I bid you for a whole night long, I'll tell you how to fill it.'

So the girl agreed, and then the frog said:

> 'Stop it with moss and daub it with clay,
>   And then it will carry the water away';

and then it gave a hop, skip, and jump, and went flop into the Well of the World's End.

So the girl looked about for some moss, and lined the bottom of the sieve with it, and over that she put some clay, and then she dipped it once again into the Well of the World's End; and this time, the water didn't run out, and she turned to go away.

Just then the frog popped up its head out of the Well of the World's End, and said, 'Remember your promise.'

'All right,' said the girl; for, thought she, 'what harm can a frog do me?'

So she went back to her stepmother, and brought the sieve full of water from the Well of the World's End. The stepmother was angry as angry, but she said nothing at all.

That very evening they heard something tap-tapping at the door low down, and a voice cried out:

> 'Open the door, my hinny, my heart,
>   Open the door, my own darling;
> Remember the words that you and I spoke,
>   At the World's End Well but this morning.'

'Whatever can that be?' cried out the stepmother.

Then the girl had to tell her all about it, and what she had promised the frog.

'Girls must keep their promises,' said the stepmother, who was glad the girl would have to obey a nasty frog. 'Go and open the door this instant.'

So the girl went and opened the door, and there was the frog from the Well of the World's End. And it hopped, and it hopped, and it jumped, till it reached the girl, and then it said:

> 'Lift me up, my hinny, my heart,
>   Lift to your knee, my own darling;
> Remember the words that you and I spoke,
>   At the World's End Well but this morning.'

But the girl would not do the frog's bidding, till her step-mother said, 'Lift it up this instant, you hussy! Girls *must* keep their promises!'

So she lifted the frog up on to her lap, and it lay there comfortably for a time; then at last it said:

> 'Give me some supper, my hinny, my heart,
>   Give me some supper, my darling;
> Remember the words you and I spoke,
>   At the World's End Well but this morning.'

Well, that she did not mind doing, so she got it a bowl of milk and bread, and fed it well. But when the frog had finished, it said:

> 'Take me to bed, my hinny, my heart,
>   Take me to bed, my own darling;
> Remember the promise you promised to me,
>   At the World's End Well but this morning.'

But that the girl refused to do, till her stepmother said harshly: 'Do what you promised, girl; girls *must* keep their promises. Do what you're bid, or out you go, you and your froggie.'

So the girl took the frog with her to bed, and kept it as far away from her as she could. Well, just as the day was beginning to break what should the frog say but:

> 'Chop off my head, my hinny, my heart,
>   Chop off my head, my own darling;
> Remember the promise you promised to me,
>   At the World's End Well but this morning.'

At first the girl wouldn't, for she thought of what the frog had done for her at the Well of the World's End. But when the frog said the words over and over again in a pleading voice, she went and took an axe and chopped off its head, and lo, and behold! there stood before her a handsome young prince, who told her that he had been enchanted by a wicked magician, and he could never be unspelled till some girl would do his bidding for a whole night, and chop off his head at the end of it.

The stepmother was surprised indeed when she found the young prince instead of the nasty frog, and she was not best pleased, you may be sure, when the prince told her that he was going to marry her stepdaughter because she had unspelled him. But married they were, and went away to live in the castle of the king, his father; and all the stepmother had to console her was that it was all through *her* that her stepdaughter was married to a prince.

The Rose Tree

Once upon a time, long long years ago in the days when one had to be careful about witches, there lived a good man, whose young wife died, leaving him a baby girl.

Now this good man felt he could not look after the baby properly, so he married a young woman whose husband had died leaving her with a baby boy.

Thus the two children grew up together, and loved each other dearly, dearly.

But the boy's mother was really a wicked witch-woman, and so jealous that she wanted all the boy's love for herself, and when the girl-baby grew white as milk, with cheeks like roses and lips like cherries, and when her hair, shining like golden silk, hung down to her feet so that her father and all the neighbours began to praise her looks, the stepmother fairly hated her, and did all in her power to spoil her looks. She would set the child hard tasks, and send her out in all weathers to do difficult messages, and if they were not well performed would beat her and scold her cruelly.

Now one cold winter evening when the snow was drifting fast, and the wild rose tree in the garden under which the children used to play in summer was all brown and barren save for snowflake flowers, the stepmother said to the little girl: 'Child! go and buy me a bunch of candles at the grocer's. Here is some money; go quickly, and don't loiter by the way.'

So the little girl took the money and set off quickly through the snow, for already it was growing dark. Now there was such a wind blowing that it nearly blew her off her feet, and as she ran, her beautiful hair got all tangled and almost tripped her up. However, she got the candles, paid for them, and started home again. But this time the wind was behind her and blew all her beautiful golden hair in front of her like a cloud, so that she could not see her steps, and, coming to a stile, had to stop and put down the bundle of candles in order to see how to get over it. And when she was climbing it a big black dog came by and ran off with the bunch of candles! Now she was so afraid of her stepmother that she durst not go home but turned back and bought another bunch of candles at the grocer's, and when she arrived at the stile once more the same thing happened. A big black dog came down the road and ran away with the bunch of candles. So yet once again she journeyed back to the grocer's through wind and snow, and, with her last penny, bought yet another bunch of candles. To no purpose, for alas and alack-a-day! when she laid them down in order to part her beautiful golden hair and to see how to get over the stile, a big black dog ran away with them.

So nothing was left save to go back to her stepmother in fear and trembling. But, for a wonder, her stepmother did not seem very angry. She only scolded her for being so late, for, see you, her father and her little playmate had gone to their beds and were in the Land of Nod.

Then she said to the child, 'I must take the tangles out of your hair before you go to sleep. Come, put your head on my lap.'

So the little girl put her head on her stepmother's lap, and lo, and behold! her beautiful yellow-silk hair rolled right over the woman's knees and lay upon the ground.

Then the beauty of it made the stepmother more jealous than before, so she said, 'I cannot part your hair properly on my knee, fetch me a billet of wood.'

So the little girl fetched one. Then said the stepmother 'Your hair is so thick I cannot part it with a comb; fetch me an axe!'

So the child fetched an axe.

'Now,' said that wicked, wicked woman, 'lay your head down on the billet while I part your hair.'

And the child did as she was bid without fear; and lo! the beautiful little golden head was off in a second, by one blow of the axe.

Now the wicked stepmother had thought it all out before, so

'That will I gladly,' answered the bird, 'if you will hang the millstone you are picking round my neck.'

So the millers hung it as they were asked; and when the song was finished, the bird spread its wide white wings and, with the millstone round its neck and the little rose-red shoes in one foot, the golden chain in the other, it flew back to the rose tree. But the little playmate was not there; he was inside the house eating his dinner.

Then the bird flew to the house, and rattled the millstone about the eaves until the stepmother cried, 'Harken! How it thunders!'

So the little boy ran out to see, and down dropped the dainty rose-red shoes at his feet.

'See what fine things the thunder has brought!' he cried with glee as he ran back.

Then the white bird rattled the millstone about the eaves once more, and once again the stepmother said, 'Harken! How it thunders!'

So this time the father went out to see, and down dropped the golden chain about his neck.

'It is true,' he said when he came back. 'The thunder does bring fine things!'

Then once more the white bird rattled the millstone about the eaves, and this time the stepmother said hurriedly, 'Hark! there it is again! Perhaps it has got something for me!'

Then she ran out; but the moment she stepped outside the door, down fell the millstone right on her head and killed her.

So that was an end of her. And after that the little boy was ever so much happier, and all the summertime he sat with his little rose-coloured shoes under the wild rose tree and listened to the white bird's song. But when winter came and the wild rose tree was all barren and bare save for snowflake flowers, the white bird came no longer and the little boy grew tired of waiting for it. So one day he gave up altogether, and they buried him under the rose tree beside his little playmate.

Now when the spring came and the rose tree blossomed, the flowers were no longer white. They were edged with rose colour like the little boy's shoes, and in the centre of each blossom there was a beautiful tuft of golden silk like the little girl's hair.

And if you look in a wild rose you will find these things there still.